BIG
BREATH
IN

ALSO BY JOHN STRALEY

THE CECIL YOUNGER INVESTIGATIONS
The Woman Who Married a Bear
The Curious Eat Themselves
The Music of What Happens
Death and the Language of Happiness
The Angels Will Not Care
Cold Water Burning
Baby's First Felony
So Far and Good

THE COLD STORAGE NOVELS
The Big Both Ways
Cold Storage, Alaska
What Is Time to a Pig?
Blown by the Same Wind

BIG
BREATH
IN

JOHN
STRALEY

Published by Soho Press
Soho Press, Inc.
227 W 17th Street
New York, NY 10011

Library of Congress Cataloging-in-Publication Data

Names: Straley, John, 1953- author.
Title: Big breath in / John Straley.
Description: New York, NY : Soho Crime, 2024.
Identifiers: LCCN 2024031158

ISBN 978-1-64129-654-0
eISBN 978-1-64129-655-7

Subjects: LCGFT: Detective and mystery fiction. | Thrillers (Fiction) | Novels.
Classification: LCC PS3569.T687 B55 2024 | DDC 813/.54—dc23/
eng/20240712
LC record available at https://lccn.loc.gov/2024031158

Interior design by Janine Agro

Printed in the United States

10 9 8 7 6 5 4 3 2 1

BIG
BREATH
IN

PROLOGUE

Several years ago, just before the last presidential election and before the Portland homeless riots, a group of jurors walked out of a well-heated federal courtroom in Seattle after convicting a defendant of murder, kidnapping and child trafficking. The small squadron of cops and social workers soon moved on to other complicated disasters, but the *Seattle Times* ran a profile, both in print and online, of the "scientist gumshoe" who had been instrumental in the case. The scientist gumshoe, they said, had broken up a small child-trafficking ring and was one of the few private investigators to have aided law enforcement since the dubious contribution of the Pinkertons during the labor wars of the 1920s. The profile outlined her career working out of Sitka, Alaska alongside her late husband, a writer and investigator himself. Just above the fold in an article featuring a color photo with her and her husband, the paper noted that she was more unique and adventurous than the fictional characters her husband had created. Even in a cynical age, the paper also noted, she had "gone against type and had done her civic duty to a T."

People who knew Delphine laughed at the characterization. It would have made Delphine laugh as well if she had read it, which of course she couldn't.

CHAPTER ONE

It was another day with a follow-up appointment. Delphine worked on her transfer memos in the morning. She wrote on an ironing board at the foot of her bed in the hotel room where she had been living across the street from the Seattle Hospital. She had not been home to Alaska for five months. Her doctor appointments and infusions came often enough it wasn't worth traveling back. Insurance did not pay for her flights, but it helped her cover the expense of the hotel. After the second month of treatment, she decided to write the memos for her students and colleagues, to conclude the story of her research.

Delphine intended for the memos to sound like a cross between a formal scientific paper and a well-researched article for a popular journal. Not a personal memoir. There would be no graphs or tables. There would be nothing about cancer or grief. She wanted her words to have the voice of mature curiosity, which turned out to be a difficult tone to maintain. She had written two memos already, one for the humpback whales and one for the killer whales, but the memo that kept drawing her mind off into the shadowy gloom of her imagination was the one concerning the myriad unanswered questions about the sperm whales. She had been trying to develop a common thread, but she was still struggling with the thought she wanted to convey.

How do animals with large brain mass and a high degree of dexterity within their dynamic environment develop strategies for getting what they want: food, breeding opportunities, safety? She split the question into two parts—how could large-brained animals gain things they wanted, like feeding or breeding strategy, and how could they avoid the things they didn't want, like predators or having cancer (there it was again) or having a dead partner at the time when she needed him most.

Delphine was not happy with her efforts so far. Diving into the murky waters of judging another creature's intelligence tempted her scientist's mind toward solipsism. By the time she finished her fifth draft of the sperm whale memo and walked to her follow-up appointment, she had decided she wanted to stick with what she had seen, photographed and gathered in her forty years of research. There was plenty there to consider.

Outside, it was early summer, and songbirds fluttered in the plantings around the hospital. Through the open window of the examination room, she could barely make out the scent of Puget Sound, while the constant traffic thrummed from the freeway and cars honked intersections to life. A car alarm blared, and a child somewhere was crying at the top of their lungs. The crying should have been distressing but it wasn't. In fact, the small calamity sounded as if it were drifting away on a balloon.

The paper on the padded examination table crackled underneath her butt. She tried to focus on the sounds outside of the window rather than the young doctor in front of her. She had grown up here, but now Seattle had the soundscape of a big city that had forgotten where and what it was. She was listening to learn this new place. The city swirled with cultural indicators of the times, like printed signs exhorting people to SUSPEND THE CONSTITUTION AND REINSTATE THE PRESIDENT. One billboard near the international district suggested that GOD IS MY PRESIDENT. The cultural divide was laid out in the blurred swirl of hand-drawn graffiti: JAIL ALL DEMOCRATS and EAT THE RICH. Other graffiti proclaimed gang names or suggested that poverty was the open door to anarchy.

"All right, big breath in now, that's a good girl," the young doctor said in his mannerly way. He had big teeth and clean fingernails.

In her three years of undergoing treatment, Delphine had never ceased to be amazed at how condescending young doctors could be. She was sixty-eight years old and almost every visit bespoke some sense of superiority, as if underneath it all, these circumstances were her fault. The nurses were almost always kind, but the young doctors made her feel guilty, leaving her mind to reel after each appointment.

Delphine had been a gatherer of data. She loved photographing animals out on the ocean, taking notes and making observations. She loved pushing her yellow skiff along the wake of a diving whale to photograph the flukes of the big animals. She had so much more work to do, more photographs to take, more data to go through, more students to foster toward their own research. She couldn't stand ruminating about her own illness.

"You have some more congestion, dear. Have you told Dr. Walters?"

"I will be sure to mention it to Dr. Walters, darling," she said in her most kind, sarcastic voice.

Delphine didn't offer up any other sort of answer because she didn't really believe the young man was listening. That and she couldn't stand the assumption that she was his "dear." Clearly, he wanted to transfer his concern to his boss so he would not be expected to do anything substantial. Most young doctors never really want to stick their tidy heads up out of the foxhole. He checked the nursing notes about when and how much medication she had been given. He could always push blame downhill onto the nurses. He wished the grumpy old woman no ill will, but these were difficult times and the hospital administrators needed her spot on the schedule.

Delphine stopped studying the young doctor. More than a thousand miles away in the North Pacific, a group of male sperm whales lay at the surface breathing, expelling carbon dioxide and taking in oxygen, watching the ocean below them, hoping to take more black cod off a fisherman's longline. Sitting on the rolled-out paper of the examination table, Delphine swam with them.

She had little respect for people who thought that sperm whales were the smartest creatures on earth—and yes, there were many who thought that sperm whales were spiritually enhanced animals. "How could we possibly know the specifics of their vast superiority," she had asked her students, "before we even know the basics of how they live, feed and navigate on this planet?"

Delphine had her gnawing doubts about human beings' capability to judge the huge mammal's intellectual supremacy. Here was a whale that made the entire basin of the Pacific Ocean its home. Males wandered the upper northern latitudes while females and calves stayed in equatorial waters. They clearly had a social dynamic. Yet humans knew less about sperm whales than they did about most other charismatic megafauna. Humpback whales were endlessly studied and photographed, and killer whales were considered demigods for their language, distinct DNA types and complex social dynamics. What made these animals almost magical to human beings, who were both humbled by the whales and tainted with the guilt of their own ignorance?

What fascinated her about marine mammals was their mystery. This was the purpose of her transfer memos to her students and colleagues: to convey what we don't know and couldn't know, and, perhaps most importantly, what wasn't worth trying to figure out. What she loved about her life was the sensation that discovery is an unending relay race of research.

It bothered her a great deal that most young students wanted to know more than anything—what is it really like to *be* a sperm whale, a mountain gorilla or a wolf? Many of them did not enjoy the hard work of trying to understand the creatures that held sway over them.

Delphine blamed the books that were so widely published for this lack of motivation: science fiction, nature mysticism, tales of the downfall of big dumb men. Students often wanted to know not just what sperm whales were thinking but what they were *trying to say* to us. They wanted to know what some thinkers call an animal's umwelt, their worldview. But sperm whales are so sensationally distant from our own experience. We hardly know what they do, the specifics of their sociality, mating, feeding or even the mortal danger they are in because of changing climate. They have been largely unobserved, obscured by their distance out to sea but also by the great depths of their world. To spend time worrying about sperm whales' umwelt is akin to planning a conversation with a space alien before you know that one actually exists.

Most idealistic young students who wanted a picture of a sperm whale's umwelt had an almost visceral disdain for understanding human beings. Being treated by modern American medicine did little to change Delphine's mind about humanity's ability to empathize. The entire institution seemed to be absorbed with its own self-perpetuated hierarchy of prestige. "I did such a good job with your surgery," the young female surgeon said right before admitting that Delphine's condition, *unfortunately*, was only going to get worse and worse. "It's lucky that your kind of cancer is relatively slow. You should have more life left to live than expected, even though the surgery wasn't effective."

Delphine thought about this as the young doctor continued reading her chart, as she considered the neighborhood around the hospital where she was living. The little hilltop community reminded her of a tide pool: dynamic and blossoming with the energy of feeders and prey. Wafting through it all were the doctors in their tunicate white coats carrying tall coffee cups, oblivious or at least hardened to the sickness around them, patients clutching on to paperwork, and now, more and more

homeless people drifting like large ungulates across the grasslands of the human-built plains. She had come to know several
homeless people during the last five months. She had tried to
buy them food rather than giving them cash. There was the
man who ate her leftover pizza nearly every night. He was
shockingly thin. There was the young couple who argued on
street corners and outside of bodegas along Madison. The
woman always seemed to be holding a different pink- or blue-
clad baby.

The young doctor left the room without explanation. Delphine remained on the examining table with her shoulders
slumped. Her mind again wandered to the northern basin of
the Pacific Ocean. She imagined sounds of whales, the hissing
of deep ocean background noise.

John, her husband of some forty years, was dead now. They
had both started out in criminal investigations; he had been a
criminal defense investigator for more than three decades until
he started writing books. John had no real expertise in any one
thing, but he had known a little bit about a million different
subjects. If you needed to know the basics of the Reid tech-
nique police used to interrogate suspects, or the effects of flame
on teeth in an arson fatality, he was your man. His one great
talent was in talking to almost anyone. He loved conversation,
particularly conversation with dangerous people. John knew
how to find things, and she missed him now like a person
buried underground misses oxygen.

They had lived most of their lives together in small
houses, some not much larger than the examination room
she was currently in. After spending the winter of 1984 in a

twelve-by-sixteen cabin where they had set out to study radio-collared Canada geese, Delphine ended up devoting her life to the study of big animals instead. When Delphine and John had arrived at the cabin on Thanksgiving, there were more than one hundred whales in the surrounding inlet. At that time, the thinking in the scientific community was that hump-backs were gone from Alaskan waters by late November. But everywhere they looked in the cove, whales blew their spouts. It was like a sprinkler system had been left on after a harvest. What were these animals doing here? When Delphine's reports began making the rounds, requests for information flooded her radio set. She began photographing the whales and identifying the patterns on the underside of their flukes. She and John never found any of the radio-collared geese, which turned out to be overwintering far up the estuary of the large creeks, so far from salt water that the radio receiver Del-phine carried in their little tin skiff never detected a single signal from their tags.

During the spring and summer of the whale years in Sey-mour Canal, Delphine and John worked on criminal defense cases together: rape, murder. They were hired by lawyers who were assigned cases conflicted out by the Public Defender Agency. At that time, there weren't many experienced inves-tigators available in Alaska. All it took was two not guilty verdicts to give them all the experience they needed. One lawyer was quoted as saying, "I don't want ex-cops. I want smart and curious thinkers who can help me tell the true story of my client's innocence. The evidence of innocence is usually the first casualty of police investigations. Once guilt is assumed, there is little else the cops need to investigate." John and Delphine kept looking for the evidence of innocence or considerable doubt right up to the end of trial.

The next winter, one year after their hunt for radio-collared geese, Delphine and John went to the Marine Mammal Conference in San Francisco and found that the leaders in the field were mostly old men. Apparently young women had nothing to say about large charismatic megafauna. The old boys acted as though the animals they studied were in fact men themselves. Hunting strategy, social hierarchy—male behavior was the order of the day. One paper presented by the most influential professor posited that toothed whales generated a powerful enough sound from their bulbous melons to injure other males or even kill them. Apparently, this possibility was discovered in meetings that started when a bottle of whiskey was broken open after a day out on the research vessel. This hypothesis was quickly named the "Saturday Night Special Effect."

"Jesus," Delphine had said at the time, "there are a whole lot of male hormones in here."

The worst part was that when they talked to the new Alaskan researchers, the old boys most often ended up talking with John.

"You know I love you," she told him back in the hotel room, "but sometimes I think you have a big floppy mouth and you talk about stuff you are completely ignorant about." John agreed, but they both realized that it wasn't really John's fault because it was his one great talent, talking with men who often weren't aware of their mistakes. But it left Delphine feeling excluded.

That night, in the cheap Tenderloin hotel, they split D and J Investigations in half. Just like that, Delphine gave up her life of crime, and John doubled down on proving up innocence.

Alaska in the seventies was a good place to forge your own odd and specific career. John worked on big murder cases all over the state. He had a reputation for knowing the docks and the fishing business, the boats and the people who worked on them. When an Exxon skipper was charged with the felony of being under the influence of alcohol after his ship grounded in Prince William Sound, the captain's legal team hired John for their defense case. He was found not guilty, and John was offered a staff investigator job with the Public Defender Agency.

Once she went off on her own as the head of the science division of their partnership, Delphine got a staff position as a marine mammal biologist for Glacier Bay National Park. She worked almost every second of every day on various marine mammal issues: interaction with cruise ships, entanglements in commercial fishing gear, population dynamics. Over time, she had accumulated one of the largest databases of sightings on the West Coast. She was the lead investigator for dozens of peer-reviewed national and international publications. She spoke to audiences in Europe, Japan and Australia. She became pregnant in the late eighties and received a master's degree from the University of Alaska in Fairbanks. If anything, her pregnancy and subsequent son motivated her to better organize her time and focus her energy. She chose not to pursue a PhD because she wanted to continue going out on the water and actually working with the big animals directly rather than becoming mired in the swamp of academia. She mentored women in the fields of study that included the life of female animals: gestation, birth intervals, nutritional needs for birthing and feeding calves. It was true that John could be a fathead, but Delphine taught him as much as she could about gathering data and about the rigorous scientific method that loved particularity and deplored contradiction. They had spent hours discussing cases until the dark hole of John's death separated them. And now he was gone and their son was grown with children of his own. Now she had cancer and she was alone on the creased paper of a padded examining table.

When the young doctor didn't return, Delphine put her clothes on. She checked with the receptionist in the waiting room and asked about her next appointment. They kept her there for ten minutes because the doctor had not yet recorded his notes for the visit. Finally, they reached him on his mobile phone. He said he had been called on a "consult" for an emergency patient and that he would make his recommendation later in the day.

"We will call you as soon as we know," the nurse said. "You will be available, I assume?"

"Yes." Delphine packed her planner into the large leather bag she carried, which was full of her medication and a smaller computer she used for her emails and notes.

"Can you give me your number again? I don't want to risk losing your info," the nurse said without looking up into Delphine's eyes.

Once done, she walked down the labyrinthine hallways to find the elevator that would take her to the south side, floor four. The hospital was built on a hillside and the numbering system of the floors had to be memorized. The fourth floor took her past surgery and out into the open air.

She liked the Baranof Hotel just because it reminded her of Alaska. Alexander Baranof had been the Russian manager of the early territory of Alaska. He had created wealth out of sea otter furs and started the first natural resource boom-bust economy in the territory: fur, gold, then oil. There was a time when salmon held the place of oil, gold and fur, but the Alaskan salmon industry was in decline. People weren't buying salmon as much as they had, particularly as sea conditions and climate change drove the price up at the dock. No amount of protesting or awareness campaigning could shift the balance of power in a state virtually owned by big oil.

When Delphine crossed over to her hotel, she saw the couple with the blue- and pink-clad children. Once again, they were arguing.

"Shut the fuck up," the man said as the woman jostled a little boy to try to get him to stop crying.

Delphine opened the old brass doors to the hotel. "He doesn't understand when you talk to him that way," the woman said. She looked exhausted. "And I don't appreciate it either. Now let's get him to the hospital."

As the doors swung closed, and their voices faded into the hush of the Baranof, Delphine heard the man say, "This is bullshit . . . I can't afford . . ."

Then Delphine was in the elevator.

The Baranof was a hot, musty time capsule. The staff worked hard, trying their best to keep it clean, but there was no way around the fact that its best days were far in the past. There were old wardrobes that were first banged together around the time of the Second World War, and hot water heat of the same period. Instead of investing in a makeover, the hospitality company simply embraced the "vintage" style, which many of the older patients seemed to enjoy. The suite kitchenettes had three clean glasses each, mismatched dinnerware and toaster ovens filled with crumbs. It was like living in the annex of a thrift store.

Delphine opened the windows, letting the smells and sounds in. Her room was on the sixth floor. She spent most of her time working on her computers, reading reports and composing her transfer memos. She had set up a little command center in the bedroom of her suite and her phone and computers on an ironing board at the foot of the bed so they could be plugged into the snaky extension cord that was in turn plugged into her travel battery system to avoid the damage from the frequent power outages. She mostly kept the TV off unless the Dodgers or the Mariners were on, in which case she watched the games with the sound low. She wanted to hear the crack of the bat.

Her son, Bertie, had left Alaska after graduating from Whitman College in Washington. He and his wife moved to California. Growing up in Alaska, Bertie hadn't ever followed a sports team, but once out of college he had fallen in love with baseball. After each Dodgers game, Bertie would almost always call his mother and they would go over the game.

Bertie had given up asking his mom to move to Monterey to be near his family—her grandson, Reggie, was just now turning four and entering preschool—and the best hospitals around Palo Alto. Delphine decided to stay in the same old hotel where she and John had so often stayed. After Delphine was diagnosed with cancer, she preferred to be away from Sitka. Sitka had only fifteen miles of main road. John had died on the only road from downtown to their house. There was no avoiding it. So she buried herself in her work at the Baranof Hotel, in Seattle.

Before setting up her computer notebook, Delphine flopped back on her bed and closed her eyes. In her transfer memo, she had been trying to spell out a research program for studying sperm whale behavior in the future, when she would be gone.

Delphine then worked for an hour and a half on what was essentially a materials wish list. She had done most of her research out of small boats based in the port of Sitka, close to the continental shelf. Sperm whales in southeastern Alaska, almost always males, had been observed near the black cod fishing grounds adjacent to the shelf. This drop-off to the deep ocean was where fishermen liked to place their longline gear, which was sometimes a mile long and laced with hundreds of baited hooks. The fishermen would lay their lines and let them "soak" on the bottom twenty-four hours before heaving the lines onto their boats and pulling their hooks, some with fish and some without. The boat would jog in and out of gear to hold position while pulling the line. It's been assumed that this underwater noise was what cued the sperm whales back to that location, where they would often hang out on the surface and consume the black cod. The big animals sometimes let the thick groundline run over their gums as they plucked the oily fish directly into their mouths. The fishermen found straightened-out hooks and shredded fish bodies. The bottom jaw of dead sperm whales often showed the marks of these black cod lines.

Here was a tremendous opportunity to actually observe these animals feeding. Delphine wanted more cameras and camouflaged waterproof housings. She wanted to perfect the camouflage, both sonically and visually. These large-toothed whales—while not appearing very sensitive to the fishing boats and their propellers scything through the surface waters, or even to being struck with sampling darts made to take skin and blubber samples—did seem sensitive to the presence of cameras in the water. Was it because of some sound being emitted by the cameras, or was it the return signal from the whales clicking on them? Delphine didn't know.

Unlike sperm whales, orcas and humpback whales are commonly seen from shore. Perhaps this is the reason their figures are so prominent in the cultures of coastal people. The more dynamic orca whale takes the largest place in the lore of Tlingit and Haida people. Orca whales are magnets for storytelling. In storytelling, they take on personalities, perhaps because of their prominent eyes when they surface. Sperm whales seem to be famous in Western lore almost solely because of one New England writer who went to sea in 1839 and wrote about it in his most famous novel. Melville's insight stems from the sperm whale's size and mystery, so much so that their size and mystery became a metaphor for our relationship with God, or perhaps awe itself. The rest of our awareness of sperm whales came to us from the industrial killing of them.

More cameras, more underwater microphones and more ways to hide them, more ships looking for the big-headed beasts were the things Delphine wanted. Knowledge of God was someone else's problem.

AFTER TWO hours, Delphine noticed that she had three missed calls from Tom Foster, a private investigator friend of hers and John's in Seattle. He didn't leave a message but after the third missed call, he sent her a text.

Hey, Del. You still in that fleabag across from the hospital? Don't forget we have a call tomorrow. Got something you might help me out with.

She flipped through her calendar on her phone and there it was. "TF TF" on tomorrow's date. TF was "telephone from" and TF was Tom Foster.

IN NORTHERN waters during the summer, the ocean often has a blue-green cast. From below the surface, during daylight hours, an object has a silver shimmer. Even at three hundred feet there is enough light for a human to see the black cod habitat. Even more clear would be the diaphanous squid shimmering through the sea. At this depth, other bioluminescent creatures distort the water with their movement. Here now are the male sperm whales, which are three to four times larger than the females. At first glance, the males appear to have gigantic heads or maybe huge noses. Sperm whales dive deep and almost directly down to the hunting depth of their prey. Imagine submarines sinking in a tight cluster. They seem to simply know where their food is, either by extraordinary sensory ability or by memory or cultural transmission. Delphine had considered all possibilities but was certain of nothing. She adds to her list more cameras, more ways to observe whales and their prey, hydrophones, sonobuoys, intel from military ocean resources.

When sperm whales dive, they dive close enough to touch each other. Like touch between a human mother and infant, touch between sperm whales seems to be an important means of communication. When males complete their yearly return to the equatorial waters to reunite with females and calves, the males lay close to the surface while the mothers dive for food, allowing themselves to be nudged and caressed by the calves and females they had so long been away from. Though it is suspected that the males vie for dominance for the attention of the females, and like to show off their ability to defeat predators, they also show off for females by demonstrating their ability to accept affectionate touch. Yes, huge males craving affectionate touch seem to be attractive to prospective mates.

They are mammals, and they are tied to the surface by their need to breathe.

Delphine was in that state between dreaming and focused attention when her neighbor, Robert, rattled his keys outside and then let himself into her hotel room. Down below on the sidewalk, the couple with the babies continued to argue about money.

"It's all my money. I'm the one bringing it in, remember." The man's voice repeated his only rhetorical flair. Soon there would be the whoop of a police siren if their behavioral pattern held.

"Delphine?"

Robert stood on the threadbare carpet at the narrow entrance. He was skeleton thin now. He had gone through his last round of chemotherapy and radiation. Delphine suspected that he was about to be "graduated" from the hospital. She and Robert understood that meant he was giving up on therapy and leaving himself to the steady metastatic whims of cancer.

"Here ya go. It's fueled up, and mechanically sound." He flipped a skull keychain with two identical keys toward her but they fell short and wide, landing on the old table in front of her.

"What's this?" she asked.

"I'm giving you my bike. I'm taking off. Jenny is driving across the mountains to pick me up. She should be here soon. I even signed the title over to you. You might want to change the plates but you won't need it to be that legal." Robert walked around the sofa slowly, taking labored steps into the kitchenette, where he grabbed a beer out of the small refrigerator. "I doubt you'll be driving it that much. You can take a few tickets before you are done with it."

"Your bike? You mean your motorcycle? Or have you been pedaling around these hills for exercise and not telling me?"

"Heck no. The Sportster. I'm giving it to you."

Robert reminded her of her brother. He was simple but kind. He was a mechanic from east of the Cascades and planned to die on some land with a cabin near Loomis, Washington. Jenny, his common-law wife, was a fair mechanic herself and always smelled like grease. They had met at a Rainbow Family Gathering some twenty years ago. Delphine had seen the photos of their small herd of dirty young boys and the maybe dozen motorcycles around their cabin. She thought it was cute, how proud Robert was of his cabin, even with all the junk and engines and frames around it. He also seemed proud of his three boys, Gudger, Ned and the youngest, who everyone called "the Vulcan." Jenny had been raised in eastern Washington. She was a rodeo girl until she went off to Washington State and became a collegiate barrel racing champion. She had always been comfortable in tight jeans and spurs, and finally, on motorcycles.

"Come on, doesn't Jenny want the Sportster?"

"Naw . . . she told me to clean out the bikes before I died, and it looks like I almost missed my chance on that. You have your motorcycle ticket, and you always said you liked the yellow tank and fenders. You know it's pretty light and it rides smooth. You will be able to tear up some shit on it."

Delphine got up slowly and hobbled to the kitchen herself. They both seemed like broken down old cowboys, except bald as cue balls. John would have liked Robert, she was sure of that.

"That's kind of you, Robert," she said. "Let me give you some money, you know, for Jenny and the kids." From the photographic evidence, Robert and Jenny's three boys appeared to be feral children. They reminded her of dogs lost on some wild cattle drive. They were dirty and apparently uncircumcised. Again, from the photos it appeared they grew up mostly naked and liked to dance around the fire pits. Wild and home-schooled, with long hair and sweet rascal smiles.

"Give me a hundred bucks and we'll call it a legal sale." Robert took a long pull on his beer.

"It's worth more than that," she said softly.

"Hey, we had some fun riding that thing and you were a good friend to me these last few months."

"Yes," she said. "You are easy to be friends with, Robert. You never got weird."

It was true. She had ridden on the back of the Sportster up and down the hills of Seattle. She had gripped his chest tight at times, but he never did any clumsy hands-on flirting with her. They sat several feet apart on her couch while they watched *Perry Mason* on the crappy hotel TV and listened to the hospital sirens split the night in half, disturbing the cries of the nocturnal homeless prowling the neighborhood for drugs or money, alcohol or the easy touch of a medical tourist who couldn't put up a fight. Robert was good at looking like he had some fight left in him. Delphine also appreciated that about him.

They heard a knock on the door and Jenny entered wearing coveralls and sunglasses. When she walked in, she put the sunglasses in her greying hair and squinted into the gloom of the room. Robert stood up slowly, then walked over to his wife and gave her a kiss. Jenny waved at Delphine over the thin man's shoulder. She cradled his bald head in her right hand. She closed her eyes for a moment, and they rocked in each other's arms, teetering like old trees in a gale. Outside, the near darkness of the late-afternoon sunset was lit by the red and blue flashing lights of a police car and an ambulance pulling through the entrance for official vehicles near the emergency room. Lights clipped the dark like birdsong in the morning. A woman was yelling angrily out on the sidewalk and a dog was barking somewhere.

"Delphine . . ." Jenny said, still holding on to her husband. "You gonna miss this old man pestering you all the time?"

"Yes." Delphine smiled as she tried to stand herself but couldn't get the needed strength.

"Don't bother, baby," Jenny said. She pulled down the top of her coveralls and wrapped the sleeves around her waist. She sat down next to the marine biologist and gave her a long side hug. On the inside of her right forearm, she had a single small tattoo:

GRL

PWR

"Delphine wants to know if you want to take the Sportster home," Robert said quietly.

"Hell no," Jenny said in her gravelly voice. "No room for one. Got the new bed, the fucking oxygen equipment and all the other tubes and shit in the back of the truck." Jenny stroked Delphine's head. "I even brought you my old helmet. Christ . . . I'm not going to ride that old horse around. We got to clean the bike crap up if we're going to sell the place someday."

Delphine recognized this kind of elliptical reference to times ahead, as if there were no death in their future. "We got no time for farting around on a bike with all the chores to be done," Jenny continued, looking fondly at her husband. "If you want another couple of scooters, just come up to the cabin and there will be more for you to ride."

"Maybe I will," Delphine said, participating in the fiction to please Jenny. Although she appreciated Jenny and her road-worn grit, she enjoyed more the absolute honesty she got with Robert: baseball, motorbikes, sunsets over Puget Sound, but no talk of future plans. In their time together, she and Robert only acknowledged the "right this instant."

"The kids okay in Wenatchee?" Robert asked, spitting up a bit of his beer. He was so weak some days that it seemed like breathing, talking and drinking a beer was just too much work.

"I got the little Vulcan with me. He just wasn't going to stay with Leana this time."

The Vulcan, their youngest son, perhaps had some kind of developmental disability that Delphine had never inquired about. He had a hard time reading and had a serious speech impediment. Jenny told Delphine that the condition would resolve itself, but it never seemed to go away. The one time Delphine had met him, she'd thought he had a beautiful smile. Big teeth, bright eyes.

"He's down the hall watching TV," Jenny said.

Delphine felt a chill brought on by the thought of the little boy by himself in a dowdy hotel room filled with medical equipment. A feeling of loneliness swept over her as if a knife had somehow pierced her "here and now" protective covering. She wanted to hold the Vulcan in her arms.

Some big-brained mammals, like sperm whales and elephants, seem to foster a type of matriarchy. Female elephants appear to take care of their young communally. From the moment of its birth, females help the calf stand on its new feet and a herd of aunties stands around the baby in a circle and builds a wall against predators with their broad backsides. Sperm whales take turns holding the calf on their backs or on their flukes while the baby takes its first breaths. An eight-foot wobbly infant delivered in midocean, as helpless as a tiny elephant plopped down on the desert where hyenas can be heard in the distance. Delphine thought of a baby human who cannot lift its head up, who can barely see its mother and likely does not recognize the separation of self and mother for months. This child is vulnerable to predators.

Suddenly, a finch flew past the bars on the windows and flitted into the room. The bird settled on top of the television, breathing hard. It had a flag of red across its head and a dust-colored beak. It did not move at all other than the billowing of its rib cage.

"Why, hello you," Delphine said softly, as if she and the house finch were the only ones in the room.

"That's a brazen little bugger," Robert said. Delphine pushed herself up off the couch using the wobbly bedside table. She smiled at Robert, then walked over and got a saltine cracker from a waxed paper sleeve. She set the cracker on the edge of the TV.

"That's a brown finch," she said. "They usually show up here in late summer. The first of July seems a little early."

"Maybe he's from the future," Robert said.

"Maybe," Delphine said again, looking at the bird. "How long you gonna be around before you go?"

"You talking to us or the bird?" Jenny laughed.

"I'm gonna miss you guys," is all Delphine said.

THE PARTY broke up soon after it was established that Jenny and Robert were going to stay a couple of days while they got all the medical equipment together and packed it into the back of the Ford truck. The brown finch was still at the cracker as the gathering ended with hugs and reassurances.

"You want me to bring you some dinner?" Jenny asked.

"No thanks. I've got some glop in a can to eat."

"That don't sound good," Jenny said. "I can heat you up some soup or run out and get a pizza from the corner."

"Aw, thanks so much. I'm good. Food is different now."

It was true, food had lost its sensual appeal. She never felt hungry, so eating was more a joyless chore of chewing and swallowing followed by a crampy kind of digestion. Aroma, no matter if it was fresh bread out of the oven or a pan-seared steak, was nothing more than the outrider of sickness.

Jenny stood in the doorway holding Robert's hand. "Yeah, I understand," she said.

Then the door was closed, and Delphine went back into the sitting room after a side trip to get another cracker. She whistled softly and stared into the pooling sinkholes of the finch's eyes.

She gave him the cracker and as she turned to sit down again, the finch fluttered back out the window.

She reached for her phone. She wanted to call John and tell him about the finch.

But of course, she couldn't.

Out on the street she heard gunshots. Three of them. A man's voice yelled out, "Yo, fucker, I see you!" There was silence for maybe three minutes, then the high-pitched whoop of a siren, then the crackle of an emergency radio transmission.

The room felt emptier than ever before. Delphine watched

the open window where the brown finch had flown out. Just out the window in the world of the little brown bird existed the soundscape of sirens, cars chugging on the freeway and people threatening each other on the corner below. Three more gunshots blasted the air in succession. Thinking of the bird, Delphine winced and balled her fists by her side.

"Shit, man. That's too close," one of the arguing voices on the street yelled.

Delphine used her walker to totter to the bathroom, which was too small for the walker. She stripped off her clothes while sitting on the toilet lid.

"Fucking people," she said to herself. Her body felt shrunken and hard. Her once-large breasts hung like pendants on her chest. She rested for a few minutes before she turned on the water and watched the rust clear through the old pipes.

The only time she really liked her female body was in the wake of giving birth to Bertie. He was just a growing, bumping thing in her belly for months, but then he was there: a squirmy, toothless mammal in her arms. *Hello there.* He took to breast-feeding almost immediately. The world pressed around them both and she was completely happy. She had John and Nita Couchman to help her, Mark and Nancy, Bob and Barbara, and Richard Nelson, the nature writer who claimed that human beings should no longer breed out of environmental concerns. But Nels was by Delphine's bed that first afternoon, as gobsmacked by love as anyone.

John was traveling across Alaska, working cases for the Public Defender Agency. The day Bertie was born he caught a morning flight from Ketchikan to be there for the birth of the little mammal. In the first years, he was gone a lot, but Delphine hauled Bertie in his car seat to Glacier Bay, where she would take him out in her seventeen-foot skiff to monitor humpback whales for the National Park Service. Even out in the world of tidewater glaciers, bears, moose and mountain goats, Bertie and Delphine found love. Nursemaids came, and other Sitkans. The nursemaids were terrific and helped keep everyone's head above water while Delphine took photos of whales arching up and diving.

Delphine loved her body then, still; she had been so physically strong. John adored her body too, and they both loved the sensuality of their lives when Bertie was a baby. Decisions, for some reason, were easier to make. The business of life, food, work, walking in the drippy rainforest and bursting across the water in a small boat was joyous.

Illness and age had robbed her of that. How did that happen? John was gone now but Bertie was still alive, living in Monterey with Camile and their new baby. They spoke every evening on the phone and sometimes they could see each other on their tiny screens. These conversations almost always came with behavioral watersheds: crawling, the eating of solid foods, new teeth, young baby Reggie wobbling and cooing at the image on the phone. Delphine loved the contact, but sometimes felt she was watching her grandchild through the thick glass of a two-person submarine. Contact with a genetic beneficiary really needed the exploration of physical proximity. Without actual touch, her relationship with her grandson felt almost academic.

Delphine had promised she would come down to live with

Bertie and Camile "after I get done with all this," which in the immediate context meant by the end of her treatments. But in specific terms, she had known all along how this situation would resolve. It was terrifying, but her big brain could not do a thing about it.

She was up now, sitting at her makeshift desk, looking at her handwritten notes and unfinished exit memos laid out on the ironing board. She had a breakfast appointment with Tom Foster, John's PI associate from Seattle, tomorrow. He had sent her another text that afternoon.

You have time for me to buy you breakfast? I'm going to ask you a favor and I think you might be more apt to say "yes" if I bought you some pancakes.

Delphine wondered what Tom would think if she rolled up on the yellow Sportster. Tom was smart and funny. She had no idea why he wanted to see her or what she could help him out with. Although she was glad for the appointment, there was a small part of her brain that dreaded what it might be that Tom wanted.

CHAPTER TWO

Delphine and Tom Foster met at an old waterfront café in the public market downhill from the hotel. Tom wore narrow-legged jeans and a T-shirt with a wool sports coat over the top. He carried a small waterproof satchel that appeared to be full of correspondence. Delphine was wearing old wool pants and a T-shirt with a drawing of Albert Einstein in a police-man's uniform saying, "One hundred and eighty-six thousand miles per second isn't just a good idea, IT'S THE LAW!" Tom's T-shirt had the words SPAWN TILL YOU DIE with skeletal salmon bodies across the chest.

Tom and John had met when John was working in Alaska on contract for the public defender. John was investigating a multiple homicide on a commercial fishing boat called *The Investor*, which was ported in Bellingham. In 1982, *The Investor* caught fire and burned almost to the waterline in the village of Craig, Alaska. Eight members of the crew, including the wife and two children of the captain, were missing. Investigators found human remains in the slurry of destruction in the bottom of the fifty-two-foot boat. Two years later, the state troopers arrested a former crewman on eight counts of murder in the first degree and one count of arson. John was brought into the case after the first trial ended in a hung jury and the crewman was retried. The case required investigation in every port where salmon fishermen were found, which was virtually every coastal fishing town in Washington, Canada and Alaska. John had hired Tom to help him. Her late husband couldn't be in two places at once, let alone several dozen.

Tom was a good investigator, smart and ethical, great at finding people and good at talking with the people he found. They had become friends, and Tom had called and written from time to time, though it had been years since she'd seen him. It surprised Delphine when Tom asked to meet her for brunch.

"How ya doing, doll?"

One of the things John liked about Tom Foster was his tendency to talk like a character in a Mickey Spillane novel. One of the things that John liked about Delphine was her ability to play along with the patter.

"Tell the truth, I've been better. I've got this damn cancer and I miss John like an amputated limb."

"Ah yeah, I miss him too, baby. Somebody like him been through so much ends up getting splattered on the road while pedaling his bicycle home from work. They ever convict that drunken mook who ran him down?"

"Yeah, but it doesn't make that much difference to me, you know . . . fucking people."

Tom squinted his grey eyes over the lip of his coffee cup. "Closure?"

"Naw . . ." Delphine waved the whole subject away as if she were flicking at flies circling her head. "How's your life, T?"

"Work, baby, nothing but work. I got a case down here that's driving me bonkers."

"How so?"

"It's a nothing case but I'm having trouble with getting people to open up to me."

"Tell me about it." She settled back in her padded booth. She missed John now more than ever, and his easy way of talking with difficult people.

"A lady in San Francisco gave up her infant for adoption to a sketchy outfit and now she has hired a lawyer to get the baby back. Lawyer hires me to find just exactly where the kid is. But this turned out not to be as easy as anyone thought. He was a newborn when she gave him up to this guy from the outfit. Hard to get an ID on someone that young, so I need someone to tell me that this baby, not someone else's baby, is the child of the woman from San Francisco. It's frustrating because the child is too young to offer up his origins and most of the other women that surround this guy are foreign nationals. Even if they did speak English, they wouldn't say a word against this guy who handles the adoptions. I get the idea that he's some kinda small-time gangster. Pain in my ass."

Tom pulled out a photograph and slid it across the formica. It showed a young man with greasy black hair and a stupid expression. "This photo comes from the file and it's more than a year old. I think the birth mother took it but I don't even know that."

"I know this guy . . . or at least I've seen him on the street," Delphine said. "He talks tough to the women who hang out with him."

Tom sat up military-cadet straight. "You've *seen* him?"

"Yeah. It seems like he's always headed to the emergency room with a baby or a sad-looking woman."

"You sure it's him?"

"Well, Tom, you know about me and certainty. But yeah . . . I've seen him."

"Wow," Tom said, "that's a big bonus."

The waitress brought her two pieces of dry toast and a Belgian waffle for Tom.

"Delphine, come on, work on this for me. I'll pay you good. Take your mind off things."

Truth be told, Tom had plenty of other better-paying cases to take care of. It would be fine to dump a nothing case like this toward Delphine. She knew enough about him not to be surprised that he would want to pawn it off onto her.

"I've got too much cancer to do."

"Come on, you won't have to miss a doctor's appointment. Probably just take a couple of days. Follow him to where he lives, talk to the women he hangs with and ask about the whereabouts of this kid. Name's Tyler Dearborn." He flapped down his phone and showed her an unconscionably adorable photo of a little baby. "The problem is, this is an old photo. The baby boy is about fifteen months old right now."

Delphine fingered her toast. A moment later, she was surprised to hear herself say, "Yeah sure, I'll do what I can." And with just those few words, she was back in the crime business.

WHEN THINKING of sperm whale behavior, it is best to consider two distinct creatures: male and female. The males, nearly four times as massive as the females, live almost completely separated from the females. Males feed, travel great distances and work at the difficult logistics of breeding. People who have observed humpback whales breeding describe the ritual as a "ballet," and the photographs seem to back up that word choice. Humpbacks, with their long pectoral fins, are very flexible in positioning their bodies. Calves are often seen rolling in kelp as if they enjoy the sensuality of it. Or perhaps they roll in kelp to clean their skin, which appears to flake off during some seasons. Of course, we don't know what goes on in their minds.

While sperm whale penises seem huge to a human, they are small in relation to the whale's body. Consider the challenge of living in the immense dark room of an ocean basin, and one of your most prominent urges is to snake that fire hose of a relatively small penis into the one tight hole of a female several thousand miles away. Then add to the task the fact that sperm whales cannot maneuver their bodies with much subtlety due to their short pectoral fins. Now, instead of a ballet, you might have a mosh pit—a ramming session. This might explain why females and males stay separated during most of the year.

LATER THAT night, when Delphine tried to unpack the reasons she agreed to Tom's offer, she determined that money was a small part of it, because she could use a little more dough, and sinking into a case would definitely take her mind off the cancer and the unctuous doctors—but mostly she thought it would make her feel closer to John. Together, they had worked every criminal case to the point of forgetting about almost everything else. Before they parted ways professionally, the world outside the facts of the case would melt away while they sat reading over files. Perhaps if she worked even a nothing case, finding a baby, she could feel John there beside her. Working on a case would almost be like being together again. She could imagine what John would say. John had always told her when looking for a single person you are not looking for the person themself, but for the person who would tell you where the subject of the hunt is. This is especially true the younger the subject is. John would say that a baby is a difficult find, because the subject does not generate any information on their own, and in a disputed baby case, all the adults could be counted on to lie.

By the time she had bathed, Delphine was exhausted. She put on her robe and lay on top of her bed feeling as if she might dissolve into the mattress. She found the motorcycle keys and held them in her right hand. She kept her eyes closed and imagined what she would do with them. Having mobility like this would certainly help her track down facts in her new "nothing" case. She would need to ride around the haunted neighborhood of First Hill and the International District looking for the greasy-haired man, Tyler Dearborn. She might need the motorcycle to run to the courthouse and look up court records.

Delphine had ridden motorcycles since she was a child. Louie Morrison, her father, had built them and kept them running. He liked riding his old BSA on logging roads up near Stevens Pass. The old Beezers were one-cylinder two-strokes, which made a good deal of noise but produced a lot of torque in any gear. Her father's people were from the French Alps though he was born in the United States and had grown up in Seattle near Green Lake, back when Green Lake was "in the country." Louie and his cousin William came up together like brothers. William was wild and adventurous, always starting speculative businesses, while Louie considered himself the levelheaded one. William raced cars and boats, went to Alaska fishing and owned a sail-making loft down in Union Bay. Louie maintained cars, trucks and a bowling alley until he became a mechanic for a bottling company. Louie worked, clocked hours, took good care of his stuff. William pieced his stuff together so he could get on to his new adventure. Louie served in the navy during World War II. William fished in Alaska. William married an artist who loved skiing and boats. Louie married Ida, who loved to gamble, bowl and cook big meals.

Delphine loved the world of the northwest. She loved the animals. Her parents had their own fish camp out on the Olympic Peninsula on Neah Bay. They put up fish and played in the sand for two weeks every summer. She loved catching fish and loved gutting them even more. Her father made her learn to tune up an outboard motor. To her, the entire project was a wonder.

None of the four kids could drive a car unless they could do all the regular oil changes and liquid checks on the family cars. Her older sister didn't do maintenance or repairs, but Delphine did. In exchange for her mechanic skills, her older sister had to drive Delphine around after school. She worked babysitting, doing chores for her sisters and brother. She worked at a root beer stand, delivering food on trays to the parked cars. She distinguished herself by once pouring an entire root beer float on the lap of a customer who refused to roll his window down far enough.

Growing up, Delphine never had a boyfriend. There was a little boy in third grade that she would chase on the playground who she called "Butterfingers." She had girl friends who were like her, smart and sarcastic, but she never felt any more romantic toward them than she had toward Butterfingers.

When Delphine got into a community college near Lake City where she had grown up, her parents did not approve. Louie didn't approve because he had never gone, and Ida did not approve because it didn't fit her worldview. Girls were supposed to grow up to be married and raise children and share in the duties of big meals. Men were supposed to work for Boeing.

But Louie bought her a red Honda 90 so she would have cheap transportation to class. They often rode together on the forest service roads above Skykomish. For most of her teenage years, the air smelled of rain, pitch from cut trees and gasoline spilled on wool coats.

After she got all her requirements done, she went to the University of Washington, where she got a degree in wildlife science from the school of fisheries. Her first professional job was as a wilderness ranger in the Pasayten Wilderness area.

The year she met John in the woods was the year William died. He had taken a small boat off Lituya Bay in southeastern Alaska with a smelt fisherman. The venture sounded exciting. But their boat was caught in big water and was pulled under by the waves and current in the narrow entrance to the bay.

Their entire family awaited news of William, and when Louie finally got the word that his cousin was lost at sea, he turned a sad face to the world. The cautious one felt he had let his reckless cousin down.

Louie did not drink and he did not play cards with Ida from then on. He bought a woody patch of ground out in Duval and spent most of the rest of his life fixing motorcycles he did not ride and splitting wood for his stove, which he sat in front of for days at a time, petting his dog and smoking cigarettes. Soon Delphine's mom started drinking on the sly and sank into her own depression because Louie didn't want to have fun anymore.

SPERM WHALES are creatures of the deep ocean. Their food is often two to five thousand meters below the surface. We know of their social interactions that occur close to the surface, but little about what happens beyond the rare pictures of them we are able to see with our own eyes. What we know of their behavior in the deep is mostly what we piece together with sonar depth finders, hydrophones and our imaginations. We need more data to say anything with certainty. We know that the deep ocean is remarkably dynamic, with many forces at work: depth, currents, temperatures, daylight changes, moon-light changes, densities of prey, the amounts of oxygen that gather in the prey at specific depths (as the ocean warms, it appears that oxygen condenses farther down the water column, which spells a critical danger if prey species range out of their biological niche), wind on the surface and wave action as well as the chemical composition of the water itself.

If reproduction is paramount to species survival, the differences between a male and a female sperm whale make it almost miraculous that breeding occurs. Their size, temperament and chosen habitat are vastly distant from each other; a male ranges almost to the arctic waters and a female ranges shorter distances but usually closer to the equator. There were likely just over a million sperm whales before the massive die-off caused by modern commercial whaling, so by the time of the whaling moratorium in 1971 there were an estimated three hundred thousand animals in the world's oceans, and their population is still growing. There is a critical need to understand this recovery. There is no guarantee what a terminal population will be. To answer this question requires a shared effort among researchers worldwide. The size of the population, just how lonely or crowded the ocean is, affects behavioral patterns tremendously.

Today, our population estimates are based on gross numbers from scattered sightings. The statistical extrapolations from catch-and-release estimates (with photographs of flukes and the back ridge as the animal is on the surface acting as a "catch") are important to management and research communities, but nothing is better for understanding both population and behavior than actual observational effort.

The first step in solving any mystery is to imagine the setting and movement of the principals. Then, to go out into the world and intercept your actors in the wild. Sperm whales locate themselves in three dimensions: the two dimensions as represented on a chart, and then at depth, since their potential habitat is the entire ocean basin.

How do they locate themselves? First, consider the tools that we know of. They have vision, but having eyes set so far apart on each side of an enormous head must pose severe limitations for navigation. They must have awareness of pressure on their bodies in order for them to understand depth. But while pressure squeezing their bulk would give them a good feeling of the depth of a dive, it would not help in lateral movements at the same depths. They are probably aware of water temperature and light penetration, and perhaps even made aware of salinity or other properties via touch on their skin or taste on their tongue. But still, how do they navigate in a huge ocean basin?

They do have their natural sonar. Most of their big skull structure is made up of a kind of sonic apparatus for emitting sound and retrieving it.

First, they can generate sound, like a sonar ping, and when it returns to them they apparently can calculate or simply know the distance from their head to the structure the ping bounced off of. The outgoing sound is generated from the front of the head, where air passes between two very thick muscles called the "monkey lips." This sound then travels from the lips, which might be thought of as an instrument's mouthpiece, to the stern end of the whale, bouncing off the hard structure in front of the skull and then through the spongy oil-soaked structure, which apparently shapes the sound, to a kind of muscular lens that focuses the sound and directs it. Sperm whales can make clicks and clangs. Clicks can be directed toward prey and clangs can be shouted out at a greater distance. The clang of a sperm whale is the loudest sound generated by any animal on earth. At 174 decibels, it is about the same energy as a thunderclap experienced directly at the source, or the explosion of the volcano Krakatoa from one hundred miles away.

It is known that blue whales can generate sounds in the deep ocean that can carry along deep-water strata for hundreds of miles. It's almost certain that sperm whales also generate long-frequency, low-register sounds at great distances aided by the chemical makeup of deep water while, more amazingly, they can generate the higher-pitched clicks and blast them through the entirety of the water column for at least five kilometers. Whales have been observed in two locations miles apart responding to each other's noises.

They also generate sounds that bounce off other animals or the bottom of the ocean, and by processing the sounds as they "bounce back," the sperm whale can sense or calculate their distance from the object. They receive the echo-like clicks on their return trip through channels of acoustic fat that lead to an internal ear.

It is possible that the entire process of perception is more wrapped up in the proximity of the organs inside this huge head than it is for humans. Humans "see" through their eyes and these impulses are translated by the brain. So too our hearing, balance and relationship to the horizon begin in our ear structure, and signals are transmitted to the brain to formulate a kind of understanding. Is it possible that sperm whales locate themselves in the ocean using this sonar system as well as a system of physical reactions we don't fully understand yet? Perhaps the sperm whale and the dolphin don't have the issue of subject-object duality that humans appear to have.

People sense and then know in the lapse of a microsecond. Perhaps the great whales know immediately. Perhaps the odontocetes (toothed marine mammals) are so much a part of their environment that they live in a moment of "is" the way two human lovers sense each other when lying next to each other.

It's tempting for human beings to think of whales as a collection of perceptive organs that send all vibrations to the brain to interpret and understand, because this is how humans themselves work. Think of a submarine with sonar, vision ports and pressure sensors that send all these signals to a central computer to print out the information on navigation, depth and location. But perhaps—and again, we don't know, but perhaps—the information flows into the body and the brain, and the animal just feels, or knows, where it is, how deep it is, where its prey is located. Its body itself is simply aware without thinking or analyzing. The whales know in their bodies that they are facing danger, like a sick woman riding a motorcycle in a big city with a lot of hills: fear rides the surface of the streets like a cold wind off the bay.

The big animals dive under a slant of light streaming into the gloom. Emptiness broken by several swimming objects. Visually the space of deep water would seem empty, but in actuality it is filled with clicks and hisses. The whales dive steeply and find the depth rich with feed, dark and clicking, squid flashing past, the pressure of deep water holding every inch of their big bodies like a strong blanket pulled tight. Clicking and feeling the clicks return. Where is the food? Where? The massive stalk of the tail pushing, pushing. The hard fruit of the lungs tight in the chest. Clicking and receiving. Seeing and at the same time not seeing, knowing where the prey is. The hissing of ocean-animal life drawing the big animal into the dark, into the pressure. An eighty-foot male weighing nearly fifty tons, floating hundreds of feet above the bottom. Weightless, knowing itself, knowing the others around itself. Knowing the sea crowded with small bodies clicking back. A complex mind living and working in the water.

DELPHINE WOKE up on the couch. She had the keys to the motorcycle in her right hand. It was four in the morning. There was just a smear of light in the sky. The world was holding its breath, and she wanted to swim out into the last of the night and feel the cool air against her face.

She squeezed the keys and stood up slowly. Robert had let her drive the bike when he was on the back, but she had never ridden it up and down the hills by herself. Once, she and Robert had dumped the Sportster when they had to stop on a steep hill coming up Pike Street. She clambered off and Robert picked it up using his back and his legs. "We're both about as weak as kittens, ain't we? If I can't get this up off the pegs, we might just slap a FOR SALE sign on it and hitchhike back to the hospital." But he got it up, turned it around, and allowed her to clamber on the back. They let it freewheel downhill until they could make a left turn, turn the engine over and come around from the south where the hills weren't that steep.

The Sportster weighed about 530 pounds fueled up. She could probably stand it up if she had to, but she didn't want to risk it. Her arms were thin now and her back was weak. She wore the old Bell helmet without a visor, but put on a pair of her dad's ski goggles to protect her eyes. She had a patched and rumpled jacket that was traffic-cone yellow. She tucked her T-shirt into old canvas pants, which were clown baggy now, and laced her logging boots up tight to give her enough ankle support if she did have to lift the bike.

Delphine really wanted to drive the bike. She wanted to feel its strength energize her body. She wanted to move, to accelerate with the suggestion of weightlessness. She wanted to feel one with the machine. But fear gripped her. What if she couldn't do it? What if weakness was going to define the last portion of her life?

Outside, the shadows in the streets were like pools of water. She smelled the old pizza in the dumpsters. The streetlamps were ringed with an opaque light because the dew point was high enough that the fog would build as the morning temperatures rose. Only when the wind came up would the fog blow off.

She approached the bike and unlocked the chain with some trepidation. It felt as if she were approaching a balky colt on a cold morning. Her wrists and hands felt weak as she grabbed the padded grips, threw her leg over the saddle, then sat on the bike. She turned over the engine with the electric starter: a wheeze and a chugging followed by nothing. She made certain that all the fuel ports were open, she checked for fuel in the tank. She twisted the throttle and tried again and the engine caught fire with the blend of air, gas and spark. A thrill rose up into her chest and sizzled her brain.

She sat astride the seat and let the 1200cc engine thrum. When she wrapped up the accelerator, the bike blared into the damp air. The sound bounced off the buildings and returned to her. She could feel it in her chest. She banged the shifter with her foot to make sure she was in neutral. Her hands were shaking as she gripped the clutch lever. Then, with the heavy toe of her boot, she shifted into first and let the bike freewheel downhill. Then she released the clutch and the engine lurched into life.

Delphine always went too fast on a big bike. The torque curled like a clockwork spring in her back. The engine screamed and echoed. She stopped for all the red lights as she headed south toward Boren. The air smelled of coffee brewing as she let the Sportster off its leash a little bit. An old Black woman was pushing a grocery cart downhill toward the Goodwill store. The cart was heaped high with what could have been rags or dirty baby clothes. She was jaywalking in the crosswalk and Delphine blasted by her like a train.

"Fuck this," the Black woman said.

"Sorry," Delphine said to herself as she rattled past.

The Sportster dipped down toward the International District. At first Delphine's lower back was tight, but as she warmed to the sensation of the bike's gravity and speed, her muscles relaxed and she laughed out loud. The colorful streetlamps stuttered by, and she took the bike down past the train station and into the area around the baseball stadium. Now she was on the flats. She opened it up some more. The bike rattled between her legs. She was doing this. Further south, forklifts crossed the streets with little heed. She swerved around one to avoid a wreck, and the forklift driver gestured with a closed fist to his face.

"Hey, what the hell, lady?" His voice was hoarse.

Her back tire broke free for a moment as she sped up to keep forward momentum. *Keep upright*, she thought. The Sportster felt as if it were going to lie down. She steered into the fall and increased her speed, stood the bike up again and watched the forklift driver become smaller and smaller in her mirror.

When Delphine came to the river, she turned back to the north. She found a freeway entrance and cranked the engine up in the early morning gloom. After a short trip on the freeway, she went down Jackson and toward the International District again. She stopped at a streetlight. Her legs felt weak, and her hands shook a bit. She stood with both feet on the pavement as she idled the engine. Now that she was stopped, her head felt numb from the drugs that clogged her system. She caught her breath, weak but exhilarated. The tank was still full. She blasted down onto the industrial flats by the sports arenas and then sped across the bridge to West Seattle.

It was almost dawn by the time she reached the shore of Puget Sound. The streets of West Seattle that ran parallel to the cobbled shore were empty. She stopped at a beach, shut down the bike and took off her goggles and helmet. Gulls cried their two mournful notes in the dark. The wind felt as if it had blown down from Alaska: cold, salty and pregnant with oceanic life.

Her hands shook as she remembered her old adventures out on the water. Her yellow skiff with the hundred-horse engine bucking the weather. Birds in the air. Seals in the ocean, damp wind combing her hair.

Just as the sun began breaking over the mountains to the east, Delphine kicked the engine over and revved it up. She ran two red lights along West Marginal Way. Drunks teetered out across the road and feral dogs sniffed the bases of phone poles. Red-winged blackbirds whirred in the cattails as she blared farther up the Duwamish River. The smell of gasoline blended with the salt water, and the mingling scents of sour beer and the first burbling of morning coffee escaped into the streets. She loved moving through the various neighborhoods. She loved the speed and the easy balance of banking into the turns. This was the opposite of dying and she drank it in.

Delphine reached First Hill again before the morning traffic began to pour out onto the streets. Medical workers were changing shifts. Tired men and women in comfortable shoes drifted in and out of the building with their identification badges fluttering on lanyards around their necks. Some held coffee cups, some carried overnight bags. Some scattered as the Sportster blared down the street. Some ducked out of the way as if the bike was a bull at Pamplona. By the time she parked at the Baranof Hotel, it was full daylight.

She had a message on her phone from the scheduling nurse telling her that she had an appointment with Dr. Walters, who supervised her treatment. Unlike the young doctors, he treated her with respect. He gave her the impression that he was genuinely interested in things other than the disease that had nestled down into her guts and was killing her. That morning, he weighed her and read the latest reports from the labs. He listened to her lungs and he noted that she was breathing a bit harder than usual and her heart rate was up. After he was done with the examination, he put his stethoscope around his neck and sat at her knees in a small chair. He looked up into her eyes and said, "You are smiling this morning. How are your spirits?"

Delphine was surprised that she had been smiling.

"Remember what we talked about, that this part of the journey all depends on you. You have lived with this disease quite a long time now. You are nearing the end. How do you feel about that? You are tough, I know, but how much fight do you think you have left?"

"I'm not sure, Doctor. I'm beginning to see the light at the end of the tunnel. I'm tired. I'm tired of thinking about myself all the time. Thinking about the cancer inside my body." She thought of Robert and Jenny. It didn't seem that they were getting much good information about his prognosis, as if his doctor just wanted to avoid the subject. "I suppose I want to move on. To tell the truth."

Dr. Walters cleaned his glasses with his handkerchief. "Want to move on as in moving on to whatever comes after this life?"

"No, I'm not so interested in the metaphysical. I mostly want to stop thinking about myself."

"Are you depressed?"

"No . . . really being sick just bores me."

"I understand that," Dr. Walters said, his sad eyes twinkling a little in the dim Seattle sunlight. "Are you suicidal?"

"No. There's too much work, too much planning. I also don't want to seem ungrateful. I had a great time this morning riding a motorcycle."

"Really?" He smiled. "And you're sure you are not suicidal?"

"Positive."

"Let me see." He looked through the files on his computer. "You have your advanced directive all filled out. You won't be brought back to life if they scrape you off the side of the road."

"That's good. But don't worry, I don't want to die in an accident either."

"How do you want to die?"

"I have no idea, really. I would just like to have something to think about before I do."

"Are you still working on those transfer memos?"

"Yes, off and on. But now I'm working on an easy criminal case for an old friend of my husband."

"Crime? You have the energy for that and for writing, and riding a motorcycle? Your work on your memos is valuable enough, it seems to me."

"Maybe so, Doctor."

"Yes . . . maybe so."

"Do you think I need to see you next week?"

"Would you like to?"

Delphine thought about his question for a bit longer than was comfortable. "How about I make an appointment tomorrow after I've given it some thought."

He smiled at her. "I'll put you down in pencil for now."

DELPHINE WENT back to the hotel and took a nap. When she woke up, it was dinnertime. She looked at her calendar and noted that she had an appointment coming up the next day with a young architect who wanted some advice on how to incorporate the ocean environment into his design for a billionaire's house out in the San Juan Islands. He had gotten her name from the credits of a film she had been special advisor to. He sounded young, but the money was good. When she made the appointment initially, she thought she might get a chance to see the house completed, but now she was not so sure.

She ate some liquid food supplement and brushed the taste out of her mouth. After rush hour subsided into the hills, she put on a fireman's coat that she kept stuffed with supplies and went downstairs to the Sportster.

Delphine always carried extra gear with her everywhere she went. Her husband used to say that she put every Boy Scout to shame. That she could make camp wherever she was. She carried knives, twine, a space blanket, extra food, water and now, of course, her own medications. And a sewing kit. When everyone else was flipping through their phones looking for transportation, Delphine was going through her coat pocket getting ready to make camp, or perform some small medical procedure, or simply survive.

The air was warm and dense with the fragrance of restaurant food. Homeless people hovered around First Hill looking to come inside the hospital to scoop up food from trays or pills out of paper cups. Those on the hill, near where the doctors and nurses worked, seemed more desperate to Delphine. Some appeared to be dressed in torn rags: poverty like you might see in India rather than the Pacific Northwest, home of Starbucks and Microsoft. She once saw a dark-skinned man bleeding from a head wound with his torn pants drooping down past his butt cheeks. He had been thrown out of a corner pizzeria. The man lay down near a bodega on Madison Street and pretended to be unconscious, hoping, she thought, to be picked up by an aid car and taken to a hospital. The red brick walls were painted with the words CLOSE THE BORDERS and BLOOD AND SOIL in different handwriting.

Delphine roared down the hill toward the International District. Clouds were coming down to the rooftops. The clouds seemed to reflect the light energy from street level up into the night air. It was as if the old earth of the Pacific Northwest street had a roof over it and the taller buildings spiked up through the ceiling. She imagined the spires, silent and alone, above the clouds.

She turned and went up Jackson Street, acceleration pulling at her arms. Then she ran a stoplight and went downhill into the bowl sloping toward Lake Washington, where stately houses looked like sad jack-o'-lanterns peering down into the brown lake water. Up over the ridge again and down onto Rainier Avenue and back down toward Jackson Square. Delphine could hear music in the street, and she thought of turning toward it.

She was stopped at a red light at an intersection, thinking of the best route back to the hotel, when she saw the man and the woman and the baby on the far corner. It was the same couple and the same baby and she knew that because the child was wearing the same knit cap with the white pom-pom. The man had dark hair and appeared to be the same person in the photo on Tom Foster's phone. The person of interest with the sketchy adoption outfit. Tyler Dearborn. He wore a

Kevlar biker's jacket and a gold chain with an actual bear claw as a pendant. The woman was the same one Delphine had seen on the corner near the emergency room. She wore an old leather jacket with a cotton shirt underneath and a fake leather miniskirt. The couple bickered in soft voices while the baby cried intermittently as if it were just waking up. Delphine watched them cross the street in front of her. They had remarkably white skin, giving them the quality of ghosts in the dark.

"No . . . I can't do this tonight," the woman said. "We're going to bed."

"You got to work," the man said.

"But the baby is hungry. The baby is tired."

Delphine turned away from the conversation, feeling in a weird way that she was intruding. It is important when watching people up close to make sure your subject is not aware of being watched. This approach is also important for snooping on big animals as well.

She then heard two short pops, one with the fleshy wetness of a punch to the face and the other the hard knock of something heavy hitting the curb. She looked back and saw the woman sprawled on the sidewalk. Blood coming from her nose, blood coming from a cut above her eye. Her eyes were closed. The baby screamed. It was still tucked in the sling around the woman's torso.

"Leigh, I'm telling you, you made me do that." The man stood over her. "That's on you."

There was no other traffic on the street. Delphine swung her leg and stumbled off the bike and the Sportster fell over, still running. Before she was even aware of making the decision to do so, she was kneeling next to the bleeding woman. She had a bandanna in her jacket pocket and was using it to put pressure on the head wound.

"Get the fuck away from her," the man said.

"She needs stitches." Delphine didn't look at the guy. She cradled the woman's head in her lap. The woman stirred and Delphine guided her hand up to hold pressure on the wound. Her eyes were open now but unfocused. Delphine took the infant out of the sling.

"Get away from her." Tyler Dearborn took two steps toward her in long strides, then began to swing his right leg back as if to kick Delphine, who reached into her pocket and pivoted her weight onto the knee closest to him.

"J-J-Jesus!" Instantly he was down on the sidewalk writhing in pain. The clicking buzz of Delphine's Vipertek 989 stun gun could be heard down the street beneath the sound of Tyler's moans coupled with the clattering of his teeth. She hit him in the big thigh muscle and gave him another two-second charge. She curled the infant into the folds of her jacket and gave him another two seconds on the ground.

"You bitch!" he screamed. "I'm going to sue your ass off. I'm going to move into your house when this is all over."

Delphine thought for a moment and said, "Get up and walk away. I will take her to the hospital."

"What is your fucking deal?" he asked, his voice carrying the sound of a mean narcissistic whine.

She held her stun gun close to her face to make sure he could see it. "Is this your baby?" Delphine asked.

"What's it to you?"

"I'm just curious is all."

The young woman in the old leather jacket moaned, rocking her head back and forth on the curb. Her fingers were painted red with her own blood. The child looked to be a little more than a year old, an early toddler. Fifteen months, Tom had said. Delphine took all three of them in to make sure that these were the people Tom was interested in. Everything about them, the pimp-hooker aspect of their relationship, the swearing, the easiness of violence, everything indicated that they were her targets.

"You were part of a loyal group of people at one time," she tried. "You had a family of some sort."

"Again . . . it's none of your fucking business." He started to get up. Delphine tapped the switch and the stun gun gave a loud crackle. An evil blue-and-white arc crossed the pegs.

Tyler stopped moving.

"There was a time you were curled up at your mother's side," she said. "Someone held you and fed you."

"Jesus Christ . . ." he muttered.

"Listen, if this is your child," and here she held up the baby for him to see, not that he was going to take his eyes off the stun gun, "and if you want to be represented at all, if you want to live past this momentary shit stain of a life you've got, you are going to want this baby to survive. It's your only hope, man."

"Are you going to let us go, lady?"

"You can go anytime. But I'm going to take them to the hospital."

On the opposite corner, a man in black leather riding gear sat parked on a large Harley-Davidson motorcycle. He stared at the scene playing out in front of him. A shadow from his helmet obscured his features. He held Delphine's attention if for no other reason than he was looking straight at her.

A taxicab rolled down the street, slowed at the stop sign and gently eased around the spilled Sportster before rolling on. The fallen woman tried to sit up. Her head wound was still bleeding so that the left side of her face from her eyebrow down to her chin was curtained with red. Blood dripped off her chin, onto her shirt, onto the ground. She had dropped the bandanna into the gutter.

"Where's my baby, Tye?" she said with slurred speech as she sat up. "Give him to me."

She called him Tye. Delphine reached into her inner pocket and took out a small pouch of first aid supplies. She separated out three pieces of gauze, a packet of bandages, and a roll of tape, then turned to the injuries while sitting on the sidewalk with the baby in the space between her spindly legs.

"That's fucking kidnapping." The thin man pulled his long slick hair back and tucked it behind his ears.

"Yes, we all have our stories," Delphine said. "You can tell yours and I'll tell mine and"—she looked at the fallen woman who was trying to take the baby back—"these cuts on her head will tell theirs." Here she looked down at his chest. Above the first button of his flannel shirt he had a big tattoo angling up his neck that read: MOB.

This she knew from John's fascination with jail culture meant "money over bitches."

Delphine thought about it for a second and even though it went against her nature to involve the police in any case she was involved in, she turned around and waved her hand in the air. "Officer!"

She had seen a cop car from the corner of her eye. Delphine finished up applying the tape and, lifting the child into her own coat, she helped the woman stand up. Then waved her hand again. "Officer, can you help us please?"

The police got out of their car slowly, without a lot of bluster. One cop made bear claw man sit on the curb, then he asked Delphine to take off her helmet. Everyone took one step back when they saw her tiny frame and bald head. Delphine looked at the far corner just in time to see the man in leather and the large motorcycle pull around the corner and disappear into the night.

THERE WERE requisite questions. A third cop arrived to pick up the bike and set it upright, on its kickstand. The police knew the couple and called bear claw guy Tye, just like the girl had. The girl was Leigh. This whole interaction was starting to have the feeling of a skid row social gathering. Tye said Leigh had fallen. He did not mention the stun gun.

Delphine stammered a bit as she spoke to the policeman. "It scared me when she fell, and I dumped my bike. I was going to get her to the hospital, officer."

"You have anything to add to this, Leigh? You want to press charges?" Leigh shook her head. Delphine took that to indicate that she didn't want to spend any more time with the uniformed men. "So, you want to go with this lady to the hospital, Leigh?" the cop asked.

Leigh looked at Tye then just back to Delphine, and she nodded her head. The second police officer asked for the child and looked the boy over for injuries. "You can't take Blue Sky to the emergency room on the bike." Leigh just nodded. Blue Sky was apparently the name of the child.

Tye stepped forward. "I'll take Blue home, Bobby." Tye knew the officers' names. "Leigh can Uber back to our place after."

Both police officers nodded and looked the group over. It must have been near the end of their shift. Milky sunlight was bleeding over the tops of the Olympic Mountains across the Sound and the cops seemed tired.

"Okay, just don't let me see any of you down here again," he said, which was understood by everyone present to be the emptiest of empty threats.

"Thanks, Bobby," Tye said, and he stepped back, taking the baby in his arms. The cops got back in their cruisers and drove away. Delphine noticed a group of pigeons circling overhead and heard song sparrows fading into the gloom. The pigeons, she thought, had likely smelled the spilled blood.

Leigh quickly walked over to Tye and grabbed Blue Sky from his arms. "No way, Tye. You heard her. We're going to the hospital."

"Let's talk about this at home, baby," Tye said softly.

Delphine felt a lightness in her head as the adrenaline wore off. She felt weak, as if she could not stand, let alone ride the baby and Leigh anywhere on the Sportster. She was grateful to the cop for standing it back up.

"You better feed the other kids when you get home," Leigh said as Tye started walking up the hill.

"Yeah . . . mother of the fucking year," Tye said over his shoulder.

Soon, he was gone, leaving the two women alone in the humming night of Seattle. Delphine was shaking now. She wasn't even certain she could continue standing. The lights along the street began to throb and the smell of grease from restaurants and car exhaust wound themselves into her stomach and Delphine thought she was going to vomit. She looked to the north where the buildings stabbed into the sky and thought she could see a large group of sperm whales swimming in the hazy light right at the rooftop of the tallest building. She took a deep breath while songbirds used their plaintive voices and gulls hee-hawed in the dark to the west. Then the whales dove straight down toward the street level where blackness seemed to be sheltering the night.

"Help me move this bike and chain it up," Delphine gasped.

Together, they got it over to the inside of a little pocket park and leaned it against a lamppost, securing it with the lock and chain from a rear wheel bag. Delphine made sure she had the key, then got out her phone and called a ride service. The boy cooed and sucked on the end of Leigh's little finger. The cooing blended with the other sounds of the night, until a firetruck blared its fat horn as it blared through the intersection like the vanguard of an invading army. Blue Sky spit out the finger and set to squalling like a calf.

Above them, close now, the pod of whales floated above the street. Delphine could hear the clicking rattle in her chest and she could see the eyes turn in their massive skulls as the whales drifted onto their sides to look at them standing alone on the ground, then flicked their tails to soar upward into the lights of the city and the distant stars.

CHAPTER THREE

At the Baranof Hotel, Delphine took Leigh and the baby up into her room. She opened the door and said, "After you get fixed up, you and Blue can stay here with me tonight. I'm not feeling well, but you can stay under one condition."

"What?" Leigh said, in a tone that indicated she expected some ominous condition.

"If I see your friend Tye, I will not help you or the baby." Delphine took out the stun gun and plugged it into a charger near her couch, where she slept. "You want me to go with you to the hospital?"

Leigh nodded. She had pressed some paper towels onto her bleeding head wound. Any movement of her head seemed exaggerated with the red papier-mâché plastered there. "If you don't mind. I know you aren't feeling well, but they will let me go a lot sooner if someone goes with me and can tell them that I have a safe place to stay. Also, they won't make a big deal out of my having a baby and want to examine him too, as long as I have a rich lady with a hotel room along with me."

"You don't think you are being a little overprotective?" Delphine said, letting her smarminess show. Then she shifted gears before she got stuck in it and blew any chance of getting any valuable information for Tom. "Okay, let me make a cup of instant coffee and get my medication." She put the motorcycle keys in a bowl on the wobbly table by the window. "Listen, I might fall asleep in the waiting room."

"You won't be alone." Leigh smiled.

THE WOMEN walked into the hospital with Blue Sky. An attendant walked over to Leigh. "Ms. O'Conner. How can we help you today?"

"I need to get patched up again," Leigh said.

"She has been assaulted," Delphine told the woman.

"Are you a relative?" the attendant asked.

"I'm a friend," Delphine said. The attendant pointed toward the big doors marked EMERGENCY.

Leigh's skin was luminous white. She had dark eyes. Now Delphine could detect a hint of an accent, perhaps Canadian, with the short *ooo*'s. It hadn't occurred to Delphine to wonder what Leigh's ethnicity might have been. Tye presented as a white man, wrapped in his own privilege. He could have been a trust fund manager slumming on a night out or a motorcycle outlaw for all she knew. He was a stupid violent man who bullied women. Delphine had no expectations of living in this world for much longer. She was disoriented, there was not enough room in her emotional storage to imagine the differences between them, Tye and herself. Leigh could be Irish or Ukrainian, Delphine didn't know what difference it made right then. Leigh just needed to get sewed up. That was all that mattered now.

"All right, let's go," Leigh said to the attendant. Her bandages were soaked through, leaving one long drop of blood to run along her eye socket and down to her neck. Blue Sky was sound asleep.

In any investigation, suspicions sit across a table and face down facts. Delphine clearly had reason to believe that Tyler was involved with the sketchy adoption agency and that the baby may have even belonged to Tom Foster's client. It was clear to Delphine that Tyler and Leigh would at least be the two people to start asking if she was going to find the baby. But it is also true that facts are hard to come by, particularly when it comes down to tough customers like Tye. John had often said that "the fact that someone is an asshole isn't proof that they've committed a crime," that is, a man might have smacked his girlfriend down on the street, but that does not necessarily prove he was running an illegal adoption agency. This was easy to see if you counted all the assholes in the world and compared that number to the number of illegal adoptions that were being arranged. Delphine would need more proof against Tyler, and she suspected that she was most likely to find the proof if she just stuck with it.

As soon as they walked into the brightly lit emergency room, the baby began to cry. There were perhaps a dozen people slumped in chairs waiting to be seen. Just as soon as they heard the first squall of crying, two men sat up and scowled at Delphine and Leigh. The men looked as if they were reaching for their guns, ready and willing to shoot at the pale white woman who was bleeding from her bandages and the other, a bald ghostly-looking woman carrying a screaming baby. An older woman in a wheelchair with an oxygen tank attached by tubes next to her sat up and looked at them with sad, sympathetic eyes. The old woman motioned Delphine to sit down next to her. Leigh went to the desk to check in.

"Oh, poor baby." The old woman reached out one talon-like finger to touch the child's stomach. "Poor, poor thing. Mommy is going to be all right."

Delphine jostled the crying child and tried to get him to suck on the tip of her finger. The baby made terrible faces when her finger went into his mouth and Delphine remembered that she had used hand sanitizer before leaving the apartment.

"Yuck . . . yuck . . . yuck." She reached into her coat pocket where, next to her knife and stun gun, she carried three suckers. "Try a little bit of this, baby." And she put the candy on a stick in the baby's mouth if for nothing else than to clear the alcohol taste from his tongue. Blue Sky was still crying; his face was red and looked like a balled fist.

Behind her, the emergency room doors hissed open, revealing the grey film of morning that was stretched tight over the dirty sidewalk. Her baldness, skeletal frame and pale skin made Delphine seem to glow in the waiting room. She watched as Leigh spoke to the admitting nurse. From their body language, she could tell that they knew each other. The nurse looked at the wound dressing. She gave Leigh a handful of tissues while she scanned the room. Leigh pointed to Delphine.

Blue Sky spit the candy out and howled. Soon enough, the nurse and Leigh came over.

"Hello," the nurse said. "Is it true you are going to help Leigh with a place to stay tonight?"

"That's right," Delphine said.

A young man with a stethoscope around his neck walked up behind the nurse. "Are you drunk?"

Delphine looked up, surprised. "No," she said flatly.

"Well, you shouldn't give candy to this baby. It's a choking hazard."

"If I were to shove it down his throat and leave it there I could see the choking danger," Delphine said. "But I didn't."

"Listen, this area is reserved for patients. I'm going to ask you to leave."

"Doctor . . ." the nurse said, "she is just helping out. There is no need to worry. Your patient is in room four." The young man walked off looking hurt because his authority wasn't recognized.

"A new intern," the nurse smiled. "Anyway, I have a clean bottle and some formula. I know this stuff is like gold . . . but I think our baby just needs to be fed. Leigh, how do you feel about your friend taking him back across the street to eat?" The nurse now looked at Delphine and said, "It's a busy night and it's going to be a few hours before we can get Leigh all fixed up and back to you." Then she looked at Leigh, and the nurse lowered the pitch and volume of her voice. "Now Leigh, your man. He is not coming here tonight, is he?"

"He shouldn't be," she said.

"Okay, good. You remember what happened last time?"

"Yes," Leigh said, then stared down at her baby's face.

"Good," the nurse said. "He doesn't know where you are staying, does he?"

"No. He shouldn't be a problem . . . tonight." She was still looking at the child, but now she showed more concern, as if she were standing on train tracks listening to the popping sound of a great weight coming up the rails.

"Okay, good. Let's get you back there and cleaned up."

"Hey, excuse me! Nurse! I've been here an hour and a half. She just waltzed in here." A man whose hands were shaking violently yelled over the sound of Blue Sky crying.

"Sir. You will see a doctor very shortly. The best thing you can do for yourself and everyone is wait here calmly. This woman is bleeding."

"Oh fine. Apparently, I didn't see the sign that this hospital was for bleeding people only."

"Sir. We will take care of you as soon as we can." It was amazing to Delphine that the nurse's voice was as calm as it was.

"Bleeding bitches with hungry babies," he said with his jittery voice.

"Sir." The nurse jerked her head toward the angry man so that a large orderly who looked like a professional football player could see her. The orderly led the man to the back.

"He's going to the time-out room," she said under her breath. "He will be happier waiting there."

She didn't say anything for a moment and all the women in their little group looked down at the baby, who was not screaming now, only whimpering slightly.

"Okay!" the nurse said as she shook herself for the task at hand. She looked at Delphine. "Here is not only the formula but some bottle sleeves and two clean nipples. You guys have fun and we'll get Mom back to you just as soon as we can. What's your baby's name, Leigh?"

"Blue Sky," Leigh said. "His name is Blue Sky."

Back at the Baranof, Delphine read the instructions on the formula can under a low-wattage light. She had walked around the block to the bodega near the bus stop on Madison and bought three-liter bottles of water. Leigh had given her a bag with the bottle-like structure to hold the sleeve for the formula. Nipples and two plastic spoons came from Leigh's coat pocket, and they were all covered with a kind of urban grit as if they were found on the pavement. First, Delphine scrubbed everything in the sink, then she boiled the nipples and bottles using bottled water and a clean saucepan from the kitchenette. She washed everything again with dish soap then boiled it all again. As she worked, she held little Blue Sky on the crook of her left hip. Finally, she took a flimsy suitcase she had discovered in the front closet out from under her bed and placed clean towels and a well-worn pillow inside of it, then more substantial pillows all around the makeshift bassinet on the widest part of the countertop so that she could lay the baby down in a place that was still visible. The child had already rejected the bed and the couch as unsuitable. Blue Sky didn't appear to be saying many words at all. He seemed small and a little behind the curve if in fact he was fifteen months old. But then again, size and weight of young mammals could be quite variable depending on nutrition. Delphine made a little bower of pillows and blankets on her floor near the kitchen. She felt better now that he wouldn't fall as he rolled around.

She put together the clean bottle and wiped the same type of urban grit from the baby's face. Then she fed him two bottles and drew a little more than tepid bath in the tiny bathtub, stripped off her own clothes and the child's and sat in the tub with him. Blue Sky burbled and burped, Delphine catching the spit-up in a washcloth, then placing it in the sink. Delphine was pleased to see a little strawberry birthmark on his right arm. Bert had had a similar birthmark as a baby. Whenever his blood pressure rose, say when he was crying hard, the birthmark would balloon up from his skin.

She loved bathing the child. Of course, she remembered washing Bertie. She and Bert had stayed in a tiny cabin in Glacier Bay the few years she was a whale biologist at Glacier Bay National Park in Alaska. Bertie was much more solid than this child. Blue Sky was thin and a bit listless. His little ribcage seemed sunken and appeared to squeeze his round belly toward his spindly legs. Bertie had always been a chunk of muscle and fat. His belly protruded from his waist like an old farmer's potbelly. He loved to laugh in the bathtub. He was almost always covered in bugbites and seemed to get great pleasure from the warm soapy water. Delphine applied an anti-itch lotion to his belly and thighs which caused him to smile and splash as he sat in the indentation of her legs. Back then, Delphine's body was thick with muscle, her breasts were firm with milk and her skin bore a silky sunburned glow. She loved the feeling of having given birth. She often thought of herself and her baby as slippery young mammals there in the tub.

Washing young Blue Sky was familiar, but not as satisfying as those baths in Glacier Bay. She was sickly, thin and bald. Both she and the baby had ribs that poked up through their skin and their muscle mass seemed wasted. Soaping the child down made Delphine sad, not just for herself, but for the baby too. But this child was alive. He had a mom who seemed willing to fight for him.

Delphine drained the water and let the child lie in the empty tub while she slowly got out and, balancing her small body between the sink and the wall, dressed in a clean nightgown.

She felt too weak to stand while lifting the baby out of the tub, so she sat on the floor, then lifted him as if ladling a big dumpling out of a bowl and into the clean towel in her arms. Delphine then crawled toward the bed just outside the bathroom, placed the bundle in the bed and pulled her own body up next to the baby. She wiped the baby dry. She had no diapers, so tied a dish towel around his waist and crotch. She noticed that the child did not have diaper rash, which she had been expecting, and this made her feel a bit guilty about the assumptions she had been making about Leigh as a mother.

Delphine then pulled the sheet and duvet up over them and curled the baby into her arms. It was a delightful feeling at this point, for both were tired, and both seemed confused about the strange circumstance they found themselves in.

A FEMALE sperm whale gestates its offspring for approximately fourteen to sixteen months. The average newborn is born at thirteen feet and one thousand pounds. Generally, birth takes place in warm equatorial waters. The infant is at risk of predation by sharks, orca whales and, until recently, human beings.

Calves have been observed being swarmed by killer whales. For protection, females surround the calf, noses in and tails out, slashing the water with their tails. The females are only thirty feet long, but their heads are still blunt and wide, which allows them to slide the baby up onto their heads to protect them from attack from below. The females' devotion to the calves leaves their soft bellies open to the orcas, whose large conical teeth are well suited for biting and ripping prey, though many of the orcas' kills are the result of drowning. There are reports of dead sperm whales being sunk to depths where orca whales can return to continue feeding, until the flesh begins to build up gas in the fermentation process and the mass floats back to the surface. This is less advantageous to the predator because at the surface, there are many more animals to partake of the bounty: birds, smaller sharks, fish and microscopic amphipods can reduce a whale to bones in a matter of days.

More study is needed of both these attacks and the survival of these attacks. In the early days of industrial whaling, this survival strategy of head in, tail out was a godsend to the whalers. They would look hard for these formations, called "daisies," along the surface so that they could ease up upon them and take all the whales at once. If predators were attacking, the sperm whales rarely broke formation, so the whalers could pick off many females before they started harpooning the orcas. Often the last to be taken were the thirteen-foot baby sperm whales who the mothers and nursemaids had died to protect.

As commercial whaling continued, sperm whales gave up this daisy behavior in the presence of whaling ships. Instead of grouping up around the young, they began to dive deep and travel laterally to get away from the ships, which was a very effective way to avoid the harpoon but less effective in staving off orcas. This dive-and-run strategy also seemed to be less effective at keeping off sharks, who had no need to work at the surface. While the orcas could continue their attack on the sperm whales, orcas were still committed to coming to the surface to consume and divvy up their catch among their own group. They needed to breathe, which made them available to the whalers again.

It is possible that sperm whales' ability to change their avoidance strategy saved them when commercial whaling brought them to the brink of extinction.

DELPHINE WOKE in the early afternoon. She had missed her morning medication regimen and she felt pain in her belly. She would have to make sure her evening regimen was right on time. Taking her pills late would push her completely out of whack, leading to nights of sleeplessness and days of extreme fatigue.

She rubbed her eyes and when she spread her arm out across the bed and felt nothing but the absence of the child, she woke with a start, sitting straight up in the bed, her feet slung over the side, without knowing she had done it. The glass doors out to the living room were open and she saw a pair of bare female feet resting on the uneven coffee table in front of the couch. Delphine cleared her throat, then took a drink of water from the glass next to her bed. As she set the glass down on the bedside table, she heard the baby fuss.

"I hope we didn't wake you," Leigh said. Blue Sky let out two hiccuping coughs and then a yawn.

"No . . ." Delphine put a robe over her shoulders and came out of the bedroom. Leigh went to the kitchenette with the

baby and poured a cup of coffee into an old café mug from an
establishment that had long since closed down. All the glass-
ware in the suite was secondhand and mismatched. She handed
the coffee to Delphine. Then she sat back down on the couch,
laid the little boy on her lap and kissed his belly.

"Thank you for taking such good care of him."

"I'm sorry I wasn't awake when you got home. We took a
bath and crashed out."

"No, don't worry. It took forever over at the emergency
room." One of Leigh's eyes was black to her chin and the other
just showed a shadow over the lid. Two butterfly bandages
covered the ten or so stitches above her left eyebrow. They both
settled into the couch and sipped their coffee. Leigh reached
down in the space between the cushions and lifted her cell
phone out. She tapped the front and scrolled, reading something.

"You hear from Tye?" Delphine asked.

"I just told him that I got held up at the hospital and would
be coming home soon."

"Do you have to?"

"Jesus, I better," she sighed. "He's alone with all the babies
and their moms. I can't bear to imagine the mess: spit-up on
chairs, poopy diapers and crusty baby food on every flat surface."

"How many kids do you have?" Delphine asked.

"I've got this one here. He's mine but Tyler has at least six
more."

"Six?"

"Yeah, he kind of collects them from his old girlfriends."

Delphine didn't speak. This information fit neatly into the clearly suspicious evidence category. It felt to Delphine that Leigh seemed to want to tell her all about Tyler's involvement, but something was keeping her from providing more facts.

Delphine kept her eye on the baby. It had been months since Congress passed the national abortion ban and litigation was stacking up. In response, many citizens wanted to mitigate the effect of more unwanted babies being born, so state and local governments had thrown money at the problem by making it easier to adopt out. There was now a bullish market in adoptions. She had read investigative articles in the last two nights that suggested that illegal adoptions were becoming a second stream of income for pimps.

"Is Tye a pimp as well?" Delphine asked without fear or anxiety in her tone.

Leigh sipped her coffee and touched her son's cheek. "I suppose he used to be a pimp. Now he seems more like a rancher."

"You should get clear of him," Delphine said.

"It's complicated," Leigh said. "I adopted Baby Blue here about a year ago when he was just a tiny baby. Tyler did the adoption, but he has all the papers. I don't really know why or how."

They sat for several moments in silence. The sun streamed in through the window and a small brown bird landed on the window ledge near the kitchen. Delphine got up and let the bird in as if she were expecting him.

"I can only imagine what this all looks like to you. But you have to believe me that I don't love anything in the world like

I love this little boy." Then she lifted him up and nestled his cheek against her own. "I just love him like crazy, he makes up for all the sick stuff that goes on in my life."

"I'm going to order some breakfast sent up from across the street. You should stay and take a shower and get some rest. Then you can go back." Delphine let her hand drift down on top of Baby Blue's head as he gurgled into his mother's cheek.

There were big emotions at play here. For a moment, Delphine imagined she could hear the clicking of a sperm whale coming from a dark gloom of night that was already on the other side of the world, somehow both in the near past and the more distant future.

"I do love him. Please believe me," the bruised-up woman said to Delphine. Leigh had picked up some new diapers from the hospital. Since the boom on poor babies, hospitals had become the central distributor of infant supplies in many big cities. Delphine tapped the plasticky material of the government-issue diaper and hummed an old tune, "You Are My Sunshine." Bertie's favorite.

"He keeps saying he is working on something big. He's got a 'golden parachute,' and he's going to cash in." Leigh's voice sounded flat and somehow distracted . . . depressed.

"Gold?" Delphine asked. "How does he turn babies into gold?"

"I don't know," Leigh said. "I just know he is working on something big. Something profitable."

"I wouldn't care how big his plans are or what his golden parachute might be. I would make a big distance between yourself and Tye," Delphine said more firmly. "He's nothing but a bully."

"Oh, I've seen worse."

Delphine shuddered, thinking that that was probably true. "Listen, give me your address so in case I need to come visit you, at least I can do that."

Leigh looked at her skeptically for a long moment. "I don't need to be saved."

"Well, you needed a trip to the hospital last night, didn't you? Are you telling me you have so many friends that you can't afford one more? You know where I live."

"All right," Leigh said. "I'm not going to be in later tonight though. We've got roommates who are taking care of the babies."

"I can always take care of the baby. I think we get along."

Leigh nodded as if perhaps she was just too tired to argue. She fished in her pockets, took out an old receipt and asked for a pen. When Delphine gave her the pen, Leigh wrote out an address and gave it to her.

"Thank you," Delphine said softly, sounding nothing but grateful, when in fact she was thrilled to find the location where Tom Foster's client's child was most likely staying.

Delphine wanted to keep Leigh talking and she decided to ask easy questions about the young woman's past. Leigh was born in the farm country west of Saskatoon; her father put up wheat with leased-out combines. Leigh played basketball on her high school team. Her mother drank to excess, and her father was always tired. Leigh moved to Vancouver hoping to get into the movie business and while she did enjoy seeing TV stars in her neighborhood cafés, the closest she got to being a star herself was working in craft services. That . . . and she started using cocaine late-night in the dance-club bathrooms. It was cocaine that brought her to Tyler. He seemed friendly and sociable at first. He told Leigh that he was working as an extra in an American police drama. Which turned out not to be true.

It was a sad story and it made Delphine think of John all the more. It had been four years since he had died, almost to the day. He had been run down by a drunken driver while riding his bicycle home from an afternoon at work.

Delphine was bottom painting her skiff when she got word. A police car came to the university and a nice female officer who used to cut hair in town got out of the car and sat on some blocking near the skiff while Delphine kept painting. "I have some hard news to tell you," she said. Delphine did not stop painting. She did not speak for perhaps forty-five seconds. The officer shifted from side to side and Delphine heard her utility belt creak. She turned down the two-way radio on her belt.

"What is it? What is the news?" Delphine asked, and the officer told her about John. There were times that she expected news of John's death. He had tried multiple medications in his last thirty years. His doctor called it "treatment-resistant unipolar depression." His father had the same thing and had treated himself with alcohol. So Delphine wasn't shocked by the news so much as surprised at the cause. She had prepared herself for the fact that he might die of a heart attack or even perhaps after being shot down by an angry client, but it made her angry that he had been run down on the side of the road. When she thought of his death, she imagined his old green bicycle pitched into a muddy ditch, the bent front wheel spinning and a scraping sound singing out into the night as the wheel hit the frame.

They had lived together forty-seven years and were married for forty-five. He loved going on her small research adventures or simply getting out into the country. As the years passed, his depression became more severe, but she was aware that he did his best not to place his sadness onto her shoulders. His depression, like most of the depressions she had seen during her life, was a distance she knew he tried to overcome. John liked to laugh, and she appreciated that, even when she couldn't understand his black melancholy.

Delphine missed him now. She loved thinking of him running their old boat, *Phalarope*, past the breakwater and past the barrier islands out to sea. He loved fishing, he loved putting his arm around her waist as the whales rose in the distance. He loved reading in the evening when the boat sat at anchor while she worked on her gear and entered data into her laptop or sorted her humpback whale photographs into her identification catalogue. She had many thousands of identification photographs, but so few shots of him. Now, she wished she had noticed him more.

They had lived apart often when he was working on cases. He once spent almost a year away while he worked on the eight-count murder case with the boat burned to the waterline. He had honestly believed that his client was not guilty, and eventually the second jury agreed. He started his own writing during long nights spent in hotels. He was a decent storyteller, but the writing added more distance to their relationship. She met his distance with her own. She worked harder than he did. When they worked together on a project, sanding and scraping, or collaborating on a book project, she would often work late into the night when he was ready to sit on the deck and stare out to sea. She would sit with him sometimes, but she always took out her notebook and noted the time at the top of one of the waterproof pages; then she would scan the ocean for big animals with her old Zeiss binoculars. She needed to work. Soon, he would be reading.

Delphine's phone buzzed.

"Oh damnit," she said. "I've got to meet this guy down the street. I've already put him off two times. I don't really want to do it, but ..."

Leigh was getting dressed in the bedroom after a shower. "I will get out of your hair," she called out.

"No. Listen, why don't you think about staying with me another night or so? We'll go out to dinner, get a good meal and maybe we can talk some more about what you really might want to do."

Leigh came out of the bedroom, put her coat on and looked down at the baby. "No ..." she said gently. "It's nice of you, but I got a thing going there with Tye." She didn't smile and there was no lift of happiness in her voice. "I mean it's nice of you and all, but Tye's not that bad a guy."

"But he is a bad guy," Delphine said, sounding more judgmental than she had intended. "Listen, I'm sorry, I'm not trying to boss you around, and I'm not trying to save you. I just saw him hit you and knock you down with your baby in your arms. You don't have to put up with that, there must be options."

Leigh did not say anything. Blue Sky squirmed in his onesie. Delphine felt a familiar kind of distance growing between them. The baby burped, then laughed.

"You love this baby, I can see that in your eyes. Let's keep talking at least. Just call me tomorrow to let me know how you are doing?"

"Okay. I'll do that."

"I want to give you some money to buy new clothes for Blue Sky."

"No." Leigh picked up her child, took a moment to check her own pockets, then started for the door. "I'll call you. You gave me your number at the hospital. I'll call you tomorrow."

Then she walked out.

Delphine stood alone in the hallway. She could smell someone frying vegetables, and far down the street she heard the wail of a siren giving the world first notice of some new calamity.

"GREAT TO finally meet you," the young man said as he stood up to kiss Delphine's hand. He wore an expensive fleece sweater topped off with a silk scarf around his neck.

He ordered himself a local beer and she asked for some tonic water and lime. They vamped on some conversation about cancer and health care until the drinks came and they ordered food. Then the young man launched into his pitch.

"Well, as I told you, I'm an environmental architect. I build homes for private clients, but I hope to do bigger projects soon.

I'm striving to bring nature into the built spaces my clients want to inhabit. I want them to feel the tremendous energy of nature."

"Okay," Delphine said, while still thinking about her new criminal case. "What can I do for you?"

He took out a folded map that he had tied with a black silk ribbon. He unrolled it by clearing a space on the table and positioning the restaurant's stubby candles on each side of the chart.

"We have an incredible site up in the San Juan Islands. When I first went to view it, I was standing on the bluff and I saw a whale jump out of the water. It was magical . . . as if it were greeting me and my project."

"What kind of whale was it?"

"I have no idea. Big, of course. I should recognize the type. I think it was mostly black and white."

"A killer whale."

"It was a baby whale, I think?"

"Was it a Dall's porpoise? Were there any other animals around? Something that could have been a family member: a mother, father? Or were there a bunch of these black-and-white animals?"

"I'm sorry, I don't really know. I was just so blown away by the greeting, I forgot to get all sciency."

"Ah . . ." she said, "sciency." Delphine pressed her fingers against her temples. "Again, what is it you would like from me?"

"Well, as I said over the phone, I was blown away by your articles and the interview you did for that French movie production. When I heard more about your reputation I thought, who better than you to teach me all about whales in Puget Sound?"

Film crews needed to work with permitted researchers in the United States by law. The French film had been well-made and garnered Delphine an improvement to her visibility in the research community.

"I did my research in Alaska."

"You graduated from the University of Alaska, but you grew up in Seattle."

She closed her eyes. "I think what you need now is to read a few books, and I'd be happy to recommend some."

"I would really like to get you and my clients together. I can't tell you their names right now . . ." And he laughed to draw attention to the seeming absurdity of the situation. "I have a nondisclosure agreement."

The waiter brought some bread which the young man ate voraciously. "But I'm sure they would love you. I'm sure you could ask them to help donate to your research." Now he leaned back as if he was finally getting to the point: the money. What was in it for her.

"They are very sweet really, but they come from Connecticut, you know, in the east," he continued, staring across the gloomy table, pausing just enough to make sure she had heard of Connecticut. "They came to me because I have built up a national reputation for my work and the way it pays homage to nature. But they don't have a clue themselves. I need you to educate them a bit and, as I said, if things go the way I hope, my couple will take a financial interest in your work."

Delphine's head was hurting now. Her stomach was tight

and the ache in her bones and meat seemed to increase the more he spoke. She thought of Blue Sky, and she thought of the baby being laid down to sleep that night within snoring distance from Tye. She thought of the brown finch flying into her hotel room.

Sometimes, she wished she had studied something common and unexciting: beetles, flies or the brown house finch. She hated acting as a kind of entertainment agent for whales. Or worse, for nature itself.

"Do you think whales have ever thought that they should be more into nature?" she asked, making the red leather uphol-stery creak as she leaned forward and backward. "Do you think they have a sense that they are separate from the water in the ocean? Do they think that they would love to get back to someplace really watery?"

She said the word "watery" with a cartoonish sarcasm. Her companion absently fiddled with what Delphine could now see was an ascot under his expensive sweater. Now he had a puzzled look as if his dog were beginning to speak English.

"No, I never have wondered about something like that." He paused and did a bit of business with his fingers at his throat. "But I know whales are incredibly intelligent, so I suppose they must."

"We are not . . . none of us are *into* nature: not you, not me, not your clients. You are not letting nature into your built spaces. We are all like a whale in the water, soaked through and through. I think it's a problem of language. You may want to be more distant from your human neighbors. We might like to live close to the ocean, or the forest, or even the landscape of a city, but that doesn't make any of us less natural.

"The problem as I see it is a matter of money and resources. Rich people can afford to get what they want. You can build them an expensive house away from other people and with big windows to let the sounds of the ocean in, but that doesn't make the owners any more into nature. It is narcissism that will or will not allow them to feel what is outside their own experience."

The anger building in her chest might have nothing to do with this pompous young man, and his documentary reverence for "nature" of which he had no knowledge or experience. It may have only had something to do with her anger toward John being so incredibly distant.

They sat there, looking at their place settings. The waiter brought their salads, and they remained silent throughout the whole fresh black pepper ceremony.

"Listen," she said, "I have cancer. I get grumpy. Your house will be beautiful, your clients are lucky, and they will enjoy their lives on the ocean. I'm sorry to be hard on you. I spent more than forty years studying big animals in the ocean. I don't need your clients' money, I won't live long enough to spend it. I won't live long enough to see the house built. I will give you a list of books and the names of a couple of researchers who could help you find a hydrophone system to pipe ocean noises into their perfect sound system."

Delphine patted his hand. "It would be a beautiful thing." She paused. "Until there are too many boats nearby . . . but that's the good thing about an underwater microphone system. You can always turn it off."

DELPHINE SPOKE with the architect about how to get high-quality hydrophones for the house's waterfront. She told him how deep they should be placed and who would know about the equipment for the underwater sound system. The young man was much more comfortable when he spoke about himself and his work.

After dinner, Delphine walked out onto the street. She was tired and feeling weak in the legs. What she wanted to do was go back to her hotel and sleep, but instead she used her phone to hail a car to take her down the hill to where she had left the Sportster. Only three white blotches of bird shit showed on the yellow gas tank and one on the tire. The bike turned over on the third try. She was able to hold the bike up between her legs even though the weakness made her whole body tremble. She used the heel of her nice shoes to pound down on the starter and she let the engine idle. Somehow, the daylight had passed by here, and the lights from the older downtown buildings squinted out into the night as if the windows had been carved out of the walls by children. Clouds were blowing in from the south, giving the city a dark grey ceiling. She knew she could die but that was an ever-present worry that had settled into her gut by now, like hunger, or love.

She revved the engine, levered the gearbox into first and pushed forward. She wouldn't drive directly to the apartment building where Leigh was living. Delphine wanted to spy on the couple without arousing their suspicion. To do this, she would need to think of the best way to get into the apartment.

She thought one, two, three steps ahead of what she might find inside. Tye was clearly a violent bully. This way, she could gather information on him without putting Leigh in even more danger. She returned to the hotel to get a chemical compound she had bought when she first moved into the Baranof to detect bloodstains and other biological secretions that would be hard to see with the naked eye. The UV light lit up the bathroom and the bedsheets and made the room look like a spook house when she first moved in, but a solution of hydrogen peroxide cleaned biological stains better than anything. Years ago, she had taught John how to make the compound from materials easily purchased from chemical supply stores: 45 mL of sulfuric acid along with 13 g phthalic anhydride and 19 g of sodium nitrate. Stir together with the temperature slowly ramped up to 110 Celsius. Once the temperature is reached, the reaction is held for one hour to nitrate the phthalic anhydride to 3-nitrophthalic anhydride. Or simply stated, luminol. Now, she no longer had to make it. It was easy to buy luminol from Amazon.

Delphine grabbed the leftover luminol from the fridge along with a small pamphlet that John had once given her, which she often carried in big cities with non-English speakers.

The rattle of the cylinders echoed off the buildings, up and out, as she rode. This wasn't a particularly comfortable motorcycle—the suspension was hard and she knew on a long ride it would be painful—but it thrilled her now that she was past the fear of dying. The thrill was the only thing she had experienced in months that was akin to a love of life.

She blared up the hill through billows of smells from the various restaurants she passed, exhaust from cars in front, the smell of coffee burning in the urns of small cafés. The bike was powerful, and its power shuddered vibrations up her legs. A small Boston terrier yapped at her from the sidewalk and its owner strained against a thin leash to hold the dog back. She swerved to the left into a bus lane to avoid having to stop, and she ran through the last moments of several yellow lights. If she crashed, she wanted the crash to be fatal. She didn't want to be laid up in another hospital bed with casts on her top and bottom.

Near the train station sat the address Leigh had given her. It was a large welfare hotel where Tye and Leigh and part of their large brood were holed up. She chained the Sportster to a parking sign across the street. She had kept her good clothes on and carried her waterproof briefcase slung over her back. As she crossed the street, she saw a black-leather-clad man idling his big bike on the northwestern corner. He looked at her for a beat too long. Long enough for her to know he was watching her with some interest. When he saw her look back at him, he turned away. Delphine now knew the man in leather was trying to hide his interest in her. He was the same man she'd seen last night, out on the street.

Delphine entered the hotel. She went upstairs and knocked on the door. A woman opened it with a crying baby on her hip, and Delphine flashed a two-sided fishing license case that had her Alaska state driver's license on one side and her fishing permit on the other.

"Hello ma'am, I am Delphine Stockard from the state

childcare licensing board. You are in no trouble at all, but I am here to do a routine inspection of the premises."

"No English. Sorry."

Delphine took her phone and John's small laminated pamphlet out of her briefcase. She pushed the pamphlet into the woman's face while the woman jiggled the baby up and down on her hip. "Madame. Look at this and pick out the language you understand."

"No English."

"Look at the writing here. What words do you understand? Just point."

"No. Sorry."

"Look . . ." Delphine waved the pamphlet open before her face.

Finally, the woman pointed to a sentence written in Ukrainian. Delphine called the phone number written on the front of the pamphlet and within moments they were connected to a Ukrainian translator.

"As I said, you are not in any trouble. I am not with the police or any immigration authority. I am here to make sure your facility is safe for children."

The translator spoke and the woman turned and walked the baby back to a small bedroom with a crib. As soon as the baby lay down, she stopped crying.

The mother walked back out and spoke in just slightly accented English.

"No police?"

"No," Delphine said.

"My boss is not here. He says I'm not to talk with anyone."

"Well, I will have to take whatever children are here to our own facility if you don't answer a few simple questions."

Here, she was thrilled a bit to be working again with John and solving problems that he had figured out so long ago.

The woman shook her head as the translator went through the motions of translating. "Hold on," Delphine said. "Ask her if she speaks enough English to answer a few simple questions."

This happened.

"Okay, what questions?" The woman sat down and lit a cigarette.

"How many children are here with you?"

"Today, five. But some babies live in other places."

"Who is your boss?"

"Tyler Dearborn. That is what he say."

"Is this child one of the children living here?" Delphine showed the woman a photo on her phone, the same photo that Tom had shown her at their meeting. She wanted to know what this woman understood Leigh's role in the living situation to be. "Who is the mother of this child?"

The woman stared down at the photo.

"I don't know. That baby went with Mr. Dearborn. Is staying with another woman. Three babies gone now. Staying somewhere else. Maybe new parents, I don't know."

"What is your name?"

The photo Tom had given her was not particularly clear. When she had first seen it, she was not convinced that the child in the photo was Baby Blue, but now she wondered. Could they be siblings? Cousins?

"No name. You no need my name."

Delphine thought a moment. "Okay then, I'm going to see that the other babies are all right. I will search the entire house or you can just show them to me." She disconnected with the translator.

They took a short tour of the place. The apartment was tidy but not really clean. The rugs were soiled and the walls had not been washed in years. There were red iron stains under every fixture in the bathroom. Delphine asked the woman for privacy in the one communal bathroom and the woman left her.

Delphine squirted some of her chemical in the bathroom. She fished out a small UV flashlight and sprayed the light on the walls. The luminol glowed around the bathtub tiles, illuminating light gushes spattering the walls. But there were flecks of blood just above the rim of the tub and down into the dirty drain, smeared off of what looked like small adult handprints. Like a woman had cleaned up while sitting in the tub.

Delphine walked out of the bathroom quickly, then poked her head into a bedroom full of cribs. There were two children on the floor, lying on a clean blanket. The caretaker grabbed Delphine's arm and led her out of the room, but not before Delphine took a mental picture of the babies. The children ranged from six months to perhaps three years old. Neither of them showed any sign of external injury.

"You can tell your boss that I will be back," Delphine said.

"You should not come back. He is not friendly. He took three babies with him." She held up three fingers in front of her face.

"He doesn't have to be friendly. He just has to answer

questions or lose his business," Delphine said as she walked to the door. "When will he be back?"

"I don't know," the dark-eyed woman answered.

"All right then, have a nice day," Delphine said, and she started to walk out.

Every investigator has an internal clock for how long a witness will keep talking. Delphine had the impression that the dark-eyed woman was very, very close to clamming up.

"One last thing." Delphine turned back to talk with the woman. "Do you know the man," here she pantomimed riding a motorcycle, "black leather, possibly something written on the back of his coat?" She pantomimed more, then foolishly said, "Vroom vroom? He come here?"

The Ukrainian mom responded with a gesture of her own, riding a motorcycle.

"Many men like that. Vroom. Motorcycle gangster men, come here. Look at babies. Now you should go."

"Today?" Delphine said. She weakly twisted imaginary accelerators with her wrists. "This man was here? No vroom vroom men today?"

The Ukrainian mom squinted and vaguely shook her head to indicate no.

Delphine thanked her and waved before walking away.

The man on the corner was not there when she went out. Delphine made it back to the hospital and chained the bike up to its original pole, where Robert had last left it. Her skull felt slightly larger and the weakness had gone out of her legs. She thought of the times John had ridden into her camps when she was a young woman. When she unbuckled her helmet, she saw Leigh standing on the sidewalk, smoking a cigarette with her hands cupping both elbows as if she were hugging herself between puffs.

"Hello, Leigh," she said.

"Yeah . . ." Leigh's voice was thin and anxious as she spoke. "You can't go up to your room right now."

"Why not?" Delphine asked.

"Because Tye is robbing your room. He is robbing everyone else on your floor just to cover robbing you. He saw you going into the apartment."

Delphine let out a deep breath. She was tired.

"Come on," Leigh said. "Let's go get a drink around the corner until he is done."

CHAPTER FOUR

"Jesus. No," Delphine said. "That little shit is not taking my money." She tried to walk straight to the door of the hotel.

"He will kill you," Leigh said. "After I told him about where I had stayed the night of my trip to the ER, he didn't trust you. He has some legal problems. He has a friend with him, a guy he calls the Babysitter."

"Are you serious? It seems kind of stupid to have some thug called the Babysitter."

"True," Leigh said. "But trust me, the Babysitter is a very serious man. He takes care of anyone in the room and Tye takes the drugs and the patches, liquids, anything that the people who are coming out of the hospital have, then he takes the cash. He doesn't want any traceable items. He leaves computers and cell phones for his partner. He remembers you and your stun gun and he let me come and warn you off him. He clearly doesn't like you. He thinks you are going to turn him in to the cops."

"Why wouldn't I call the police? I know who he is. Why shouldn't I call them right now?" She pulled out her phone.

"Listen, he has got an issue with a group of parents who don't want to abide by the agreements they made with him. They are tough people. I don't know where he gets this stuff, but he really believes you are going to snitch him off somehow. He's paranoid, I tell you."

"Then why is he robbing me? Paranoid people are not suited to being thieves."

Leigh flicked the end of her cigarette with her thumbnail. "He wants to see what's in your room. He'll look through your computer, but he won't steal it. And what the hell are you doing going to our apartment?"

"I wanted to see where you and Blue Sky lived."

"I would like to trust you. You know I would; just tell me what you're up to. He is genuinely mad about this. He could end your life."

"I don't have a lot of life left," Delphine said, raising her voice.

"He thought you might say that, so he told me to tell you that if you called the police or made a fuss it would be bad for the children. That's why I'm here asking you not to."

"Come on! Is he really the kind of sick bastard who would threaten to hurt a child?"

"Not really, but this involves me too. I don't need him threatening my baby just because of you. He thinks you disrespected him down on the street last night and that you are working for one of his dissatisfied customers."

"Disrespected him? He punched you and put your baby in danger."

"You tased him out in public, where people could see the both of you. It's bad for his reputation to have a sick old lady take him down."

Delphine was too weak to argue. She had her hand on her

stun gun in her briefcase. The only decision to make was to either go up to her room and face them down ... or not. She was furious, but her arms were shaking and her legs felt like unsubstantial twigs. She clearly didn't want to get into a fist fight with a couple of young thugs.

They went to the bar around the corner. Leigh ordered a beer and Delphine had a cup of herbal tea and a glass of soda water.

Leigh brushed back her hair and sat up straight. "There are fifteen rooms on your floor. He knows they try to keep most of the medical rentals on the same floor. He figures that most of the rooms have people who just had operations, so there will be painkillers. There will be fentanyl patches. Cancer patients will have marijuana and perhaps morphine. All of those things sell well on the street. He says he needs the cash for his golden parachute. Besides, he is pissed at you."

The bartender brought their drinks. Delphine had her elbows on the bar and cradled her chin in her palms. Her eyes were closed.

"Look, Tye knows what he is doing. He is not a child. He goes to the basement and picks one of the housekeepers' lockers. He takes the universal key card to open the doors. He walks in and starts robbing, and if there is anyone there, the Babysitter puts his big hand over their mouth and explains the situation. He takes their phones and computers, not for the dough really, but just to prevent them from contacting the police. The Babysitter isn't afraid of stealing electronics. That's his cut. He takes them to a fence in the International District close to where we all live. They wipe them and get them sold quickly. Tye empties out the pill bottles into plastic tubs he carries in his backpack. He leaves the pill bottles scattered across the floor. He has nothing with him that has a possible victim's name printed on it. If he gets caught with the buckets of drugs, he says that he got them from someone else. He is just a holder, someone to hold the goods until things cool off. Not a burglar. Not a distributor . . . just a mope. The Babysitter makes sure they don't come out of their rooms. He's big and ugly like that. Most sick people and even their family members don't want to mess with him. I'm telling you this because I kind of like you. I'm telling you this to warn you."

"Why does he threaten you?" Delphine asked her. "And threaten your kid? What will it take for you to turn him in?"

"It's crazy, I know. But it's hard being all alone on the street. Especially with a baby. He makes a life for me. There are always some good people around. He keeps a roof over my head, you know? Besides, he holds all the papers."

"Your life can't be that good. I promise I will help you get a new life started for yourself and Baby Blue."

Leigh smiled and drank from her beer. "Come on, I'm in a hard spot here. Tye saw you go into our building and he already thinks we're conspiring. He doesn't like you and he won't trust me if he thinks I've thrown in with you for some reason. Tye is so much better than he used to be. He stopped taking meth and crack. He's off all that now. He takes ketamine sometimes and that just chills him out. He just needs . . . we just need to sort out this mess with the dissatisfied customers."

Delphine drank some soda water. She tried to focus on

getting the information that Tom needed for his client, the dissatisfied customer. What would she have to do to discover where the child that Tom needed was living? "What do you mean that there are always good people around?"

"Tye's got lots of friends, both men and women. They're always helping out with the kids; they help out with food and laundry."

"How many kids are there really?"

Here, Leigh scrunched up her face and started tearing the label of the beer bottle with the long painted nail on her index finger.

"He's got twelve kids now, scattered around town ... at least I think ... I don't know for certain. He didn't have that many when I met him. Ever since they made abortion illegal, and King County started paying more for childcare, he's got a lot more."

"How many mothers?"

"'Bout eight moms. He consolidates the expenses, and they help out."

"Help out how?"

"Any way they can. He is legally in charge of each child's finances now and he collects the welfare money, but the girls all pay what they can." Leigh was stripping a long tendril off the label. She drank another sip and she closed her eyes as if she were either savoring the taste or wanting to escape this conversation.

Delphine decided to lay some of her cards on the table. "There is a woman from San Francisco who wants her baby back. Is that one of the dissatisfied parents?"

Leigh burst into tears. "Please . . ." she sobbed. "You can't tell Tye that you know about that. I will never tell anyone. For the love of God, drop this. Drop it now. It won't help."

"You're in real trouble," Delphine said as she put her hand on Leigh's forearm.

"It's just me and Blue. Tye is not the father. Blue is my baby, nobody is going to take him away. If he even suspected that I would turn him in to the cops . . . It would be very bad for me. Very bad for Baby Blue."

"You happy with Tye?"

She didn't answer for some moments. The barmaid came by and asked if they wanted any more drinks.

"No, sweetie, thanks," Leigh said. "Happy . . . ? Like I said, I like where I live. It's mostly women, and we take care of each other. He doesn't dare hit one of us when any of the others are around. I like it, though, I do. We try and eat together; we save food money that way. We plan meals. We try and eat good. One of the girls used to work on a fishing boat, one works at the market downtown. I mean we eat fish, and vegetables, it's not pizza all the time or food thrown away from grocery stores. I'm not saying we are above dumpster diving but . . . you know. We usually get only the good stuff."

"Who is taking care of Blue right now?"

"Oh, one of the girls in the other house. She's cool. She's just out of rehab, she takes good care of her own kids."

"So you can go out and rob my hotel room?" Delphine stared straight at Leigh.

"Listen, I'm sorry. But what were you doing in the big

apartment by the train station? You were nice to me when I got hurt. I didn't want you to get hurt. I could only imagine that you would get in a tussle with the Babysitter."

"Are you threatening me now?"

Leigh started crying in the dark bar.

Finally, Delphine finished her soda water. She hadn't touched her tea. She looked at the clock on her phone. "How long is it going to be?"

Leigh looked at her cell phone. She tapped the screen a few times. Delphine could tell Leigh was checking her texts.

"What's up with Baby Blue's name anyway?"

"Sometimes when we travel, we tell people we are a commune that is way into this band. We use hippie names so nobody gets ahold of our real names . . . like this woman who wants her baby back. Are you working for her lawyers?"

"Did you kidnap this woman's baby? I found blood in your bathtub. What's up with that?"

The battered woman seemed to think for a long moment, then said, "Right at this moment I have no reason to believe that any of the children are in danger." Her phone dinged and Leigh looked at the screen. "Cheap bastard won't buy me a decent phone." She snapped the phone shut. "Listen. You can go back to your place now. I will cover these." She waved her hands over the drinks.

Delphine stood up slowly; every bone in her body seemed to ache. She had tears in her eyes, for herself, for the girl and for her baby.

"If they messed up my room. If they took my computer . . ."

"I told them not to. I told them you were a scientist and that you had years of work on the computer. I saw how important it was for you. Really."

Leigh's eyes were wide now. She reminded Delphine of a little girl getting caught at something naughty by her mother.

"If he's messed with my computer, I'm going to call the police and tell them everything I know about you and Tye."

"Please don't," Leigh said, tears still in her eyes. "I swear, Tye didn't want me to talk to you. Didn't want me to warn you about walking in on them. But I had to warn you."

Delphine tapped her key card on the bar. "Leave your man. Let him go. I have friends, we can get you and your child set up." She was not worried about what they would find on her computer. All the information from Tom Foster was on her phone and that had been safely in her bag.

"I would but he's got all the adoption papers on my baby. He owns Baby Blue."

"He's your pimp, isn't he?"

"I wouldn't say that. Why would you make him sound worse than he is? He genuinely likes me. He doesn't make me do anything I wouldn't do myself to feed the baby."

"Jesus Christ," Delphine snorted. Then she walked out of the bar without looking back.

BACK ON the sixth floor, the hallway was chaos: women in their nightgowns and men in sloppy big pajama bottoms were standing around in their slippers. Cops stood at doorways with their notebooks open, nodding while people listed things that were taken.

"They had no weapons, but the big guy made it clear he

would hurt us. It was weird . . . because he seemed kind of nice . . . I mean that was the funny thing. Polite, kind of; he was polite," a woman in her housecoat with a scarf over her bald head told the young scribbling cop.

"Excuse me, ma'am." Another older policeman touched Delphine's arm just as she turned to put her key in the lock. "You were out earlier; would you mind if I went in first just to make sure no one is hiding in there? We've had some break-ins on this floor."

"Sure," Delphine said. "Come on in." She still wasn't certain what she was going to do. She didn't really think that Tye would hurt the child, but he would certainly find out she had snitched on him soon enough, and before he went to trial or got put in lockup he would have plenty opportunity to come back anytime, day or night, and exact his revenge for meddling with his reputation.

The officer walked in first, looked around the rooms and the closets and bathroom. Delphine walked straight over to her ironing board command center and switched on her computer to make sure it was okay. It opened straight up to her email.

"You're lucky," the cop said. "Other people are missing their computers. Take a look around and see if anything is missing."

Delphine walked into the bathroom where she kept her big white cotton bag with a drawstring on top. It had been full of the medications that she didn't carry with her. Now it was on the floor and full of empty bottles.

She held the bag up in front of her as if it were a trophy fish. "All my meds are gone."

"Can you make a list of them along with the amounts and the name of your doctors?" the cop asked. He had a slight Southern accent, as if he had been from Texas a long time ago. Like Huckleberry Hound, except not so Deep South. He looked tired and sad. His eyes sagged as if he needed to sleep, and he looked as if he was trying to be kind to her but he just couldn't muster it. That, and he looked pissed off.

"It's not a long list," Delphine said. "I had only one bottle of painkillers, and one bottle of pills to help me sleep. I had one fentanyl patch if things got really bad. But I don't like to take opioids, they raise hell with my guts."

"I understand," the cop said, and he offered her his card. "Well, you still have a computer so maybe you can send me a list of what you had tomorrow in an email?" She took his card, and he finally managed a good smile for her. "We will investigate this. We will post somebody outside for the next week to make sure they don't come back. But I wouldn't hold my breath for us to make a quick arrest."

"Do you have any descriptions of the guys who broke in?"

"They jumped in on two couples while they were still in their room. Two males, Caucasian. One small and dark, dressed in a black hoodie, another one large, about six five, wearing a colorful Hawaiian-style aloha shirt."

The cop was reading from his notebook, then he took all of Delphine's details: name, phone number and the name of her doctor. He slapped his notebook closed. "You have any idea who did this? You see anyone suspicious hanging around, or anything that might help us catch these guys?"

"No," she said, then she paused and took a deep breath in.

"I mean, there are a lot of strange-looking people hanging out on the street late at night, but I didn't see anyone like those two . . ." She stuck to the basic truth even though she wanted to tell the cop everything she knew, but she thought of that dirty little baby she had bathed the night before.

"Anything else?" the cop asked.

"No," she said. "I will send you the list of my medications tomorrow. If I remember anything I will send it in the email."

"Good," he said, and he tipped his hat, then walked out the door.

His absence left a draft of cold air in the hallway. She felt lonelier than she ever had.

DELPHINE WOKE up to a violent knocking on the door. She was tired, and the sun was out, and the morning temperature was already starting to build to a smothering heat. She opened her eyes and the first thing she saw was a little brown bird sitting on the ledge of her kitchen window. The pounding continued and Delphine could not figure out for the life of her how this bird could be making all that racket.

"Just go away!" she said to the bird. The bundle of feathers flitted off and disappeared into the empty space just off the sixth floor. The bird was gone and the pounding had stopped, so Delphine stretched and looked forward to going back to sleep.

Someone slipped a key into the lock and opened the door. Delphine's yellow coat was hung on the chair next to the bed. She reached into the pocket and took out her stun gun. She slowly stood up and just as she turned the corner out of her room, she ran right into Leigh.

"Jesus ..." Delphine said. "What, did you come back for the food in the refrigerator?"

Leigh's eyes were red. She was backing up, away from the stun gun. "Hey ... no ... listen!"

They each took several steps back, as if a little bit of distance between them was going to guarantee some additional safety.

"What's going on now? How did you get in here?" Delphine lifted a bony finger and pointed at the red-eyed woman.

"I need help. I'm sorry. Tye is going over to Eastern Washington to turn over his drugs. He is going to confront the group of parents who are not satisfied with the agreement. He took some other children as bargaining chips."

"How did you get in here?"

"Tye threw away the passkey he used last night and I dug it out of the garbage. But listen, he's got my baby and two others. He took off in his rig."

"Give me the key. You can't just walk in and out of here." Delphine was angry now. She was weak and she was having a hard time focusing her eyes. She hated the idea of someone creeping in and out of the place where she slept. "Why come to me about your man turning his stolen drugs, my drugs included, into more saleable drugs?"

"He doesn't trust me after I talked to you and insisted that we not take your electronics. He's super pissed off; he's got it in his head that you are some kind of cop. He said he'd kill me if I snitched him off."

It crossed Delphine's mind that Tom may have done something clumsy and had already been made by Tye. Her stomach cramped up with this new worry.

Tears were starting to leak out of Leigh's eyes. All the lines on her face seemed to turn down, her shoulders slumped, and her knees buckled as if her bones were made of sugar and she was melting.

"So come with me. We'll hide so deep no one will be able to find you," Delphine said.

"Listen . . . I'm sorry," Leigh said. "Just now you are the only straight friend . . . you know, a regular type of citizen, I know."

"That's sad. It really is, but—"

"He hasn't left yet. I talked to him just around the block. He says I can go with him if I want. I'm supposed to meet him at the hotel in half an hour if I want to go with him. He is going to take Baby Blue whether I come or not. He is arranging possible adoptions for two other babies. He says this is all about his parachute thing. He's been getting paid in gold."

"Gold? Why?"

"Tye's got a thing about gold. He tells me he needs to convert these babies into something of tangible value. He converts all his assets into bullion. But something is happening to the gold. I don't know. He won't tell me."

"Let's get Blue Sky back right now, tonight. He is in real danger, you must know that." Delphine stormed around. She should have been taking her medications, but of course they were gone.

Leigh tumbled to the floor in tears, great heaving sobs of tears, as if she were having a convulsion of sadness and disbelief.

"Oh please, please, please . . . you helped me before. You didn't have to, but you did. I just thought you might be different and you might help me again." She was almost shrieking. Her chest was heaving and her hands covered her mouth.

"Take it easy," Delphine said in a more patient tone than she had used before. She started to draw closer to Leigh, holding her hands out. Leigh sat up straight and stopped moving. Then she vomited on the rug.

"Okay . . ." Delphine said, and she walked around to the kitchenette and brought a wastebasket and a clean dish towel over to the girl. Then she went back and got a bottle of water from the refrigerator, unscrewed the cap and gave it to her. In a way, the scientist was grateful to see the vomit. Here was something she could do that would be more useful than talking or listening.

"Okay. Start over. Where is Tye now?"

Leigh was still on the floor but now had her back against the couch and the waste can between her legs. "He's going over the pass to someplace near Yakima to meet with some prospective parents."

"When does he leave?"

"He wants me back in half an hour. It's two forty-five now. He doesn't trust me anymore. He's worried that I'm going to turn him in. These adoptions aren't exactly . . . you know . . . legal."

"I know that already, honey." Delphine encouraged her to drink some bottled water. The girl was breathing easier now and spitting into the wastebasket.

"Will you go to a shelter when we get the baby back? Stay away from Tye until you can sort things out? There is money for women in shelters now. You would have to stay away from him for a while."

"I will stay away from him." The girl looked up at the older woman. Leigh's eyes were red and she had a string of mucus hanging from her nose. Delphine handed her a tissue.

"Then let's go and grab little Mister Blue and bring him to the hospital. You have a relationship with someone in social work there?"

"Yeah, I do, but you can't go to my house right now. He's still there . . . I've never seen him quite like this. He says he's going to give Blue Sky to someone else. I can't tell you any more."

"Really?" Delphine helped Leigh to her feet. "I found blood in the bathtub. Whose blood is it, Leigh?"

"Like I said, he's pretty angry. It could be anybody's blood. I hate to think. He wants what he wants and nothing's going to get in his way."

"And what exactly does he want right now?" Delphine asked.

"He wants wealth. Substantial, primal, don't-give-a-shit-about-anybody-else . . . wealth."

Delphine checked the pockets of her old fireman's coat. In any investigation, there is research and rumination, but then there are moments when the rumination stops and events start to drive the train and the investigator has to take action of their own. Delphine, in spite of everything, wanted to ruminate a little more.

"Let me go and get Blue and I will meet you at the train station," Leigh said. "The main waiting area. There are a lot of people around there. He won't suspect me going there and if he catches us there, he won't make a scene. Then we can catch a ride back to the hospital. Or we'll take a train trip." Leigh was picking up her water bottle and looking around for other things she might forget, but she hadn't brought anything else.

"I will meet you there at three-fifteen," Leigh said. She didn't look Delphine in the eye.

"Three o'clock," Delphine said. Then the door shut and once again she was standing alone in the narrow hall to the door. She could smell food cooking, and the ever-present sirens sang close on the street.

DELPHINE WAITED in the main concourse of the King Street station from three to four. A few travelers waited on the pew-like wooden benches. The atmosphere of the place was clean and bright but felt right out of an old movie. White marble gleamed up almost three stories. The doors sparkled with brass handles, and red-capped men in their train company uniforms moved luggage in and out. Two little children, a boy and a girl, probably not yet ten years old, hectored their tired-looking mom by bouncing a rubber ball and laughing when it skittered away, rolling quickly on the stone floor.

"Stop that!" the mother hissed. A soldier smiled from down the line of seats.

"I swear, you aren't getting any lunch if you keep this up," the woman said, shaking her head as she looked down at her actual paper book.

Had it all been a ruse? Delphine thought to herself. Perhaps Leigh had done this to draw her out of her hotel room. Maybe she would go back to find not just her electronics gone but the entire place trashed.

She got up to walk outside to call her doctor again to make sure that she was going to have new prescriptions at the pharmacy, and was put on hold. This was the fifth call she had made on the subject since Leigh had left her room earlier that day. Her doctor needed a police report for the painkillers. Delphine needed a list from the doctor to send to the police in order to get a police report. She wasn't worried; she hated taking the pain medication. Pain meds felt like the early onset of death itself.

Soon enough, she was chaining up the Sportster in front of the welfare hotel where Leigh and Tye lived. And there on the corner was the biker dude. His helmet off. A bandanna over his face. Delphine began to march over to him and ask him just what the hell he was doing. But she stopped.

Suddenly, three police cars lined up in front of the hotel along with a SWAT van and an ambulance. Cops and EMTs were soon bustling about under the canopy of the hotel entrance.

She walked as quickly as she could. The leather guy ducked away, perhaps more afraid of the cops than he was of a possible confrontation with Delphine. She ran across the street and up the three steps. She fell in line with the cops and EMTs and rode a rickety elevator up to the sixth floor. When the door of the elevator wheezed open, she let the responders out first, as if she were going on to a higher floor, and stepped out just as it started to close. She and John had always talked about how it was much better to be thrown out of somewhere than it was to be denied access.

The hallway was a torrent of activity. Babies crying, women talking in the burbling vowels and consonants of languages she didn't understand, and cops—three men and two women speaking in loud English trying to ask questions, pens hovering over open notebook pages. On the floor was a smeared pool of blood that appeared to Delphine to be from a head wound where someone had at first dripped down into one spot and then crumpled on top of the spilled blood.

Delphine pushed her way inside the cramped apartment.

"Hey!" a female cop burst out at her back. Delphine waved over her shoulder.

A red-haired woman was standing by a window holding a baby blanket and a feeding bottle. She was crying. Delphine was wearing her own coat, which looked enough like a first responder's coat that it did not draw attention to her, and a black stocking cap to cover her bald head. She reached into her deep pocket and took out the laminated pamphlet again. She held it out to the crying woman and flipped through the pamphlet. Delphine pantomimed that she wanted her to look at the pages. The woman did, and within seconds she chose the page with the Russian writing. In big letters in English were the words, "Do you speak Russian?" with the same thing written in Russian just above the English.

"Yes," she said slowly and in a thick accent.

Delphine called the number on the cover and within a minute they were on the line with a Russian translator. A bill would come to Delphine's email address under John's name in a week.

The female cop who had yelled at her came up behind her.

The cops had sent out for a translator after scouring the apartment for an English speaker or anyone who was bilingual.

"You ..." the policewoman said. "I have some questions for her."

The translator asked the Russian woman if she wanted to talk with the police. The Russian woman shook her head vehemently in the negative. After some wrangling and a vague untrue promise to share information with the police, Delphine had cleared a little area by the window where she held her phone, which was on speaker now.

"I am a friend of Leigh's. I am not a police officer or an immigration officer," the translator said in Russian.

Then, after the woman spoke, the translator said, "Leigh ... yes. I know Leigh. Tye hits her hard. Very often." The translator was a man with an impassive voice.

"Where is Leigh now?"

"I do not know."

"Where is Tye?"

"He took three babies. My Juris, Baby Blue and one other. An older girl went with him. Christina. Babysitter, I think. Leigh too might have gone with Tyler. I saw her walk out just after Tye went outside. Leigh does not have good sense."

"Is Tye headed east?"

The woman started crying. "I do not know. Someplace far away, I think. I may never see Juris again. Visitation." She said the last thing very slowly and in a broken kind of English. "Visitation ... what mean?" she said.

"Going to visit," Delphine said. "Sometimes one parent gets to visit a child after a divorce."

"We're not married. I'm not married," the translator said for the Russian girl. "Yakima . . . Yakima? Does that make any sense to you?" the woman asked, looking fiercely into Delphine's eyes.

"Did he take the babies to Yakima?"

"I do not know," she said through the translator. "I just heard the word, Yakima, said over and over. He kept saying his gold would be there. I don't know. Something about eighty-eight. The eighty-eight. I don't know. I don't know."

Gold again. The cops were coming toward her now. "One last thing. Can you show me where Tye keeps his paperwork?"

The Russian girl, who did not want to give her name, looked up and saw the police walking toward them. She darted from the window, and they walked toward the front door. Down the hall was a large bathroom and shower room which apparently served the entire floor. The cops were held up at the door of the apartment where a policeman, apparently in some kind of supervisory position, stopped them all and demanded a situation report.

In the bathroom, the girl showed Delphine to a stall and opened the door. Inside, the toilet was clearly out of order because there was no toilet at all. There was a large green filing cabinet. It was locked.

In her magic pocket was a small ring of sledge keys for lock picking and an assortment of bobby pins. Sledge went in first, then a bobby pin to tickle the wedges up above the sledge.

The translator had hung up. "Hammer?" Delphine asked slowly and stupidly. Then she made a hammering motion. The Russian girl looked around, confused, and then took off one of her heavy and tall-heeled shoes. Delphine gestured to the lock where she now had both hands employed. The girl swung her shoe and hit the end of the sledge, the button went in and the cabinet was unlocked.

Police shoes squeaked on the linoleum outside. Delphine grabbed a handful of files. She pulled the girl inside another bathroom stall where they stood on the toilet that apparently did work. The hall doorway to the bathroom door swung open, and the cops scanned around quickly and called out for anyone inside to turn themselves in. Then they backed out and continued their search.

Just then a young blond woman poked her head in. "Is there any cash in there?" she asked in unaccented English.

"Christina!" the Russian girl yelled. "Babies! Where babies? My Juris. Where is he?" she yelled.

Christina came into the stall and ducked down. "Fuck this, I got to get out of this. I got to get out of here. I want out. Where is his money?"

"Let's look," Delphine said.

The three of them went through the contents of the cabinet. They found no money, only legal-looking file folders. The folders contained forms, all on amateurish letterhead, that read "Dearborn Adoption Service: Eighty-Eight Babies a Month." Tye's first and last name, date of birth, and social security number appeared on the forms under "Adoption Supervisor." Delphine held folders for five children. Some were processed years ago, some were as recent as this summer. Thankfully, there was nothing to suggest there were as many as eighty-eight adoptions per month.

In the bottom drawer were three large chunks of lead. Delphine tapped on the three of them with her tools. The metal was soft and black—yes, clearly lead. There were also tools to etch metal, and gold paint. What troubled Delphine the most was that there was a large swastika embossed on each of the supposedly gold bars. They were badly faked Nazi gold bars. She had seen photos of actual Nazi gold on the History Channel.

"This has got to be worth something." The blond woman took two lead bars and ran out of the bathroom. "I'm done with this fucking guy."

"Wait," the other woman said. "Juris, my Juris!" She ran after the blond.

In the paperwork, there also looked to be billing invoices, but instead of dollar amounts were notations for ounces or pounds. Fake Nazi gold? Drugs?

There was one file that contained the names of five prospective parents wanting adoptions. The file folder was marked "Rolling 88's."

The Russian girl rushed back in and looked at Delphine. "Tye . . . he took Leigh. Carried . . ." She was pantomiming lifting something in her arms. "Blood . . . all over. Lifted. Babies were . . . ah . . . down." She pointed down. "Maybe in car with . . . the Babysitter. They have my Juris."

She waited to see if there was any light of understanding in Delphine's eyes. "Blood? Carry? Babies in car?" she asked hopefully.

"The Babysitter is a man?" Delphine asked just to be certain she was not crossing into some language tangle with other possible babysitters.

"I no like the Babysitter man. Yes, he is not good."

"Good. Thank you," Delphine said, holding both her shoulders. "We should both go and try to find them." Delphine hugged the woman, then walked away down the back stairs where blood spatter lit the dirty concrete like drops of fresh paint.

The first floor gave way to the stairs that led to the small parking garage below, where she ran into a very large man wearing a Hawaiian shirt and holding on to a baby—Blue Sky. The big man had blood on his hands and was trying to wipe the blood off the small denim blanket the baby was wrapped in. This was not the man in leather with the motorcycle. Delphine was guessing he was the Babysitter.

"Give me that child," Delphine said.

"Slow down now," the Babysitter said in a deep voice.

"I said, give me that child."

"I don't think so," the big man said.

Delphine walked up to him and reached for the child. He shouldered her and backed the thin woman against the wall. "You're the snoopy woman with the stun gun. Listen, don't worry. I'm going to get this little guy back to his mom."

"Where is Leigh? Whose blood is on your hands? Hand the baby over to me, it's simple."

"You have no idea what you are talking about, lady. Nothing about this is simple."

The big man turned a corner and walked down into the parking garage. Delphine could hear the little boy squawking like a chicken, and then the echoing cry down in the gloom of the car park. The big man must have been running, for the sound of the baby keening was fading like the light of winter. She followed it.

On the first floor of the underground parking garage, Delphine saw a large dumpster next to a staircase door. She heard a car door slam and baby Blue Sky's voice muffled behind another closing car door. Doors opened, doors slammed, an engine started and tires squealed in the echoing distance. Delphine stopped. At the lid of the dumpster was a bright smear of red. She walked over and lifted the lid.

Slumped in the near-empty receptacle sat Leigh's lifeless body. She was badly bruised, with a substantial screwdriver driven into her right eyeball, clear up to the handle. The expression on her face was of faint surprise.

DELPHINE WENT back to the apartment and found a cop. She was certain that it was now time to involve someone with more law enforcement authority than her and Tom. She spent the rest of the afternoon telling various police officers everything she knew about who Leigh was and what she might have been involved in. But Delphine did not give the cops any details about Tye, not a name, not a description. Not anything. If the cops scooped up Tyler in the next couple of days, Tyler would use the babies in trade. He would barter each one of them for a better legal outcome. The babies could end up in some uncertain foster care setting. She did not give the cops any of the files in case she was going to need them to help her if she ended up being charged with a crime. This too was something she took from John. "We don't do anyone any good if we end up in jail," he had often said.

Delphine was in deep, but she knew she needed to be the one to find Tom Foster's child or else Tom would never find his baby.

A fat male policeman said he was going to let Delphine go for now, but told her to answer her phone if they called. "Don't leave town." She said she wouldn't and then headed for her hotel to pack the motorcycle for a trip east.

CANCER IS like a broken copying machine. A mistake appears in a cell and when it is fed back into the copy machine, more mistakes are added and the healthy cells are soon overwhelmed by errors. There are two types of treatment. A doctor can try to erase all the mistakes with poison; essentially, this is the traditional chemotherapy. Another treatment introduces new cells that try to fix the copier so it doesn't add any more mistakes. This is immunotherapy and it is effective for some cancer patients but not for others. If the cancer is not caught early, most patients will experience both. So, while some of the cancer cells are being killed, doctors are trying to fix the copier and catch up with the production of problematic cells.

The pancreas produces bile and other hormones that aid in digestion. When the pancreas is overwhelmed, the patient usually shows signs of jaundice. Whites of the eyes darken. Appetite worsens, patients will have pain in their abdomen, and the liver and kidneys might become sick, sore. Even if the patient can eat, their digestive system does not transport energy or nutrition to the rest of their body. Patients are tired, and though they are not necessarily hungry, they are wasting away nevertheless.

Death comes slowly, usually after a long starvation. Energy lessens, muscles atrophy along with the vitality of life. Patients disappear into their withering bodies. Patients who eat food supplements to boost digestion and energy can gain some temporary relief. But ultimately, it's like putting high-octane fuel into a broken motor. Some alternative therapies, like coffee enemas, have short-term effects. They make you feel energetic but do nothing to fix the engine. A person can live a long time with pancreatic cancer, but if the treatment does not stop the production of the cancer cells, then the patient dies.

Delphine had lost seventy pounds since the onset of her disease. She once had loved the sensuous pleasure of eating good food. She and John had gone to Paris for her sixtieth birthday. They went to see their favorite band, the Mountain Goats, in a small theater near the Sorbonne. They didn't go to a single museum, but had wandered through Paris until they were thoroughly lost. Then they sat down in a café to eat and look at their phones to try to figure a way back to the houseboat on the Seine where they were staying. French food, with its musky palate of fat and sweetness, had surprised and delighted her.

But now Delphine was looking forward to eating half a power bar and swigging down her pills with a fruity sports drink. She exited the hotel with the files from Tye's hidden cabinet stuffed into the inner pocket of her coat. She needed a nap but was determined to leave Seattle on the hunt for Blue Sky. The police wouldn't get too excited about solving anything unless there was someone holding their feet to the fire: the press or some intangible politics that directly affected the police. She knew she had to take care of this herself. Even if she didn't find Leigh's killer, she would still need to find Tom's baby before the child got swallowed up into the legal system. The drugs, the ones meant to replace those Tye had stolen from her, had been delivered to the front desk. All of them were there except her pain medication because the pharmacist insisted on waiting for the police report before processing the pills.

Once in her room, she laid out her basic supplies. She had a bivvy tent with a sleeping bag and pad inside of it. She had a lightweight tarp. She had a parachute cord, a water bottle, a fuel bottle and tiny single-burner stove, an aluminum cup that could act as a bowl or a plate, a basic tool kit and a waterproof fabric bucket. The Sportster had two saddlebags and she could tie a pack to the passenger seat. Her clothes and medicine would easily fit in the bags, and she would put the camping gear over the bags on the rear of the bike. She had some good boots and rain gear, plus a lightweight sweater.

Delphine didn't mind sleeping out. She was used to living out of her twenty-three-foot skiff, sleeping under the tarp that covered the bow. She could travel for two weeks like that, looking for humpback whales along the inside waters of southeastern Alaska. She would sometimes travel from Sitka to Frederick Sound, north up to Juneau and then farther north to Glacier Bay, photographing whales, making recordings of their vocalizations and taking blubber samples with either a crossbow or a pneumatic rifle.

Her chest hurt worrying about what Tye and the Babysitter would do to her if she found them. But still, she was ambivalent about making the trip. She was dying now, she was certain of that. What good would it do anyone if she got out on the highway and died along the side of the road? Why not turn everything over to the cops? As she had recounted everything to the police, she had realized she couldn't make a case as to who had killed Leigh.

She knew nothing about the Babysitter. She knew he was more than unsavory; he was dangerous. She considered not going, but then she thought about how she would spend her time if she stayed. Every second, every minute in pain and helplessness. Even if she died doing this, at least she wouldn't have died in this hotel room, sequestered away with others held hostage by death.

She would go north and over the Cascades. If it turned out that she was not strong enough for a long trip, she could duck in to see old friends in Winthrop or else she could go to Robert and Jenny's cabin to the east, near the Canadian border, before she turned south toward Yakima.

It was seven o'clock and Delphine lay down on top of her gear. She knew she was going to fall asleep, but she didn't know for how long. If she had died right then she would have had few regrets ... but still, as she drifted off, she wanted to go out and find the baby. Finding the baby would give her some purpose. Something other than herself to think about before dying.

CHAPTER FIVE

Delphine was packed and ready to rattle across the Cascade mountains by nine the next morning. It was a Sunday and the Seattle traffic was not horrendous. She was weak still, but the momentum of the bike on the concrete soothed her. She was not going to stop until she got off the freeway near Mount Vernon and got on Highway 20, where she would rest, eat and get some gas.

She would ride through the neighborhood where she had grown up, in Lake City. Past the streets where she had organized her childhood bike gang, the Blue Angels, with playing cards on clothespins through her spokes. She rode in formation with four or five other girls down the nearly empty streets and wandered through the neighborhood while her mom worked at Grandma Mile's restaurant on Aurora. Her skirts flew high while she biked with the Angels, adjusting the barrettes in her short brown hair. Even though it was not the most direct route, she would drive north into the mountains surrounding the Pasayten Wilderness area, down into the Methow Valley, and then southwest, skirting the great basin of Eastern Washington and, finally, down into the rich farmland surrounding Yakima. Both Leigh and the young Russian mom at the welfare hotel had suggested that Tye was off to Yakima.

Once, when she and John were visiting with a drug client at Lemon Creek Correctional Center in Juneau, they got locked down in the attorney room. The lockdown lasted a full two hours. John spent the time in an off-the-record conversation about the dope business in the Pacific Northwest and the client had waxed eloquent on the story of the drug trade in Yakima. Yakima was one of the northernmost pump stations on a drug pipeline run by two Mexican cartels. Up from Mexico came heroin, fentanyl, oxycontin and cocaine in industrial quantities; from there, the drugs were traded for cash on the deserted lots and back streets. From Yakima, the drugs sprayed out in all directions via smaller loads and more independent agents. Yakima wasn't Casablanca, it was merely a place where the handful of heavy hitters in the drug trade could do some anonymous deals and then blend into the background of the honest fruit pickers and stoop laborers who plied their trade in the cheap labor of American agribusiness.

The weather was cooling by the time Delphine passed through her old neighborhood. The young man who had befriended her father in his last years—"the kid" as her father referred to him—was living in the old family home her father and Uncle William had built. Even from the freeway, where commercial trucks and recreational vehicles clattered along the seams of pavement, she could get a sense of the country opening up the way she remembered it as a child. Seattle had lost a sense of itself as a lumber and fishing town. No longer did it seem like the ramshackle Hooverville of the depression era. Hobos had given way to the hordes of homeless people who camped under the freeway overpasses. Hobos were working men who had no jobs, and the homeless seemed to be a new form of underclass marked by drug addiction and mental illness. Hobos lived in camps along the railway, often surrounded by blackberry bushes and willow trees. The homeless were now structurally a part of the city itself. Concrete gutters ran with their urine where they gathered, and the night sounds of discontent and violence against women replaced the train whistles, fog and the singing birds. But north of the city, there was still some open ground near the saltwater sloughs. While leaving Everett, Delphine saw there was still a field where someone used to raise mules, though the mules were long gone. The Sportster buzzed and rumbled farther and the sky opened up. The feeling of being on a flat plain that ran to the Pacific Ocean pressed in, and the freeway itself started to feel like a river of commerce in an open landscape. The timber industry was fading in this part of the world, and Everett no longer smelled of pulp mills, but of overwhelming vehicle exhaust. Soon, the mountains started easing closer and the strip malls, gas stations and weed-strewn lots for equipment storage became fewer.

Just under a sign for a boat storage lot was a billboard with a full-color photograph of a fetus. The text read, WE WILL HELP YOU FIND THEM A HOME. There was an 800 number on the bottom. Below the structure of the sign was a biker in black leather, scanning the road. His head turned on a swivel as she drove past.

Delphine had seen enough of the mysterious biker to recognize his profile in her rearview mirror. In a few minutes he was about five car lengths behind her. He was tall and thin and was clearly not the same build as the Babysitter. She slowed down along the side of the road and was about to pull over to stop on the interstate when the biker gunned his engine and passed her. As he passed, she saw the lettering on the back of his jacket: ROLLING 88's. She remembered the mention of the Rolling 88's in Tye's paperwork.

Now, she dropped the Sportster into gear and sped off to follow the biker for a change.

She followed him off onto Cook Road and blustered past flower fields and old farmhouses, now bought up by holding companies. Here red-shouldered hawks sat on the telephone lines. As she approached the Skagit, she saw two bald eagles worrying the bottoms of clouds above the river.

All she learned from the internet on her phone was that the Rolling 88's were an outlaw motorcycle gang based out of several locations, most notably northern Idaho and Eastern Washington. They were closely affiliated with the Aryan Nations prison gang. The papers she had gathered up in the Seattle hotel suggested that Tyler too had some affiliation. But she was surprised that the online trail was very short. She would ask Tom about the 88's when she called him later in the evening. And she was going to need to follow this one member rumbling down the blacktop in front of her.

Delphine remembered the feeling of first opening search engines and following their leads wherever they were sprinkled in the virtual world. It seemed thrilling, as if a whole era of investigation was laid out at her feet. Later, she and John discovered the best and most secure information was hidden behind either government web pages or well-protected sites with expensive paywalls. Official criminal information was hard to come by legally. Court records were often open to public access and could give good clues as long as the police investigation had led to actual litigation. LexisNexis could offer up some public-access information, but very little could be found through "Inspector Google." The more violent the crime, the less reliable information could be found on free online sites. The real world of addresses where mail was delivered and garbage was thrown out was still the best way to find good information. Unless you had a lot of money for decent subscription services. But John and Delphine enjoyed following people and, if necessary, collecting up their juicy trash.

She had helped John follow people of interest. But truth be told, they were not as experienced in tailing people as someone like Tom Foster would be. Tom was a big-city operative and in big cities, three people could follow one suspect easily: two behind the suspect and across the street from each other and one in front within radio or phone contact to take care of unexpected turns. But Alaska was mostly small-town work where a stranger on the street stuck out like a marching band. There were no secrets in small Alaskan towns, even if people were dead wrong about what was going on. It didn't matter; followers were conspicuous. The only question was when the inevitable confrontation would occur. So too, it seemed, with Delphine and the Rolling 88. They had both been made—but when would they acknowledge it and how dangerous would the confrontation be?

John had often said, "Getting your ass kicked is always bad for business and should be avoided at all costs." It was best to

keep your distance and always leave a way out. Either that or
just stop short and ask whoever was following you, "Hey, what's
up? Why are you following me?" The strategy always came
back around to avoiding an ass kicking.

The Rolling 88 stopped at a gas station near the one good
barbecue joint on the highway in Marblemount, and she did the
same. He bought gas, refusing to look directly at her across
the lane. The handle of the gas pump was cold in her hand
and as she filled the tank, her legs became weak. She paid with
her credit card just seconds after he left the station. She
gunned her bike to catch up, but suddenly lost the strength in
her arms. Her hands shook on the grips until she knew she
couldn't drive fast enough to catch up to him. She rode to a
rutted track that ended in a pullout by the river and placed her
bike against a poplar tree so that her kickstand wouldn't give way.

The hiss and rumble of river water rode on top of the cool
air that drifted down from the rocky course. Delphine untied
her sleeping bundle and laid it in the shade of the trees, where
she was out of sight. As soon as she lay down with her head
propped on her rolled-up jacket, she was asleep.

She dreamed of bumblebees, fat and lazy, bobbing on the
warm air around her. Her stomach hurt with cramping, and
she vomited just one time in her sleep. Her hands shook as she
slept, but the river seemed to hold her in an affectionate
embrace, its cool air brushing her cheek.

When she woke up, it was twilight. Next to her was the
man—the Rolling 88—silently watching her. She reached for
her stun gun but didn't have the strength to sit up quickly. She
operated the taser so that blue and silver arched across the

contact points. The man had his helmet off and his bandanna pulled down. He held his hands up as if he were surrendering.

"Whoa now. You all right?" he said.

"What are you doing?" Delphine asked in a voice that betrayed her weakness.

"I'm going to Yakima to find Tyler Dearborn." She could now see the man's distinctive facial hair, which was cut in a kind of scraggly Vandyke. "What are you doing?"

"I want those children out of his hands," she said.

"You want to travel together? Or I could just meet you in Yakima at the information fair."

"I can find my own way," she said. "Do you have any tattoos reading MOB?"

"All right then." He smiled and shook his head, then kicked over his modified Electra Glide, pulled down his helmet and pulled up his bandanna. Then he was gone.

"Fucking men," she said under her breath.

DELPHINE BOUGHT a sandwich and sat out on a graffiti-covered picnic table and listened to the birds sing off in the woods. She threw up again and then found a motel nearby that rented refurbished farmworker's cabins. She showered and listened to the radio while she fell asleep.

In the morning, she looked out the rippled glass of her single-pane window to see a small black bear nuzzling the lid of a chained-up garbage can that she was too small to open. She waddled down the edge of the lane, which led to the highway. The bear gave the impression of meandering without purpose. Suddenly two small cubs came bouncing up behind her. The big-eared cubs had to run to keep up. Black bears and homeless people always had a way of finding whatever food others didn't appear to want. Delphine took a deep breath and slipped her coat on, trying not to worry about the bears approaching the highway.

She ordered a cup of hot chocolate and a cup of coffee from the hotel café. She drank a little from each and then used her spoon to mix them together. In the café was a truck driver who had filled his thermos. He wore cowboy boots and his big belly hung over his dinner-plate belt buckle. He was watching some right-wing talking head on his cell phone, listening to the rant on full volume. It was bad manners, and she could tell the young family in the other corner was uncomfortable listening to the tinny voice listing the failings of avaricious and menda-cious leaders of the "Demo-craps." The husband wore waterproof sandals and cargo shorts. He grimaced at the trucker, while his wife tried to distract her child using a color-ful board book that was apparently about baby bears. They too had seen the bears this morning.

Delphine thought of Baby Blue. She was haunted by the image of Leigh lying in the dumpster in the parking garage. She didn't know for certain who had ended her life. The Babysitter had Blue Sky in his arms and wouldn't have had enough time to take care of the problem with Delphine fol-lowing him down into the parking garage. Not enough time to kill Leigh and dump the body. He had blood on his hands, of course, but it bothered her that she couldn't put the timeline together. The mysterious Rolling 88 rider seemed way too relaxed to be outrunning a murder rap. Instead, she suspected he was simply an unhappy customer of Tyler's. Or perhaps, like a salmon born in a gravel bed far upstream, this rider was just making his way home and their paths had crossed by accident.

Of course, she still wanted to find Tom's child, but somewhere in her sick gut she was beginning to feel that Tye knew exactly what was going to happen while she was flailing around in the dark. *What the hell am I doing?* she thought to herself, and she didn't have an answer. But she was married to the idea of solving the riddle.

Delphine ordered some wheat toast and a side of bacon. Fruit plates arrived at the table of the husband, wife and child. Delphine would keep going down the highway; she would find the babies. She would get them away from Tyler and the Babysitter. If only she could live long enough.

DELPHINE THOUGHT of John all the more. He loved mystery and would hunt down anything. He would know how all these things were connected: Leigh's death, the Babysitter and the Rolling 88's.

They had met in the wilderness in 1973. John was leading a string of nine mules to Hidden Lakes, over the log bridge over Diamond Creek. Down by the banks of the stream where she'd made her own camp, she was preparing her dinner in a blackened cook pot over a wood fire when she first heard the footfall of the animals on the planking. She looked up. From his viewpoint, he was looking down on a lovely blond woman squatting by the fire. From her viewpoint, she was looking at the belly of a smelly mule. When she hiked into Hidden Lakes the next day, John was there, and he seemed determined to make an impression on her. He had good manners, saying "please" with every request, and even calling her "ma'am" twice. She started in as soon as they met, teasing him about how bad he smelled, about what TV shows he had watched as a child. "I don't think I've ever met anyone who watched *Bonanza*," she commented. They washed the camp dishes together that night. When his fingers touched hers in the cooling dishwater, she saw that he was a flirt and decided she didn't like him.

Later, Delphine heard from friends in the Forest Service that John had "lots of girlfriends." This made her uncomfortable. She was twenty-one and never had a real boyfriend before. Men were distant creatures to her. Boys always seemed to like her, but they were dopey. Delphine was completely unaware that boys were naturally attracted to her, and this was the reason for their dopiness. Back in Seattle, she and her friends hated the pretty girls at Nathan Hale High. They loved to make fun of the rich girls who had nice cars that they had no idea how to maintain. They spoke of the vacuous boys who lost all sense of humor when they came around those girls. They hated jocks and were irritated by the smart boys who seemed to condescend to sit next to them at lunch and wouldn't make jokes. These boys looked offended at being teased. But the boys were always there, sending notes, acting horribly uncomfortable and nervous. She assumed they were snobs and they assumed she was "weird" because she sewed her own clothes and had dirty hands with grease under her fingernails. She didn't need boys, but they were always around.

John hung around her in the months after they met. She

always thought he was lying to her, telling her she was beautiful, yet he always seemed happy to be in her presence. She didn't mind getting ready to go see him—she liked her handmade clothes and enjoyed washing her face with unscented soap and not ever wearing makeup, which was the most fake thing she could think of. But when she looked into the mirror, she saw her father's bulbous nose, and she knew that she was hideous compared to other girls. She had been born with a defect in her left leg that made her walk with a subtle limp, and the limp and the nose were all the boys were really looking at. The blond hair and her big breasts were just another sign that she was shallow. Not to be taken seriously.

But Delphine couldn't shake the cowboy who was rumored to have had sex with lots of women. He hated to hike, but would ride a horse some eighteen miles round trip at night to bring her fresh fruit, candy and the homemade pie that the camp cook made for paying guests. She would hear his horse come into her camp in the middle of the night and throw back her tent flap, and John would be there looking tired and dirty, saying, "I thought you might like some fresh food." She would sit inside her sleeping bag and eat greedily with the single spoon from her kit, making him sit or squat in the door of her little tent. As the sun began to rise in the east, she would zip the tent flap and thank him with as much kindness as she could muster. Soon she would hear the horse snuffling against the bit and the rattle of stones along the ground as the tired horse went up the trail and disappeared into the breaking dawn.

John was frustrated she would not let him in the tent. Her friends suggested that it was the horse that was the problem.

Horses would pee anywhere in camp and Delphine resented the lingering smell. She was tough and a hiker by nature. This is what prompted John to try hiking in to see her. But no. John ended up sleeping in a tent with the male ranger after dinner. John was ready to either give up or take the hint that the strong woman with the beautiful face just wasn't going to sleep with him.

Delphine was a virgin. She felt that being a virgin was somehow, like the limp and all the hiking, a disqualifying factor for her and the smelly cowboy with the brown eyes that seemed to scan his boots when their conversations lagged into silence. But John never saw it that way, apparently. He asked her to dinner toward the end of summer on a night when they were both in town. He cooked her a meat loaf with baked potatoes and a green salad, which he would do often in the next forty-five years.

John lived in a tiny white house that sat near the irrigation ditch in the back of a sixty-acre hay field. He had spent most of the day washing himself down, as well as every surface of the kitchen and bathroom. As he cleaned, John was beginning to see the merit in her concerns about his cleanliness. He wrestled his old electric stove out of the kitchen and onto the dusty apron of the field so he could take the whole apparatus apart to clear the mouse nests from the insides. Some of the nests actually had little pink baby mice curled together in the remnants of his paper towels along with the hard peppercorns of their little mousy turds. His shower and tub were caked with a rind of soap, trail dust and whiskers from when he shaved in the shower. He scrubbed and banged on the electric range so the little mouse pups could wriggle off into the field. He bathed outside because he was afraid that the mouse-turd stink would follow him wherever he went.

A coyote slunk across the dusty drive. The coyote stopped suddenly, watching the grass in front of him, then hopped straight into the air and buried his snout in the alfalfa, bringing up a mouse in his teeth. The coyote snapped it down headfirst so the tail flipped over its gums like a pink spaghetti noodle.

Something good for the coyote had come of all this cleaning, John thought to himself.

The little white house smelled of dust, alfalfa, and the bite of cold water from the irrigation ditch by the time Delphine arrived with a bottle of expensive bourbon and a can of her favorite body powder, which they had discussed when they met out in the woods. The powder helped prevent the chafing and smell she herself had experienced on the days when she had to lug her hundred-pound pack some fourteen miles. When she handed the can of powder over to him at the door, John could not be sure if it was a joke or not.

They ate sitting on the tailgate of his pickup. They drank the bourbon with cold water from his well. They listened to early Tom Waits records as the stars began to appear. Night in the North Cascades was deep black, broken only by the shattered fragments of the Milky Way. A red-tailed hawk swooped down from the hillside and landed on the power line to his house. They allowed themselves permission not to talk while they watched the hawk fold its wings and settle into itself, then silently scan the field for food.

John tasted ketchup and Wild Turkey on her tongue when they first kissed. The hawk stirred, dropped down, then glided off into the alfalfa. Delphine shook as if she were freezing when they started kissing. The sides of her torso were taut with muscles and her lips were soft. She seemed to enjoy kissing but each time he put his hands up to touch her breasts she shimmied away from him. They were alone in the dark, and the light from the little white house spilled like cold milk out onto the dust, and soon they gathered up the dishes and took them inside.

BACK ON the road, Delphine snaked up the west side of the Cascade Range. The air was clear and clean. Dogwood fluff sparkled in the light. The highway curved up steep hills, and recreational vehicles plugged up the passing lanes. Not many commercial rigs liked this twisty road that crowned out at Rainy Pass and tumbled down into the Methow Valley, which had once been her and John's home long ago but was now mostly the scenic little community for Seattle's wealthy. She still had friends in the Methow, old friends from her wilderness rangering days who were still obsessively active in their sixties, but she wouldn't stop. She was aware that her health was an awkward subject for them. Or perhaps it was she, Delphine, who felt awkward. She didn't enjoy their troubled expressions during mundane conversations. They too felt awkward about their gratitude at not being sick. Her friends owed their good fortune to their country lifestyle of diet and exercise, while Delphine's deepest thoughts were occupied with the question of why she had gotten cancer, at least until the pain in her back and belly became so intense that it robbed her of the ability to concentrate. Though now, she didn't think of how her cancer had started, but how it was going to end.

Delphine didn't mind pulling in behind the slow-moving rigs with their oversized travel trailers. Once she found the right gear, she could pull into their blubbery slipstream and watch the lines on the pavement and relax into the curves. When the travelers pulled over for a pee break or a photograph, Delphine would shift through the gears and feel the full push of the wind against her goggles. Once, a timid doe started easing out into the road and instead of slipping past her, Delphine pulled over and stopped. The doe poked her nose out, sniffing the air, always looking ahead when her instinct should have been to look for cars coming along the highway. Her gait reminded Delphine of swimming. Throwing her nose and neck ahead and pulling her back and legs along to ease forward. Delphine shut her bike down and listened to the doe's cloven feet touch the pavement until she disappeared into the trees on the downhill side.

Delphine kept thinking about the wisdom of her trip. One part of her, a small part, wanted to be working on her transfer memos. But now she had to find the babies that Tyler had taken. Delphine had a nagging feeling that she had let the children slip through her fingers back in Seattle. The blood in the tub could be the child's blood. But given what she knew about Tye, the blood could have been almost anyone's.

Of course, whales too died long and painful deaths. She had observed it herself. Whales entangled in enough fishing gear that they would succumb to infection and wasting, using all their strength just to bring their heads to the surface for air, until they couldn't anymore and drowned. Their big brains, their big dexterous bodies that had once served them so well, were of no use. But she didn't want to think about that now. She only wanted to find the babies and mark this case as solved.

THE ROAD downhill from Rainy that became Washington Pass was thrilling and familiar. She liked the pull of gravity, appreciated the quiet of easing up on the engine and coasting. She did not see any more big animals, but some ground squirrels ran across the highway. Delphine had not made an appointment to see her doctor or to go to her last chemo treatments. She was now thinking of graduating herself from all her treatments. She thought of this when she saw the squirrels pause in the middle of the road ahead, stare at her bearing down upon them and then scuttle away to the side of the highway.

"The hell with it," she said to herself. "I'm not going to park myself in the middle of the highway and wait to get run over. I'm going to just keep moving."

Delphine made it through the little tourist town of Winthrop and went straight up the hill to drive past her friends' house. She just wanted to see if they were home. She had many good memories of being with them and with John, here in the valley: swimming holes on hot days and sleeping under the stars in the bed of a truck. Nostalgia for her past made her depressed now, as long as the child was still missing.

The old friends lived on a dead-end road and when she drove the Sportster by their pristine new house, she saw her friend out in her garden with a large straw sun hat on. She was bent over a raised garden box gathering what looked like fresh carrots, with long greens swinging in her hand before she flipped them into a bucket. She was fit and tan. Her husband was pushing his electric lawn mower around the lawn. They were living the future Delphine would never have. Tears came to her eyes, and she eased past their house to the end of the road where she turned around and drove back out to the highway. She stopped at a gas station.

Delphine's hands were shaking as she filled the Sportster's tank. She took off her heavy coat and her helmet, nauseous. The sun was hot but somehow the dry air felt cool on her skin. She drove south toward the town of Twisp and found a campground near the river.

She asked the campground attendant if she could find a place to just lie down in the shade for a few hours. The attendant, a thin boy who looked like he had just gotten his first summer job, looked at this bald old woman for a few moments before asking her, "You sure you wouldn't like to get a hotel room or something? They got some nice ones just here. Ones with air-conditioning and everything." He had a sweet, concerned expression, his eyebrows arched with his big eyes crinkled at the corners.

"No thank you," Delphine said. "I just need to lie down for a bit. I've got to be going."

He took her over to a little flat spot under a pine tree about a hundred feet from the river. He said he wouldn't charge her, but if it turned out she wanted to stay the night to come see him. Delphine agreed. The boy even helped her untie her sleeping bundle on the back of the bike and they both carried it to the shade and laid it out.

"You gonna be okay here?" he asked.

"Of course," she said. "If I'm still asleep when it starts to get cool in the afternoon . . . or if you need to rent this spot to someone, you come to wake me up. Okay?"

The boy backed away from her as if he wasn't quite sure what he was supposed to do. But after a few steps, he turned in the direction of his tiny log cabin office. He walked through the grass where the rainbird sprinklers were chip, chip, chipping the water through their nozzles and jogged out of the way of the water falling around him.

Delphine lay down and the gravity of the earth felt like a weighted blanket across her shoulders. She liked the lazy sound of the sprinklers, and the dry air sparkled with the smell of cut hay and dogwood bloom.

She fell asleep quickly and she dreamed of her own son, Bertie, and wanted to call him on the phone, but something always kept them from connecting on her end. In the dream, either her phone was lost or when she found it, it would not work. Her heart yearned to see him, to hold him in her arms. She dreamed of bathing him as a baby back in Glacier Bay, when she was young and healthy, and he would cackle at her touch. The dream morphed like the weather and soon Bertie was a dolphin swimming next to her, then he was a sperm whale calf easing to the surface where she lay waiting for him in the sea. Aunties crowded around them, lifting him out of the water. He rode her back for a moment, then flippered away toward the waiting snout of another nursemaid. She dove and her huge body was weightless. The surface of the sea was a rippling mirror above and as she dove, her body compressed. She could hear the clicking sounds of the nursemaids keeping track of her baby as she dove down to find something to eat, darker and darker, the pressure pushing against her body, the volume of air in her lungs seeming to harden as she descended. In the background was the clicking of her family rising above her, rising toward the diffused light of the bright surface.

She felt something moving across her legs, then up on her chest. She wasn't sure if it was a part of the dream or something new. Pressure and then a musty smell like a rodent's cage. When she opened her eyes, she recognized a mottled grey and brown snake moving up her torso. As she sat up straight, the snake began to fall into her lap and she grabbed the reptile just under the head. The fat king snake opened its mouth and wriggled like a pressurized garden hose let loose. She did not see fangs.

"Hello, you," Delphine said to the king snake, then she stood up and walked over to the grass by the river and let it go. She was awake. "Go on now, sweetheart. Find your own bed for the afternoon." The snake didn't waste time getting away from her.

Delphine lay back down on the nest she had made for herself. Her phone sounded a short tone. She took it out of her pocket and read the text that had just come in.

Robert died this morning. His heart gave out. He was home in the bed where he loved to sleep. I will let you know once we decide on any memorial. The kids are sad but okay. Jenny.

Delphine clambered slowly to her feet. She laced her boots tight and repacked her gear. She kickstarted the Sportster and rolled out of the little campground by the river. As she did, she imagined the fat snake wiggling through the tall grass littered with river stones and pine needles. Alive, alive for however long fate would allow.

THE WAY up to Jenny and Robert's cabin was as simple as the flow of water. Once she got to the river she headed north, leaning her bike into the curves, first one way, then another. The world smelled of dust, fresh breeze off the river and dogwood bloom. She lost track of time and only noticed the blackbirds on the phone lines and a coyote slinking across the road. Yakima was still several hundred miles away.

She turned on a shaded one-lane road near the national forest boundary and rode until she reached a log cabin surrounded by motorcycles covered in tarps. Two men were working on two different bikes, and three little boys in shorts and dirty T-shirts stood around the men, watching. The littlest one, "the Vulcan," stood alone in some tall grass. He was whipping the flowering tops from thistles with a piece of wire. About fifteen feet away, a teenage boy with long hair and a bike shop T-shirt stood watching his little brother, sucking on a leaf of grass.

Delphine shut down the bike on the edge of the tall grass. The Vulcan walked slowly toward her, continuing to whip the grass in front of him.

"Hey there, buster. Is your mom around?"

"She just got back fwom town. She wode in the 'bulance when they took our dad away."

"Yes. I understand that he died. I'm sorry about that."

The Vulcan swiped at his runny nose. "He had cancer and that's bad." He kept beating the grass with his piece of number nine wire. "They gonna burn him up now, I guess. We gonna throw what's left of him up in the hills. That's what everybody says." Snot hung down from his nose. His dirty legs were covered in bugbites he had scratched until they bled and scabbed over.

Jenny came out of the cabin and the screen door slammed shut behind her. "Well that was fast. I only texted you a couple of hours ago. What, did you drive it at two hundred miles an hour?"

"I was on my way to Yakima. I was in the Methow when I heard," Delphine said.

Jenny came over and wrapped her arms around the tiny bald woman.

"Oh my Lord. Yakima? What the hell you gonna do there?"

"It's a long story. Can I sleep on your floor?"

"I've got a nice comfy bed that just opened up." Jenny sniffled into the nape of the dying woman's neck, and her strong arm curled under Delphine's arms and practically lifted her up the porch steps and into the house.

CHAPTER SIX

They drank a case of beer between the two of them. Neighbors brought food for the boys but didn't stay too long because Jenny seemed most keen to talk with Delphine and hear the tale of the sketchy adoption agency, the lowlife man who stole a child and the medicine of the patients in the Baranof Hotel, and the blood that spattered behind him wherever he went.

"I have to get as many of these babies out of his hands as I can." Delphine stared hard at Jenny with an apologetic look in her tired eyes. "And I'm afraid that I can't do it without your help."

By the time they started drinking the tequila, Jenny had decided to go to Yakima with Delphine. Then Jenny went out in the yard. The two men who had been working on the bikes when her guest arrived were sitting with their own beers on the tailgate of a truck. She talked with them both about her own bike and if it could be ready tomorrow. No one argued with her or questioned the wisdom of it. Then Jenny invited them up to have some sliced ham and scalloped potatoes. The grieving food was piling up on her table with each truck that stopped by the cabin.

It appears that big-brained animals, when faced with the impossible fact of death, use their imaginations to realign their reality. Instead of grieving or organizing a memorial, Jenny would take off on an impossible adventure with a woman who had been a friend of her late husband.

Jenny decided all four would make the trip—her and the boys. The oldest one, Gudger, would drive the chase car, their old Ford truck with the battered aluminum canopy on the back. They would all camp together. She couldn't bear to leave them now, and she couldn't bear to see Delphine break down and have to be taken away in an ambulance. It was foolhardy of Delphine, as sick as she was, to be riding that rattly hard tail as far as she had already. Delphine did not look like she had many more miles left in her and Jenny was not in the mood to leave Delphine dead on the side of the road. She was going to need her oldest teenage boy to drive and help with the two other boys, Ned and the Vulcan. But Gudger was going to be a sulky little bastard about being made to come on the trip. He was seventeen and had recently dropped out of high school. His dad's sickness and now his death had sapped most of his strength to face the future. If he had applied himself in history or in English, he might have described his present emotional situation as an existential crisis. But being who he was, he simply said, "Yeah, what the fuck ever," to all or any of the myriad wonders, the hundreds of thousands of possible futures, that might be offered to him. "What the fuck ever." He said it with a certain gravity that bothered Delphine, as if he were describing his own version of the Augustinian prayer. "Late have I loved Thee, O, Thou beauty ever ancient, ever new."

"What the fuck ever."

But to their surprise, when Jenny mentioned driving the chase vehicle to Gudger, his eyes brightened a bit and he only said, "Whatever," and, "Can I ride the hard tail sometimes?" Jenny agreed. Then the rescue mission for babies he had never met moved to the planning stage.

DELPHINE DIDN'T want to sleep in Robert's bed. She laid a flimsy camping mattress on the floor and made a little nest of pillows. Ned gave her a well-used Hudson's Bay–style wool blanket. Neither boy asked why she wasn't sleeping in the bed.

Jenny came in with a plate of ham and scalloped potatoes and kneeled by Delphine's nest. Delphine was counting out her pills into five daily planners she had opened on her lap.

"I'm glad to see you have your meds. I plan to throw all of Robert's out. I didn't want Gudger to get into the pain meds and try and sell them to his skeevy friends."

"Pain meds are almost more trouble than they are worth," Delphine said, watching as the little jewelry boxes filled up with brightly colored pills. "Maybe I just don't hurt enough," she muttered, while the fact was that she was in a great deal of pain.

"God, Jenny." Delphine sighed and looked up at her, thinking of Gudger driving the chaser and the boys coming along on this mission. "I really have no idea what I'm getting into . . . or really why I'm getting involved in this." She struggled a bit to sit up straight. It was a struggle to even look into Jenny's eyes.

"This girl I don't even know was murdered by a bad man who apparently just steals babies and disappears. What the hell am I supposed to do about that?"

She gestured with her hands to her own body. "I mean, I'm dying for Christ's sake, why should I go? Why should I care?"

There was silence. No one spoke during the uncomfortable pause. Gudger came into the room with an armload of wood for the stove.

"Maybe you're going because you are dying," he muttered in that insolent teenage tone.

"Gudger!" his mother blurted out.

"I'm just saying . . ." He clattered the wood on the brick hearth that the big iron barrel stove sat on.

"But show some sensitivity, Gudger," Jenny said.

"Mom, she started it. I didn't bring up the fact that she was dying . . . I mean, fuck."

"Language! Gudger . . ."

"Oh, so we're not cursing now?" Gudger did his best to stomp out of the room, which was difficult because he was wearing low-top, thick-soled skater shoes that were virtually silent on the wood floor.

"Kids. I mean, come on," Jenny said. "You're lucky you only had one."

Delphine pushed the plate of food away. She liked the numbing buzz of the beers, but she couldn't stand the thought of putting the ham and potatoes in her stomach.

"Thanks, Jen. I'm just not hungry."

"Sure, I get it. How is the pain?"

"Truthfully, bad."

"Take the medicine?" Jenny asked.

"Naw . . ."

The boys roughhoused around outside. One was chasing a goat around with a loop of rope, and the two oldest ones were throwing rocks at beer bottles.

"So what's the plan on finding these kids?"

Jenny cleared her throat and offered what she could. "Robert had some friends who rode for the Jokers at one time. They can always turn us on to some bad boy types. From what you said of him, it sounds like this Tyler runs with a rough crowd. These old friends of Robert's would know what's up with the White Covenant and the Aryan Nations boys."

"Why do you think they're involved?"

"You said he was white. The girl is white and all the women at his place were white. He was stealing pills, and if there is something sketchy happening with white boys around here, those assholes are involved."

"You sure you want to take your boys along?" Delphine asked.

"This isn't anything they haven't been exposed to already," Jen said. "I mean after all this foolishness with our former president, the Aryan Brotherhood is like the chamber of commerce around here."

"Really?"

"Delphine, my mom used to warn me about boys wanting to play folk music and have sex with me. I warn my boys about men who play death metal and try to recruit them into armed revolution against the Zionist Occupied Government. I mean, what the fuck?"

Delphine laughed weakly.

"I'm serious. This close to northern Idaho, there are more

weapons and ammunition in the hands of delusional paranoids than in the hands of the National Guard."

"Was Robert into that stuff?" Delphine asked, with a bit of fear in her voice.

"Naw ... Robert just liked to ride, you know. He smoked a little pot and thought it should be legalized but he wasn't political beyond that. He liked his life here. These new political nutbags are upset about things they run across on their computer. Robert just turned the damn thing off. Nazis just keep online trolling and compiling their never-ending list of enemies."

Delphine closed her eyes and sank into her pillows on the floor. "We'll run down to Yakima and see if we can find this Tyler. I'm not going to rope him up for the killing of his partner or girlfriend or whatever. I just want to find the babies he took with him. If, after a couple of days of looking for them, it looks like they are long gone, then we'll load up and come back home."

"Promise?" Jenny said.

Delphine started to drift away to sleep.

"We've just had our fill of dying around here. I tell you, sweetie, I'm going to take you to the hospital if I think you are going to die. I'm not fooling around. My boys don't need one more death to deal with. They'll feel responsible."

HOW DO scientists know the relative health of a dynamic system, like an ocean basin or even the microscopic ecosystem of a human body? How do you assess the health of something you cannot really see, or tease out the history of a patient, whether it's the ocean basin or a human being? The questions you might ask a human being are much different than the questions you would put to the ocean. Then the scientist needs a background in the complexities of the organism or ecosystem. How have they behaved in the past; how are they behaving now? In the case of an ecosystem, the questions must be honed down and expressed directly, for the answers have to be inferred. The ocean basin cannot tell you, "Something is wrong. I feel sick and I didn't feel like this before." To find out the health of an ocean, one has to have a history of close observations and keep track of the changes.

When Delphine went to the doctor and said her gut hurt and the pain reached around to her lower back, the doctors used all their diagnostic talents to discount some pathologies and find a specific pathology that fit all the symptoms. The lucky circumstance with human health is that there is a person to ask. It is a relatively simple case for the medical detective.

But in the ocean, whales die en masse, temperatures and oxygen levels shift, and the food pyramid that sustains larger animals collapses.

"How are you feeling?" the scientist asks, but no one answers.

In the early twenty twenties, a die-off of humpback whales occurred. The calving rate seemed to drop precipitously. Earlier, there had been sightings of emaciated humpbacks with white skin discolorations. It may take many hours of observation to identify a systemic problem, let alone understand it.

"How you feeling?"

Eyes out on the water. Delphine had been photographing the animals and keeping track of individuals. She observed fewer females returning with calves each year.

"I feel sick."

Delphine read the clues of who was getting sick and when, and began to suspect that there was a problem in the humpback's primary food source: herring.

Now, it's hard to imagine that the economics of a Japanese spring festival and a quirk in the way the Alaska Board of Fisheries categorized the little silvery fish could actually be a matter of life and death for the whales.

Kazunoko is a highly prized traditional dish in Japan. Herring roe cut from a female herring still in the delicate membrane of her womb is marinated in dashi and soy sauce and eaten during the traditional New Year. For the Japanese, eating this crunchy and oily caviar symbolizes prosperity and the wish for many offspring. But of course, the Japanese are not the only ones who like it. The coastal Native people of Alaska love herring eggs as well. In the spring, people set hemlock boughs in areas where herring will spawn, and the little silvery fish encrust the branches with the white eggs. Herring eggs are still traded by Native people all the way up into the arctic for king salmon, caribou, or moose meat.

In a healthy and prosperous ecosystem, big predators rest comfortably at the top of the food chain. Japan in the 1980s was among the most prosperous nations, so the symbolism of the golden caviar became a necessity. Japanese customers were willing to pay almost anything to have them delivered to their cities. Herring roe, bait herring and herring for food consumption became a huge cash flow for fisheries. One boat could easily earn a million dollars in a weeklong fishery.

In the early nineties, salmon fishermen began to worry about the impact of taking all these little silvery fish out of the food chain. They called them "forage fish." Only fifty boats had permits to catch herring for their roe. One permit was worth hundreds of thousands of dollars. The Sitka herring roe fishery became a wild horse rodeo. Millions of tons of fish were caught in a few days, fortunes were made in a single set of a purse seine net.

The Alaska Board of Fisheries protected all forage fish, but herring were somehow not defined as a forage fish. Some Fish and Game biologists made the argument that in small units, herring introduced less energy into the food chain than other forage fish. Individually, they weren't as dense with energy as the other forage fish . . . individually . . . but this was a cynical argument. If you listened to the old people, herring came in shoals hundreds of feet thick, covering thousands of miles of coastline. But the testimony of old people was discounted. So, all the other important forage fish were protected from commercial harvest. It was just bad luck for the Native fishermen who ate the oil-rich eggs, the humpback whales and all the other top predators.

Humpbacks, whose population had been building up, started to decline.

The North Pacific had a serious illness. Without the large dense mass of oily fish, the whole system had become weaker. Delphine had been working on this problem, trying to document little pieces of the picture. The decline couldn't be seen from an afternoon out with whales in the bay. A decline must be seen from multiple angles and areas, and by adding up reliable sightings and looking at the numbers over time.

Eventually, just as she was getting sick, the sickness of the North Pacific was becoming clear in her mind. The herring fishery was just a part of that picture: warmer waters and changing climate contributed, too. The part they played in the health of grey whales and even sperm whales made her head hurt.

The whales are sick, and there is no agreement on what to do about it.

DELPHINE WAS thinking about sickness as she showered the next morning. She was feeling more and more sick. But what to do? She was already feeling too sick to ride the bike back to the hospital. Like it or not, she had tied herself to this mission, the mission to finish her closeout memos for her colleagues, and her mission to find Tyler and however many children he had put into peril. She was swarmed with worry now, and it occurred to her that her memos were simply a neurotic attempt to hide from the death of children. While the boys were eating their pancakes and kicking each other under the table, she was hoping that finding Tye would be relatively simple. She was hoping that she would be able to talk him out of the three babies he had with him and get them back to some safe port. Then maybe she would call Bertie and ask him to come get her in the next couple of days. Maybe she should allow him to rescue her.

Jenny had made a little nest in the back of the truck for

Delphine. Gudger would ride the Sportster the first leg, and this made him happy. Jenny was going to ride Robert's old Road King and Ned, who was fourteen and had his permit, would drive the truck down off the hill and the rest of the way down the highway to their first camp spot, which was about twenty miles out of Yakima.

The road down the mountain was rutted. The lurching in and out of potholes hurt Delphine's back, but once they were down the mountain on state roads, the ride was much better. Young Ned did a fine job driving. He drove nice and steady and never pushed the speed. Delphine tried to sleep as she lay on her back on the piles of mattresses and sleeping bags. She watched the wires through the grimy windows and read the birds on the wires as musical notes. She called her son's phone and left a message asking him to call her. Then she slept.

DELPHINE DREAMED that the hissing of the tires on the old blacktop was a cold river. Her body felt cold and the light surrounding the truck was white. Her stomach hurt and she was certain she should not have drunk the beer and tequila last night. Jenny had put an old mop bucket within arm's length of Delphine and several times Delphine had to vomit into it. White light pulled around the inside of her skull. She felt something rising from her stomach even when she didn't have to vomit.

The hissing all around her felt white, and she dreamed that she was flying through this whiteness just a few feet above the ground. When she opened her eyes, the welded seams on the roof of the old canopy throbbed with the same energy that wanted to rise up out of her chest and out into the whiteness. She couldn't keep her eyes open for long, and it occurred to her that she might be about to die.

Delphine was not afraid. By this point dying seemed to be a kind of relief. Maybe Jenny could handle Tye and the babies. With her eyes closed, the world seemed dark to Delphine, but the sizzling light continued to burn in her skull. The light changed shapes; sometimes it was perfectly round like a wheel, sometimes it was a running horse, then it became a hawk push-ing its wings and starting to soar. Perhaps this was the red-tailed hawk she had seen on the wire. Even though she didn't actually hear music, she imagined a kind of baroque piano dictated from the black spots of birds on the power lines. She was asleep and not asleep as the truck gained speed on the highway.

She was dreaming now of her own burial. People were pull-ing her out of the back of the truck. A brown-skinned woman was at her head. Jenny and her three boys carried the four corners of a sheet. Delphine was happy that she was going to be buried within earshot of flowing water. A few small birds split the hiss of water, and when she opened her eyes this time she was sinking beneath a canopy edged by the spiky tops of evergreen trees. She lay still, letting the pull of sleep take her into a deeper kind of rest. They gently laid her into the damp ground and she sank back into her body. She felt a hot pain in her arm as if from a bee sting. She felt as if she might wake up, but then there was the warmth of sleep sitting on her chest like a heavy quilt. Her sleepiness made her happy, for all Del-phine wanted to do now was escape all of the pain she associated with continuing to be alive.

She woke up. She was in a reclining deck chair thirty feet uphill of a running creek. She could smell the sweet cool air that was running over the top of the water. She could taste water that was frothy with minerals, then lightly flavored with the sap on the trees. Her senses were so heightened that she believed she could also taste dust and ice there along the streambed. She seemed to be held in the palm of a little bower of trees. If this was going to become death, it made her happy.

Just next to her sat the youngest boy. The Vulcan was patting the top of a small dog's head. The dog looked directly at Delphine as if he were hunting her. She began to sit up, and the little boy straightened up on the flat rock he was sitting on.

"You awen't gonna die then?" he asked seriously.

"Not right away," Delphine said gently.

"Mom told me to come get her if you was gonna die," he said.

"Well, I guess we can just sit here together for a bit. Who is this boy then?" Delphine stretched and lifted her hand, putting it next to the Vulcan's in mid-pat on the dog's head.

Delphine saw for the first time that she had an IV in her arm. A clear plastic bag was hanging on the chair next to her. "Did you put this thing on me?"

The little boy was back to scratching the bugbites on his legs. "Noooo," he said gravely. "Jenny did that. She had lots of pwactice with Poppa." Delphine noticed that he had a hard time saying his *r*'s. "Jenny said that you were dehydwate . . . hmmm . . . . that you were needing water. She mixed some medicine in there too. Stuff she said would make you feel better. This is Boosta." He kept his hand on Delphine, and Booster seemed happier about life for having two people's hands on top of his head. "My dad named him. He said it was for Boosta Wocket."

"Well I'm glad your mom put this thing in my arm. I do feel better. How do you feel, Booster?"

"Boosta likes to be petted," the boy said.

"Well, I like to pet dogs," Delphine said.

"Me too," the boy said. "Do you have a dog?"

"I do, but I can't take care of her now that I have to be in the hospital so much."

"That's too bad," he said. "What's your dog's name?"

"Dot. Like Dorothy but just Dot," she said. The boy scrunched up his face, not really understanding the tie between Dorothy and Dot.

"Is she little like Boosta?"

"Oh no, Dot is huge. She weighs more than a hundred pounds."

"Wow," the boy said.

They both looked down at the river where a cow and a calf were pawing the surface, looking as if they wanted to cross over to their side. In a few moments, Gudger came walking down the other side of the river above the cattle. He had a long stick and rousted the animals back up out of the creek.

"Cows awn't allowed on this side of the cweek," the Vulcan said.

"Where are we anyway?" Delphine asked.

"We are at Wose's Cantina and Campgwound. She is a fwiend of Jenny's."

"What do you like to be called?" Delphine asked.

"My name is Dwayne but I don't mind being called the Vulcan."

"What do you want me to call you?"

"You can call me Dwayne if you want. My dad used to call me Down the Dwayne, and he would laugh when he said it."

Tears ran down his cheeks, but the little boy smiled like a dandelion in the morning. He had no idea why his dad thought his joke was funny, but he smiled anyway. Smiled and cried.

"Oh honey, come here," she said, and she hugged him. It was a little awkward with the IV line. Delphine shaded the sun out of her eyes and wiped her own tears. "Well, Dwayne, I want to say that I'm grateful that you stayed here to look after me. I would have been scared to wake up here all alone by this creek."

"Scawed . . . why?" the boy asked.

"I thought I had died. So I was glad to see you and Booster here. You are too young and tough to be dead."

"Gudgew is tougher than me," he said.

"Maybe so," Delphine said, "but he's older and not as polite as you are. I'm glad you were here to take care of me."

Dwayne smiled down at his feet and kicked at some rocks on the hillside. Booster jumped up into Delphine's lap and she hugged the homely dog in her arms.

"I bettew go tell Jenny you are awake . . ." He paused a moment, trying to think of what to say. He bent over and picked up a stone and threw it right into the deepest part of the creek, where it landed with a thunk. "Is that okay?"

"Sure, but wait a minute. Why don't I remember Booster from the trip down here?"

"He was widing up fwont of the truck and you were in the back."

"Ah . . ." Delphine said. "You be sure to come back quick. You are a good man to have around."

The little boy blushed and shook his head back and forth, not knowing what to think or feel. He threw another rock, listened to the thunk, and ran off as if just the two thrown rocks were a clever comment he had thought up all by himself. Booster leapt off the sick woman's lap and followed the boy.

Black-capped chickadees worried the brambles. Delphine watched a water ouzel dipping like a wind-up toy in and out of the water. Sunlight pooled in the shade of her little bower, and she felt uncommonly good to be there and alive.

Soon enough, Jenny came down the trail to where she lay, followed by a Latinx woman close on her heels.

"Hey, D. You look a lot better."

"I feel a lot better. What you put in this concoction?"

"Ah, you know. A bit of this. A bit of that. Mostly just standard saline water. You were dehydrated and your fuel tank was empty. We got you some sucrose to pep you up and just a little bit of the evil painkillers you seem to hate so much."

"I just don't like what they do to my guts. Seems like they usually make me dopey and then I get crampy."

"Taking drugs is an art form. I helped Bob find the right balance to feel good. Don't worry, doll, I'm not trying to turn you into some kind of redneck junkie. It's medicine, not a carnival ride."

"Good thing. I almost always get sick at carnivals."

Jenny stroked Delphine's hair.

"Thanks, Jen," Delphine said. "Are we any closer to finding Leigh's killer and her baby?"

For a moment, Delphine was overwhelmed with the memory of Leigh's body in the parking garage: screwdriver in her skull, blood as black as paint on the cement.

"Honey . . . D?" Jenny's voice cut into her own brain. "This is Rose. She says we can stay here."

"Thank you," Delphine said.

"Of course," Rose said. "Come on up to the place. I have a couple of friends coming over to talk. Apparently, they know this Tyler and his business. I offered them some food and they are on their way. But let's get you up there."

Jenny took Delphine's arm and Rose handled the IV bottle and the line as the three of them made it up the hill to the parking lot of the cantina/campground.

The wooden building with the dusty porch was a fairyland of white Christmas lights and two flashing neon-red beer signs. Jenny's sons were sitting at a picnic table playing a dice game with a cup and drinking from huge cups with straws. The Vulcan saw Jenny and stood up, then ran-skipped over to her, acting solicitous. "Was it okay that Jenny and Wose came and got you?"

"Of course, honey." Delphine brushed his hair off his dirty forehead.

"But you told me to be wight back." Dwayne was genuinely concerned that he had not pleased her.

"No, that's fine. If you are close, I'll know that I'm safe."

The boy blushed again, and Booster slowly crept back up

in her lap. "Hello there, you old flea bag." Delphine hugged the mangy dog and tucked his head under her chin.

A BLUSTER of four big American motorcycles—customized Electra Glides rolling on fat tires and cushions of big cylinders— entered the little fairyland, easing around the road and pulling up to the cantina. Men wearing denim jackets scrawled with the words COLOMBIA JOKERS drove all four bikes. Two of the men had a female passenger on the back of each of their bikes. The jackets included a stylized, and somewhat demonic, image of the joker from Bicycle playing cards. When they took their helmets off, Delphine could see that all six appeared to be of Mexican heritage. She could tell not only from their faces but from many of their tattoos: fine art detail, an eagle gripping a snake, and dark-haired babies.

"Carlos," Jen said as she put her hands in the air and walked toward the oldest and most densely tattooed man. Carlos lifted her off the ground in a hug. Rose walked quickly to the porch and greeted all her guests in Spanish. She scooped up menus with one arm and gave side arm hugs and gestured them to a corner table with the other. A waiter brought out pint glasses of tap beer.

Carlos looked over Jen's shoulder at Delphine, who was sitting at a garden table with her IV bag elevated in a small olive tree next to her and a dog with a prominent underbite on her lap. He looked her directly in the eyes, turned to the woman who had been his passenger, and exchanged a few words with her before walking in Delphine's direction. First, he came to Jenny and hugged her, told her that he and his family were sad to hear of Robert's death.

"He was a good dude," Carlos said. "I respected him, you know. I respected that he didn't want into the life, but he was smart and he was honest. He could fix anything, and I trusted him . . . as I do you, *mi amiga*."

"Thank you, Carlos." Jenny kissed his cheek and turned to her friend. "This is the person I was telling you about. She is looking for this guy, Tye."

Carlos turned to Delphine and looked directly in her eyes. He had salt-and-pepper hair and deep brown eyes. "You must have known Roberto in the hospital. I'm sorry for your suffering as well . . . but y-y-yes . . ." He stammered, broke eye contact. "I know this man. *Malo* . . . a racist bastard."

"First, thank you for your concern." Delphine was aware of her formal diction. She didn't want this meeting with Carlos to take on the tone of a diplomatic summit. "Tell me what you can about him. He has three babies traveling with him. They're the ones I'm most interested in, plus a child whose mom is in San Francisco."

"Tyler claims to run an adoption service. He advertises mainly to racists who will pay money for white babies . . ." He paused and scuffed the ground with his boot. "He is only interested in white babies. Pure white. Tested and certified clean of any brown or Jewish blood. He likes Russian Orthodox, but don't let them slide over too close to Asia. Of course, he likes German Christian, Protestants, Catholic, it don't matter."

"All babies?"

"*Sí*, under four years old. Blue eyes are a premium."

"What does he do with them?"

"He sells them to the highest bidder."

"And there is enough of a market for these babies?"

"Yes, there is plenty of demand. But most of his potential buyers are peckerwoods without a lot of money."

"So what does he do about that?"

"He wants them to pay him in gold. He tries to get the ones who deal in drugs and guns to convert whatever they have into gold. He will take cash, but he is crazy for the gold, and he converts it himself." Rose brought a pint glass over to Carlos and he took a long drink. "But if he has a premium baby with all the paperwork, blond and blue eyes, he will take drugs or guns straight across. Some of these guys want to trade in ammunition. Different calibers are like different denominations in bills. The .22s are like nickels, .308s are like a buck ... not straight across trade in value, but that's how they talk."

"What is a premium baby worth?" Delphine asked.

Carlos finished his beer, set the empty glass on the arm of his chair. Then he touched her wrist with the tip of his finger. "So, a boy, blond, blue eyes, paperwork in order. Health papers and health records of the biological parents. I mean really legit for these *pendejos*, they can go upwards of a pound of gold, or a shipping pallet of ammunition. Drugs are another matter, that gets more complicated. Your Tyler deals in small amounts of pharmaceuticals. I think he just does it to know the market."

"So, he's not what you call a serious drug dealer?"

"Oh, he is serious. He's just not very good at it. He does it just so he can keep up with what the various drugs are worth."

"Why gold?" Delphine asked.

"It's a primal thing. Like the time before money, gold is

from the earth, *señora*. It is the source of real wealth for these peckerwoods. The racist bastards see gold as something eternal. It's as old as the desire for the golden calf. I stay clear of gold. Bad things happen when white people get around gold."

"What happens to the women? The mothers, what do they get for their babies?"

"This I'm not sure," Carlos said, and he was brought another beer. "I suspect they get what Tyler gives them. Most of them are undocumented and they don't have much legal ground to stand on. If they go to the cops, they are instantly investigated for the disappearance of their babies. Then immigration detains them and deportation begins. Tye holds all the paper-work. Often, they are delivered privately using nurses and a midwife that Tyler knows. He often registers the child with himself as the father."

"He owns the baby," Delphine said with a sad voice. Then, "Where can I find him?"

"There is a gathering," Carlos said. "Kind of a meeting of like-minded bikers. I would not be welcome." He pointed at the exposed skin on his forearm. "Too dark and from a shit country, according to them. But I can show you where the gathering is. Tyler will be there. I hear he has a small amount of drugs to sell. But you should be careful. These men are not respectful. Do you understand?"

"Yes, I think so," Delphine said.

Jenny stepped forward and put her hand on Carlos's shoulder. "We will be careful. All we want to do is talk with this Tyler."

As if on cue, Boomer let out a soft woof.

Delphine said, "I met a man on my ride over here who mentioned something about an information fair. Is this thing you are talking about the same thing?"

"Yes," Carlos said, "probably . . . literature and anti-government propaganda."

Delphine went to the truck and brought back the folder of papers she had stolen from the cabinet at the welfare hotel in Seattle. Carlos agreed to take a look.

"What's this mean, you think?"

The dark-haired man looked up at her. His eyes were sad. She imagined that Carlos didn't like thinking she was mixed up with Tye.

"I think this means that Tyler is in big trouble if he was in business with the 88's. They love gold the way their women love their babies and nobody . . . nobody will ever forgive a debt."

DARKNESS CAME. Rosa prepared a wonderful meal for everyone. Dwayne and Ned carried plates of food out from the kitchen and to the tables under the trees draped with white lights. Gudger helped in the kitchen, frying tortillas and stuffing them with spiced pork or shredded beef. Rosa carried pitchers of beer and the air smelled of woodsmoke and boiled chilies.

Delphine ate sparingly. She did not drink the beer, but drank fresh apple juice that Jenny brought to her. She was feeling much better by the time she went to sleep that night. Jenny unhooked her IV. The boys had set up a bug-net tent that had a rain fly over it. The tent was set back from the cantina where the Colombia Jokers continued to eat and laugh. Delphine lay in her well-padded cot, where she could hear the rush of water from the creek, and shut her eyes. She could smell the food and heard the boys laughing as they helped with the dishes. Grackles flitted and made urgent guttural gesticulations in the trees. Just downstream, cows lowed in the field while someone stretched barbed wire from fencepost to fencepost. Some tired farmer working late, no doubt. After a certain point, what is the use of worrying about the future? Cows will always get out. No matter how well you build your fence.

The hiss of the stream no longer made her think of death now. Just like the rich soil they had ridden over, the germinating seeds pushing their way up toward the sun, the stream, the light, the call of the birds, life seemed to be floating up through her body, giving her being a feeling of rising. Either she was experiencing something akin to the opposite of depression, or Jenny had put some ketamine in her IV.

CHAPTER SEVEN

Breakfast was scrambled eggs wrapped in freshly made tortillas. It was decided the boys should stay behind at the campground. Rose had agreed to give them work to do. It was only thirty miles to the meet. Carlos would come to the cantina by nine to show them the way to the biker gathering. The GPS on their phones would not read the little back roads and trails that had largely been scabbed out of the dust. Jenny would drive the truck, and Delphine was grateful not to be banging down the improvised roads on the Sportster. Jenny left the keys to the bikes on the picnic table after extracting a promise from Gudger not to go beyond a twenty-mile circle around the cantina. She even drew the circle on a map and showed it to her oldest son. Ned and the Vulcan were gathering eggs with Rosa, and Gudger studied the roads within the circle on the map as Jenny pulled out of the campground. The gentle hills and valleys began to level out to the great arid plateau as they drove southeast.

After about forty minutes, Carlos pulled over next to a fencepost with a paper plate stapled on it. The number eighty-eight was scrawled on the plate. Carlos pointed to the right and there in the distance, dust was rising. Delphine heard the thumping of very fast heavy metal music.

"Here," Carlos said. "You be careful, *amiga*. You have my number? Don't use it unless you need an army of angry Mejicanos. Okay?"

Jenny nodded and they parted ways.

The day had turned hot. As they came closer to the gathering, Delphine described her interaction with the mysterious biker who had followed her out of Seattle. He might turn out to be a complicating factor for their hunt, but there was nothing to be done about it now.

Jenny unbuttoned her shirt so that the top of her sports bra was open to the breeze. "Give the animals what they want. You aren't a woman if you don't show your tits."

"I guess I'm not a woman," Delphine said, looking down at her shrunken chest.

"You'll be fine. You got that crazy skinhead look these bastards love. We're not doing anything wrong. We're looking for Tye. If we don't find him here, someone will tell us something so we can find him in town."

"Jen?" Delphine asked.

"Yeah, doll?"

"What's with the number eighty-eight?"

"Oh Jesus, that's their clever jailhouse code. *H* is the eighth letter of the alphabet. Eighty-eight stands for HH."

"For?" Delphine rubbed her hand on top of her bald head.

"Heil Hitler."

"Really?" Delphine asked.

"Yep."

The old truck moved closer and closer to the swirling circle of rising dust. Delphine didn't quite know how to feel.

These men were convicts and surely some of them were dangerous. Their politics were noxious to her. But there was an element of humor—sick humor to be sure—among the white nationalist culture in the American West. Humor begins with tension and there is plenty of tension between the left and the right.

The dynamics of group formation had interested her since high school. She had never felt associated with any group, other than perhaps her family. She wasn't one of the pretty girls, she wasn't a jock, or a brain bound for an exclusive university. She had made her own clothes, she liked to read books, she worked hard to earn money because her family had little. She wasn't a hippie, or a nerd, or a dork. She felt singular. The one girl who floated around the outside, without even the distinction of being a "loner." She had friends. Like her, they were smart enough, pretty enough to avoid harassment, but essentially unrecruitable. She joined clubs and helped foreign students with their issues, for they themselves were outsiders. She, like them, felt temporary in her situation.

Orca whales on the west coast of North America are divided into at least three separate groups that are so distinct they are sometimes referred to as three different races of killer whales. Resident killer whales eat fish and generally travel in large groups. When feeding at the mouth of the large Alaskan river systems, they move slowly and methodically as they harvest the king salmon out of the ocean. Their vocalizations are distinct. They may recognize the sounds made by the others, but their language, if it is a true language, is different.

Transient killer whales eat other marine mammals. They

have complex hunting strategies that use features in the ocean to corral or block a mammal, sometimes even using the presence of a boat as a backstop to kill dolphins, sea otters, seals and other whales. They have a strict social hierarchy in which they share food with their young and become involved in distinct training activity. After a kill, adults will sometimes throw the corpses of smaller prey back and forth in the air, taunting young ones to chase the dead dolphin or seal. Sometimes an adult will trail a streamer of flesh from its jaws and swim among the rest of the group, getting the young whales to strike at the bloody prize. Transients move quickly and avoid time on the surface while hunting. Their language is distinct, and they will even maintain "radio silence" while they sneak up on their prey.

Offshore killer whales are also hunters, but because they are offshore, less is known about their social life or hunting methods. But like the others, they are unique. All three groups have unique DNA signatures, but what is interesting is that while they could interbreed—their bodies bear only subtle differences in the coloration and shape of the white patches on their hides—they don't interbreed. Resident youngsters have been seen moving alone into bays where transient pods are hunting. Of course, this is dangerous because it exposes them to other predators large enough to take them on: sharks, whalers, fast-traveling ships. But instead of mounting more extravagant strategies like the sperm whales' daisy circle of protection, a resident killer whale adult will break off and nudge the young one back to their pod. Transients have not been documented to kill and consume residents or offshores, but other orcas simply choose to remain genetically distinct and stick to their own genetic profile.

The fish eaters travel in much larger groups and maintain interrelated family patterns among the large groups. Transients appear to travel in smaller family-affiliated packs. Think of a caribou herd and a timber wolf pack. There is no real hatred there.

Of course, human beings affiliate in many different groups. Such groups can be as large as a political party or as small as a book group. Delphine and Jenny were just then driving toward one particularly tight group of outlaw bikers who shared a great deal of prison culture among themselves: a kind of uniform, slang, codes and entire blocks of racist ideology. It could be that the racist ideology served as a prophylactic strategy against male violence in prison. Everyone had to belong to a set while inside. This appears to be the only way to stay safe.

Humans appear to like to belong to large group affiliations or small group affiliations for different reasons. A large group, when acting as a group, is more powerful. The Democratic Party can move initiatives to change laws. Gangs in prison can move prison policy by violent action. This is a large group affiliation, a benefit, but an individual's influence or benefit from within the large group gains can be small. So, all groups look for that sweet spot where there is benefit to individuals while they remain in a powerful, large group.

Jenny drove through the parking area toward the single opening in the ring of vans and a stage setup. Most of the men were wearing denim coats with the sleeves cut off and no shirt underneath. Delphine noticed that the older men had dark tans, grey hair, big bellies and arms that had once been immense but now sagged toward their elbows. Many wore black bandannas around their heads and steampunk-style round sunglasses. Their vests were tight over their bellies, but still all their flesh shook to the rumble of their big noisy American bikes. Many had swastika or shamrock tattoos, which had become the Aryan Brotherhood trademark. Phrases like "Jews will not replace us" and "14 words" covered their bodies, along with a slurry of Nazi insignias and numbers.

Jenny parked the truck and they entered the inner circle of activity. A man with a long beard and big belly stopped them before they got two feet. The speed metal band was thumping and the singer was bellowing the lyrics to "Tomorrow Belongs to Me."

"NO TOURISTS, LADIES!" he yelled above the din.

"Not tourists, bro. We are here with Tye. I got to see if he's got a home for little Martin!" Jenny yelled back. The big man simply pointed across the circle to a table labeled BOOTH TWENTY and waved them in.

Then a girl in riding gear with a short shotgun slung across her back and the word SECURITY embossed on her leather jacket took them aside and swept a metal detector over both of them. "I'm sorry for the intrusion, ladies. You are welcome to keep your guns in your ride, but we are all here for a fun weekend of music and information, so no weapons inside. I'm sure you understand." She had glittering blue eyes and jet-black hair. She had a nice smile and would have seemed friendly if it wasn't for the riot gun on her back.

The band took a break and the mosh pit boys headed toward the beer garden. Jenny swept Delphine along. It could have been a rural music festival with the beer and fried foods for sale. Couples wandered the booths: women with halter tops and men with no shirts at all. Dirty skin with dark tans indicated a lot of miles on the road and exposure to sun reflected off hot black pavement. Booths sold T-shirts and CDs, even cassette tapes featuring, apparently, the latest from neo-Nazi bands: Adam Waffen, Lone Wolf, the New Black Shirts, the Landsberg Prison Orchestra. The T-shirts were the usual fare, with Nazi slogans as well as memes from the far right, and red, white and blue shirts with MAKE AMERICA WHITE emblazoned across the front. Bumper stickers read: ABORTION IS MURDER. THINK ABOUT THAT! One T-shirt had a strange slogan: 50LBSAU. There were prison reform booths, booths selling leather goods, booths promoting websites on 4chan with portable computers set up with satellite connections and people there to help newbies find their communities on the dark web. There were lots of handmade knives marked with upside-down runic letters, copies of Nazi daggers and Nordic berserker swords. There was an electronics booth selling devices to sweep a room or phone line for bugs, as well as sophisticated bugs themselves. They sold micro-recorders that came in black leather sleeves and looked like cigarette lighters. There was a large area that was a used bookstore. They sold leather-bound copies of *The Turner Diaries* as well as annotated Bibles that directed the reader to racist, homophobic, anti-Semitic or possibly anti-feminist scriptures.

Then there was Tye. He was standing at the "Dearborn

All-White Babies Adoption Service" booth. The phrases underneath read, ALL 100% LEGAL WITH UNBREAKABLE CONTRACTS, WILL STAND UP TO ANY SHYSTER LAWYER and YOUR BABY WILL ALWAYS BE YOUR BABY. He was dressed in brown slacks, a blue rayon blazer and a green button-down shirt, like a businessman from a seedy firm.

"Hey! Bug Zapper. What the fuck you doing here?" Tye yelled out, pointing at Delphine. She walked up to the booth as Jenny ducked back into the crowd. Delphine's gut felt like it was packed with dry ice.

"Where is Blue Sky?" Delphine demanded.

"Jesus Christ," Tye muttered. Then he said nothing for a long pause. Elsewhere, a man onstage was giving information for small workshops to be organized on lone wolf tactics and procedures.

"Blue Sky doesn't concern you," Tye said. He looked at her as if she were throwing mud on his nice slacks.

"Where are the other two babies? Getting them back to their moms concerns me now."

He paused a long beat, rigid, as if he was holding himself back from doing something against his own interests. His shoulders were tight and the veins on his neck bulged.

"Look . . ." he said. "I don't want anything to do with you, but I tell you what." He bent over, took a pen out of his shirt pocket and wrote on the back of one of his brochures. "The babies will be at this address at about ten tomorrow morning. Be there then and you can check them out. Don't be late because I'm not hanging around here long."

"What is happening at this spot at ten in the morning?"

"It's a meeting; the children will be there but it won't last long. All these children have new homes with loving parents who value their culture and heritage." He leaned over his booth and whispered to make sure no one else heard this respectable manager of an adoption service say: "You can see my clients' children tomorrow at ten. If you don't want to wait around, then fuck off." Then he started to try to reel a passerby in to conversation. "All children are one hundred percent healthy and free of disease or cognitive defects."

Delphine grabbed the brochure and wondered if Tye even knew how he sounded. Hearing his voice made her want to vomit.

She turned to meet Jenny near the center of the circle, where she was talking with a girl who was wearing leather chaps and a tank top with the words LIVE FREE OR DIE scrawled across the chest.

"Will the babies' new parents be at this meeting?" Delphine shouted back at Tye.

"I don't know what kind of daycare situation the new parents may have set up on short notice. But I imagine the new parents will be at the meeting."

Jenny grabbed Delphine's arm and pulled her in close. "This is Starlight," she said. "She saw you talking with Tye. She says he is bad news."

"To be avoided at all costs," Starlight said. "I'm riding with the Grease Monkey Dykes out of San Francisco." Now she bent close and looked around, whispering, "We aren't into this scene, you know. We are pretty hard-core, but we're not batshit crazy."

"What are you doing here?" Delphine asked.

"One of our sisters had a baby and sold it to that asshole. Now she wants him back."

"Do you have a plan?" Jenny asked.

Starlight backed away as if trying to bat away her words. "I'm just here gathering information and getting ready for a meeting." She bent over and reached into her right boot and pulled out a Nazi dagger. "I bought this here. I'm taking it to my meeting with Tye."

"I think we might be working on the same case," Delphine said and held up the photo of Tom Foster's child of interest.

The woman biker did not look long at the photograph and tried to act like she didn't recognize the child. "You cops?"

"No. Lord no. I'm private and I was hired to find this child."

"That's little Hank. That's our member's baby boy. She will do just about anything now to get her son back from that psycho. It's going to happen either tonight or tomorrow morning at ten."

"We've got our own problems with Tye," Delphine said.

"Who doesn't," Starlight said.

A big white man with Nazi tattoos walked by the group of women. "Well hello ladies. Are we gonna party or what?"

"Fuck off," Jenny said.

"You need to learn some manners. I mean, you gonna kiss me with that mouth?" the big man said.

"And I suppose you're the guy to teach us manners?" Starlight said.

Before he said anything in response, Delphine said, "We're not in the market, thanks."

"I'm nasty and I can teach you some nasty moves." He walked up to Starlight and tried to grind his crotch against her chaps. Starlight bent over, giving him a good look at her cleavage. Then she stood up quickly and just as quickly dropped to her knees and stabbed her brand-new dagger into the middle of the big man's foot. Delphine could almost feel the blade go all the way through the foot and down into the sand beneath the sole.

Simultaneously, Jenny and Delphine backed calmly away and into the crowd. Starlight sprinted past them toward the entry, melting into a group of three other women who exited to the parking area.

The big man was down on the ground and screaming, pointing toward the entrance and shouting, "Stop those dyke bitches!" The woman who had checked Jenny and Delphine in to the venue was on her walkie-talkie and striding with purpose toward the injured man. She told the radio to "send medical" and scanned the crowd. Saw the group walking Starlight out. Saw Jenny and Delphine milling by the used bookstore. By accident, Jenny caught the security guard's eye in a direct stare. Then, after a pause, the security guard jerked her head toward the exit as if to say, "Get out. I'll try and stall as long as I can," before turning back to the fallen big guy.

"All right, make a hole here, we got medics on their way. . ."

Surprisingly the toughest-looking men were not responding but, by instinct perhaps, were walking away and trying to make themselves invisible. But outside the circle there were some brothers running around looking for some kind of retribution . . . whatever retribution there was to be had.

"Frog got himself shanked by a little dyke," Jenny heard someone in the crowd say, to a smattering of laughter.

"Excuse me, ladies?" someone close to Jenny and Delphine said. "Ladies, stop!"

Jenny turned around and saw four men wearing filthy blue jeans and gang colors on their jackets running towards them. She looked around for the truck, and there next to it stood Gudger and the Vulcan with her own Road King. Behind them was Ned with the Sportster.

"What the hell are you boys doing here?" Jenny yelled.

Gudger was nearest the front wheel. Behind him, the Vulcan was holding on tight and Ned was revving the Sportster.

"Mom!" Ned yelled. "They made me come. I didn't want to but they made me bring the Sportster."

"You big baby," Gudger said as he kickstarted the Road King with Dwayne on the back.

"You get that child off that bike!" Jenny screamed. She walked over to the big bike and pulled Dwayne off into her arms. The men who were chasing after her came to a stop, apparently dumbstruck by the rage of a middle-aged mother who did not meet the description of a "little dyke."

Delphine had taken off on the Sportster and Jenny suddenly had control of the crowd. She ordered five of the bikers to help her load the Road King up into the back of the truck. They horsed the big bike up a ramp she kept in the Ford and soon it was strapped into the back and her wild young boys were riding in the front.

Jenny turned to the men with swastika tattoos and said, "Kids . . . I tell you."

The big men smiled and shook their heads.

As the Ford pulled out to the blacktop road, there was a lot of yelling in the truck: "What were you thinking?"

"I just followed these biker guys. I figured they were going to the same place you were."

"Gudger made us come along."

"Mom . . . you know I didn't mean to have them ride along. These babies were going to cry about it all day long if I didn't let them come."

"You know it's not safe to ride those bikes."

"It was fine."

"Yeah, we did good."

"Dad would not be so mad about it."

"Don't start with that," Jenny said in a pissed off mom tone.

Not a conversation, just a lot of hollering. Soon it stopped. Ned pointed out toward the horizon. There in a wide pull-off was a herd of big bikes with women sitting astride them. Their leathers were multicolored as was the hair that hung down from their helmets. There were tattoos of goddesses and many piercings into skin. What the boys saw could have been a gathering of tribal huntresses from all the savannas of the world. In the middle of this herd sat Delphine on the Sportster. She wore the fluorescent yellow fireman's coat, a bulbous old Bell helmet that Gudger had made the Vulcan wear and some safety goggles that made her look like Adam Ant.

"Jeepers, Mom, who are they?" Ned asked.

"I believe these are the Grease Monkey Dykes."

The boys didn't say a word.

And just at that moment, Booster the dog poked his dirty face up from below and whined to get up on the driver's seat.

"Now where did he come from?" Jenny demanded.

"Boosta wode with me and Gudgew on the big bike."

"Oh my God," Jenny said, almost completely exhausted now.

CHAPTER EIGHT

Some philosophers say it is our interior *reason* that allows us to extrapolate and bind all information of our senses, and feel as if we are living in a world that has continuity. Humans, like other big-brained animals, have an extraordinary range of senses, and some philosophers believe it is that range and our evolutionary biology as hunter-gatherers that gave birth to our ability to reason. Another explanation is that our big brain gave us an interior moral voice to help us make our next move. Even more simply: animals with complex functions have brains that produce a type of consciousness, if and only if they live in a stable and predictable environment. If the environment is sick, so too will the consciousness become ill.

On the other hand, ticks survive with a very simple brain. We know that ticks can smell mammals, that they can sense the correct animal to feed on by sensing temperature and deciding to drop down on them. That's all ticks have to do. They don't see, really, they don't feel, hear or taste as we understand it. They have no need to develop reason to work out their survival. They don't have any other choice. A tick's consciousness would be a dull interior existence. There would be nothing like imagination that allows them to preplan an experience.

Humans are not superior to ticks, they only have more

sensations to deal with, and they evolved with a lot more opportunities to survive: the big brain, the opposable thumb, the forward-facing eyes with the ability to focus at a distance and up close, sensitive skin and sexual urges that give some free agency to mating.

But we are still stuck with the problem of the mind. Do we really know what we are doing, or are we operating on a much more sensitive set of urges that are giving us the answers when we think we are working them out for ourselves? What if you were sitting out on a boat with the oars crossed in front of you, and you were as aware of your surroundings as possible—the water lapping against the side of your boat, the loons singing their mating call, the motion of the boat rocking back and forth? What if all of that, your sensations of the world, *was* your consciousness? The world is your environment, and your environment is the substance of your consciousness. If this really were true, don't you think we would take better care of the world?

Perhaps our minds are no more complex than a tick's at the root. Maybe our brains are just much bigger. If that were the case, how much more difficult would it be for Delphine to decide what to do next as she sits on a motorcycle along the side of a rural highway, thinking she probably has Tye and a cohort of murderers blasting down the road intent on killing her? How does she decide on the wise thing to do? Does she really decide anything, or does she just react to what the environment tells her to feel?

"WE'RE GOING to go into town and get a hotel. They gave me a name. Then, we are going to go to discuss this meeting with the babies," Delphine said. "The Grease Monkey Dykes all believe that something very bad might go down. Something that would keep them from getting their baby back."

"All right," Jenny said. "Give me the name of the place and you can follow me."

Delphine did. Then, not murderers, but a lesbian motor-cycle gang blustered down the road. The procession of thirty-five women and three young boys moved down the highway like a mob of starlings.

Jenny didn't have the heart to punish the boys for their reck-lessness. She was happy enough to have them safe and unhurt there in the truck. But still the boys mounted their defense.

"We've ridden three to a bike ever since there were three of us to ride," Gudger insisted.

"I know," Jenny said as if she were already beaten.

"It was fun, Mom. Gudgew is a good widew."

"Uh-huh," Jenny grunted. "Ned, you want to say anything?"

"No Mom," Ned said. "But it was fun and it was cool seeing all those Fat Boys on the road."

"Okay. Anything else?"

All the boys remained silent.

"Can I speak?" Jenny said after the pause.

"Yeees," Gudger said, rolling his eyes.

"Thank you. Okay, we just lost your dad. It's hard on all of us. I know that. But we are together in this. We are a family. A little tribe, a team, a unit."

Gudger, Ned and Dwayne sat still on the bench seat of the old Ford. They didn't squirm and they didn't say anything smart-mouthed back to their mother.

The tires whined and the old frame jostled around on the uneven pavement. They rolled over a dead snake in the road. "And I love you all so much. I really think that I would lose my mind if anything bad happened to any of you. I don't even want to think about how crazy I might become if any of you goofballs got seriously hurt with these shenanigans. *And* I know that I am part of these crazy hijinks Delphine has gotten us involved in. I know it's crazy . . . but she is a friend . . . and she can't help that she is going to die just like your dad. It just feels to me like helping her with this thing . . . with finding Leigh's baby . . . it feels like being able to do something for your dad, I guess."

"It willy is kind of cwazy, Mom . . . but I'm with you."

Jenny was crying now, and she snorted when her youngest son spoke both like her husband and his little child self.

"Thank you, sweetheart," she said.

They bumped along the highway without speaking as blackbirds swooped down from the wires into a field and dead snakes lay motionless along the centerline. Most of the Grease Monkey Dykes had found their hotel down the street.

The neighborhoods on the outskirts of Yakima could have been little favelas in any part of Latin America or Mexico. There were no sidewalks on the streets and footpaths were beaten between the houses. The streets were a patchwork of squares looking more like a community garden than a North American suburb. It was late afternoon and families were gathered out by their concrete steps. The small cottages were transplanted worker's shacks from the big farms, hauled in and put together haphazardly. Every fifth tree had a tire swing in it. The roads were unpaved, and the edges of the blocks were rounded off as people cut the corners in their cars or on their bikes. Grills were being lit, and the air held the gassy smell of lighter fluid and charcoal smoke. Big men carried coolers full of ice on their shoulders, girls carried old milk boxes of toys and notebooks. Boys carried boom boxes. Soon enough, the air was spiced with music just as it was with cumin on cooking meat. There, in the middle of a makeshift block, was not a hotel but a guesthouse where Starlight and Delphine sat on their oily motorcycles waving the old Ford down.

The place where Jenny's little troop was going to stay was made up of three single-wide trailers laid out in a U, making a little courtyard in the middle. In the center was an inflatable kids' wading pool and two folding chairs. There had been two other chairs, but they lay off to the side with one broken leg each. Between the trailers were two portable dog crates. One crate was filled with clothes and the other held a placid-looking mutt asleep on his side.

The boys jumped out of the Ford and ran frantically to the pool and immediately dabbled their fingers there. Dwayne peeled off and picked up a long blade of grass, then walked to the dog crate. He touched the tip of the leaf of grass to the tip of the dog's nose to make sure he was alive.

"Hello, fella," Dwayne said while down on his knees. "You all wight in thewe?"

Jenny checked in. Starlight kept talking with Delphine. Her real name was Estrella. She had been born and raised in Indio, California, near Palm Springs. She went to Arizona State on

a full tennis scholarship. When she broke her ankle skate-
boarding, she dropped out of school and moved to San
Francisco. She had small jobs in the drug transportation
industry and had a few minor convictions but had avoided any
felonies. That's not to say she hadn't committed any. At the
end of the conversation, Starlight held up her cell phone next
to Delphine's and they exchanged numbers. She walked to her
bike, turned back and yelled out, "Tonight then?" and Delphine
waved as if agreeing.

The truck was unpacked quickly, and the boys got into their
shorts and flopped out in the soft and dusty pool. Gudger ran
and got a bike pump from the *señorita* who rented the place and
hardened up the pool. His brothers were laughing and splash-
ing as Ned put more water in the pool from the hose. The
water was cold and tasted rubbery. Dwayne screamed as he got
squirted. Delphine and Jenny sat in the two good chairs. Jenny
was drinking a beer and Delphine had a glass of nutritional
food supplement.

"Your drink could use a little bit of rum in it," Jenny said.

"Oh God," Delphine said.

Jenny took a little airplane bottle out of her beach bag and
poured a bit of rum into Delphine's glass.

"Starlight said we'll go check out where our meet is supposed to be. They are coming along. This is their meeting with
Tyler, too. He wants us all there. We'll all go tonight to check
out the spot. You could unload everything from the Ford and
come along?"

"Sweetie," Jenny said, "I can't leave these boys here alone,
and I can't bring them with. Not after today."

"I know, but we could take them out to dinner first. The Dykes are going to have a barbeque tonight and we've all been invited. I'll take Dwayne on the Sportster. You guys could come in the truck or Gudger can drive the truck and you take the Road King with Ned. Now tell me they wouldn't enjoy that!"

"Oh Christ." Jenny closed her eyes. "You're right. They would dig it. The Dyke barbeque would be a blast. Good for my oldest son, that punk, and it would be best if we stuck together." She took a long drink of her beer and stretched out in the warm sunlight. She reached over and took Delphine's hand. Delphine was nearly asleep already. Jenny reached into the pocket of her shorts and pulled out some loose pills. "D, take these."

Delphine felt the fat oblong pills in her hand and was about to refuse, then she too lay back, popped the pills into her mouth and closed her eyes.

"Hey listen, you ruffians . . ." Jenny spoke to the dirty little boys in the inflatable pool. "If I fall asleep here for a second do you promise not to go out and rob a bank or something?"

"Wob a bank?" Dwayne shouted. "Are we gonna wob a bank?"

"No . . . you half an orphan . . . we're not going to wob a bank. She wants us *not* to wob a bank!"

Dwayne started crying harder and faster than anyone expected.

"What's wrong, Dwayne?" Delphine opened her eyes a bit, struggling to keep awake. "Why are you crying?"

Snot began to roll as he sat at the far end of the flimsy plastic pool, his shoulders shaking hard.

"What's half an owphan?" he finally spit out. He literally didn't know but it scared him.

"Oh, come here, baby," Jenny said, and she threw him a towel. He got out of the pool all hunched up and shivering, crawled into his mother's lap and buried his face in her shoulder.

"It's okay. There is no such thing as 'half an orphan.'"

Then Gudger got out of the pool and walked over. "Yeah Dwayne," he said. "I'm sorry. I was teasing but there is no such thing."

"Okay," the little boy sniffed. "I'm awight."

THEY SLEPT out by the pool until the woman who checked them in came up to them, slowly walking through the dead weeds of her yard.

"*Quieres comer, señora?*" Jenny's eyes fluttered. "*Poquito . . .*"

The woman asked if they wanted to eat a little. She held out a little plate of deep-fried tortillas with melted cheese and hot sauce. "*Poquito.*" Just a little bit to eat. The little tribe roused themselves, showered and put on clean clothes with long pants, then followed the rock and roll music coupled with the smell of cooking on the barbeque.

As they followed the sweet smoke of the party down the block, Delphine saw what looked like an old airport shuttle bus rolling down the street toward them. She couldn't take her eyes off the driver. The Babysitter was driving the small bus away from the Dykes' party. Delphine pivoted on her heels and waved for the bus to stop.

To her surprise, the Babysitter pulled over.

"What are you doing here?" Delphine demanded.

"I told you I was returning a baby boy to his mother." The big man blinked dumbly toward Delphine.

"Who killed Leigh?" Delphine demanded.

"I have no idea what you're talking about. That girl Leigh is back in Seattle as far as I know."

"Whose blood were you trying to wipe off your hands when I saw you in the parking garage?"

The Babysitter shook his head almost as if he sympathized with Delphine. Then he slammed the bus door shut and took off down the road.

THE GREASE Monkey Dykes knew how to party. Three grills were burning out on the pool patio of a high-end motel just three blocks away. Two refrigerators sat at the end of a complete outdoor kitchen. Long tables were set up where women were making many kinds of salads. Women were drinking beer, wine and cocktails. There were tables dedicated to vegan dishes, two women with short hair and coveralls were working on nothing but sauces, meat cooks were cooking wild-caught king salmon, black cod. A fifty-gallon plastic drum that had been cut in half and filled with ice was overflowing with Dungeness crab. There were buckets of chips and salsa, and one table was dedicated to baked goods. There were a few kids carrying reusable plates with overloaded hamburgers and potato salad sliding around on them. The women laughed and hugged one another when meeting. The vibe was fun and friendly, with the feel of a reunion.

Starlight had changed into a fringed leather jacket and some clean tight jeans, along with expensive cowboy boots. She wore her hair long and her bare arms were tanned. She looked more like a sun-damaged Sheryl Crow than a lesbian road warrior. She was standing by a horse trough filled with ice and champagne bottles, having her glass filled. The sweating bottles were almost too cold to hold on to.

"*Salud*!" Starlight yelled as she held both hands aloft with fresh glasses. "I'm glad you came."

They met over by a table laid out with different seafood salads and a large pot of paella.

"Quite a spread you have here," Jenny said. "It's not like any biker barbeque I've been to."

"We're out of San Francisco, girl. We are diverse, you know what I'm saying?" She handed them both a glass of good French sparkling wine. "Help yourself."

"These are my boys, Gudger, Ned and Dwayne."

"Hey fellas, get yourself whatever you want to eat. You are welcome here. If someone asks, just say you're with Star. No one will ask though."

"Thank you vewy much," Dwayne said.

"Of course. Try some of that crab before you bloat out on dessert."

All three boys took off into the crowd of partying bikers.

Starlight scanned the crowd and then stopped. She pointed at a stocky woman in black leathers with close-cropped hair who was walking around the party. She was wearing a modern-looking leather baby carrier in front, with what looked like a baby covered up inside the leather cocoon.

"Here, come meet mom and baby."

The mom, Shirley, had thick forearms and the sturdy build of a house framer. She was wearing a Hawaiian shirt under her jacket. The baby was covered up in her carrier. Introductions were made all around. Shirley took off her jacket and Delphine could see a well-made tattoo that had the female symbol on her left biceps. Surrounding the symbol was a banner with the words "Deeds Not Words" flowing down it. Shirley had been raised in Oakland in a large family of boys who mostly ended up in the earthmoving and site-preparation business.

"Congratulations on recovering your child." Delphine shook Shirley's hand.

Shirley said, "I'm just so happy to have my boy back. I was foolish to ever let him go to that guy."

"How did you ever get him to give the baby back?" Jenny asked.

Shirley looked around the crowd. She had an intense stare.

"With a guy like that, I think there isn't a problem that money can't solve. My parents and the Grease Monkeys helped me raise the money. I think my mom thought keeping the baby would magically make me straight." She kept squinting into the crowd and raised her eyebrows, like a western gunslinger.

"What's his name?" Delphine asked, and Shirley leveled her stare back on the thin woman in the fireman's jacket.

"His name is Hank," she said. "The adoption people had some crazy hippie name for him." And here Shirley pulled the blanket back and leaned back to show off her child.

Delphine's blood pressure rose.

"Jesus," she said.

"What?" Shirley said defensively. Just then the baby reached both of his arms toward his head. Little Hank had the small strawberry birthmark on his right arm.

Delphine had suspected, but now she was certain. "This is Leigh's baby. This is Blue Sky."

"The hell you say," Shirley said, and then Delphine's world went dark.

SURPRISINGLY, THE party went on rather smoothly after Shirley slugged Delphine in the face. Starlight and two other Dykes pulled Shirley back. There was some yelling back and forth while Jenny cradled Delphine's head in her lap. The three boys came running with their plates filled with chocolate torte. Dwayne put his palm on Delphine's forehead much in the way his mother had always done when checking for a fever.

"She's okay, sweetie. She just offended someone, and they got mad at her."

"That's just not nice," Gudger offered. He was standing with his chest puffed out, but his chin was smeared with chocolate.

"Stop it," Jenny said. "We are not in a situation to fight anyone. It was just a mistake on Shirley's part."

Shirley stood over them now, spit flecking off her mouth. "I may not be a good parent for getting rid of him in the first place. But that baby is mine, I gave birth to him and his name is Hank."

Jenny waved her hand toward Shirley. "You punched a woman who is dying of cancer and that is the only thing that concerns me now."

"Well, tell her to mind her own business when it comes to my family," Shirley said.

"We got a family too," Dwayne called, puffing out his chest like a little terrier looking for a fight.

"Yes we do, sweetie, let us handle this now," Jenny said. A bruise was rising on Delphine's cheek and her eyelids started to flutter. "That girl really coldcocked you," Jenny said.

"Little Hank was Leigh's baby," Delphine mumbled.

"It appears there is some dispute about that and anyway . . . Leigh is dead now, right?"

"I know, but still." Delphine was beginning to stir more and more. "All I know for certain is that the child we just met was Baby Blue and Leigh wanted to keep him and now Leigh is dead. Leigh is dead and Tyler has more money than he was planning on."

Starlight leaned over. "I'm sorry, ladies. Shirley is having some big feelings right now."

Delphine struggled to her feet and as soon as she got upright, she doubled up and vomited.

Starlight started walking Shirley back to the hotel. She was crying hard. "I'm never letting Hank go again. I'm his mom. Nothing is going to change that."

JENNY AND her tribe of chocolate-smeared boys helped Delphine back to the trailer. They made her a bed of old chair cushions by the inflatable pool.

The boys had managed to take some crabs and cream puffs from the Grease Monkey party. Delphine didn't want to eat, but Jenny made her a glass of artificial food and medicine, stirred some crushed banana into it and watched as she drank it down. Delphine was ghostly thin by now. Her hair was starting to grow back because it had been some time since her last chemotherapy treatment. The boys cracked crab and slurped it down. They splashed each other from the pool, being careful under Jenny's watchful eye not to get Delphine wet.

Two hours passed and the sun made a lazy arch in the sky. The heat held them all like a blanket, but eventually, cold started to creep in around the edges. Small birds tittered in the brush and dogs barked in the distance.

Starlight appeared with a bottle of champagne and a plate of chocolate-covered strawberries. She walked into the circle of waders and cleared her throat. The boys looked up and each of them had their hands balled into fists but none of them took a step toward her.

"Boys!" Jenny said. "It's okay. I don't think she wants to fight. Look, she is bringing gifts."

"That's right," Starlight said. "We had a meeting, and the entire corps of Grease Monkeys wants to send our apologies for one of our sisters attacking you." She was looking down at Delphine, who barely had her eyes open.

"They sent me to explain that we have spent a lot of the club's money getting the baby back. But it breaks our hearts that there may be a woman out there who feels like little Hank is her child. There is no one to blame but that little shithook Tyler."

"Well said . . ." Delphine mumbled from her cushions.

"We hope that even if you can't forgive us, you will not seek to take some kind of revenge."

"I forgive you and the person who hit me." Delphine raised herself up on one elbow. "We don't need to make this complicated. I don't want to take anyone's baby away. All I have ever wanted is to find the three babies who were taken from Seattle. Leigh, the woman who was taking care of the baby, was murdered in Seattle. I doubt that Leigh had agreed to give her baby up, and I suspect that Tye killed her for it."

"Jesus," Starlight said. "We are not conceding anything about who the baby's mom is. Shirley is the biological parent. But we'll help you find Tye, because it has to be clear we had nothing to do with what happened to this other woman. We had nothing to do with her murder."

"What are you thinking?" Jenny asked.

"We'll talk by phone with the lawyers tonight. And you guys and I will go to where Tyler said the meeting was to take place and see if there are any clues as to where he might be, because it's pretty clear to us that Tyler Dearborn won't be at any meeting."

"What do you mean, where the meeting was supposed to take place?" Delphine asked.

"Tyler said he would make the exchange tomorrow afternoon. He came back to us and said he would bring the baby out here tonight. That's all I know."

"Good . . . we will go to the meeting tomorrow and see if either the Babysitter or Tyler shows up."

"Of course," Starlight said.

The boys shivered now as they walked, dripping, from the pool. Dwayne stepped forward and took the plate of strawberries from Starlight's hand.

CHAPTER NINE

Delphine slept soundly through the night. Booster slept on the bed with her. The dog would lick her face periodically, as if sensing the pain in her cheek.

Delphine dreamed about bears circling her old house in Sitka. The big animals were taller at their withers than John was tall. Their breath steamed out of their nostrils like an old locomotive. The bears grunted in a low register, snuffling around the edges of the doors. The rotten smell of their breath, fetid with the smell of their own filthy hide, gradually filled up the house. In the dream, she opened the door to confront the bears and John stood in the doorway, smiling. He was as thin and handsome as he was when they first met. His hands were calloused from work and his shirt was unbuttoned down his chest, where beads of sweat gathered. He had been working in the heat and he had come for a drink of water. She was happy to see him, but when she went to him for a hug, he spoke in the impossibly low tone of a bear. "I'm sorry, I can't stay." The tone was so low it made her guts shake and she withdrew. Just then, Booster licked her cheek and Delphine startled awake—away from the bears, away from John. Her hands were shaking. She was cold.

Booster wiggled his small canine body next to hers. The dog's breath stunk of canned dog food.

"That's okay, Booster," Delphine said aloud, and she stroked him back to sleep.

The next morning, she was up by six. She drank strong instant coffee as she walked through the weeds in the lot. Three dogs who appeared not to have permanent homes walked side by side around the periphery of the yard. They were of indiscriminate breed, and they were thin as war babies, all ribs and teeth. Gray jays dove on a plastic bag of garbage down in a ditch. The coffee made her jittery and she was a bit haunted by the bears of her dreams.

The boys and Jenny came out of the trailer and announced they were off to a local fast-food joint for breakfast.

"I've got your breakfast drink on the counter. I'll be back in a minute. We should get to the spot by eight. The actual meet isn't supposed to be until later in the afternoon, but we should check out the spot early to make sure there is nothing sketchy about it," Jenny said. The boys all gave sleepy waves.

"Okay." Delphine waved back. Booster ran across the yard and jumped up on Delphine's legs.

"Hey, lover," she said.

At eight thirty, she pushed the starter over on the Sportster and Jenny swung her leg over the Road King. They ran by the motel where the Grease Monkey Dykes were staying and kept their engines running. Within seconds, Starlight came out and started up her Fat Boy and stood next to it drinking her coffee from a travel cup that fit behind her seat in a well-machined clip. As soon as the Fat Boy started running smoothly, she threw out the coffee dregs, clipped in her mug, jacked her leg up over the saddle, squared herself and then let the throttle roar.

Delphine followed the directions on her phone to the meeting place. It was a vacant lot on the far margins of the town. The weeds were ground down by tire tracks. It looked as though vehicles came off the street in pairs, as if many people had pulled in to the lot to meet other cars and talk to one another. Delphine noticed that sandwich papers littered the ground alongside lidless paper cups. To the far eastern corner of the lot, a blue tarp lay curled in more weeds, which grew wild on the periphery by the fence.

The three women shut down their vehicles and sat for a moment, letting the silence seep back into their ears.

"I don't know what we thought we would find here," Jenny said as she walked to the far eastern end of the lot. Jenny kicked at the bits of food wrappers and cups to see if anything small might be hidden there.

"It is set up for drug meets," Delphine said. "The drivers come here to talk and exchange stuff. See the tracks and the trash? Someone comes first and waits. When both are here, the cars are facing opposite ways down the road. They can see anyone coming from either direction. It's kind of a squirrely place."

Jenny came running back from the east end of the lot. Her skin was pale. "You two have to help me. There is something in the blue tarp and I don't want to open it up by myself."

They met in the corner and Delphine stepped on the blue bundle. There was something heavy there, something that gave to the touch.

Starlight walked to the other side and found the edges of the tarp.

"Grab the middle and the other side," she told the other two.

It was hard for Delphine at first and as they got the package to move, the unmistakable smell of butcher paper began to escape. Sour blood smell. They pulled harder and out tumbled the dead body of the Babysitter, shot twice through the center mass with a high-powered rifle.

DELPHINE WAS not a fan of the term "orca whale." She thought of them naturally as killers. She had spent months of her life taking her yellow skiff and hunting for the transient killer whales in Alaskan waters. She had gotten close enough to the animals to shoot darts into their flesh from a pneumatic rifle or a crossbow. The darts would hit the skin and pop off, then float on the surface of the water for her to recover with a long-handled pool net. The blubber sample was about the diameter of a pencil eraser and perhaps an inch long. The samples, once analyzed, could give back a great deal of information about things including diet, sex and specific genetic typing that would help reveal the nature of divisions in the population. She had witnessed dozens of kills of otters, sea lions, seals and other whales.

Transient killer whales hunt as a pack. Sometimes, they appear to kill not for nutrition but as a training exercise for their young. She once watched a pod of killer whales use the bottom of her thirteen-foot inflatable raft as a barrier to block a herd of Dall's porpoises from getting to the surface as the whales snatched them in their jaws. Later, she observed the adult whales throwing a dead porpoise back and forth with their snouts, allowing a young whale to chase the dead animal.

When the training appeared to be over, a large male threw the dead porpoise high up onto the beach.

When large whales are killed, it is an opportunity to understand the condition of surplus. Killer whales have been observed killing and partially consuming large baleen whales. Delphine had personally observed killer whales taking humpbacks. But there have been many reports of killers taking grey whales as well. Baleen whales use their tails to slap at the surface to defend themselves. They also use the top of their heads, which have a bony structure, to defend a stricken whale, like warriors encircling a fallen comrade with their shields. The slaps and bumps, the lunging with their superior bulk, can often stave off an attack. But often the defenders' soft bellies remained exposed for too long and they tire under the attack. Often the killer whales will rip into their sides and eventually pull off enough chunks of blubber to gain access to the internal organs.

If the attack takes place offshore, the killer whales will eat the tongues out of the bigger mammals. The kill and the eating produce a lake of blood, which is neutrally buoyant, turning the sea red in the area. The dying animals succumb to death in a pool of their own blood. The dead, tongueless animals are abandoned. At first, the corpse remains at the surface, where it faces predation by birds, sharks, and many other fish that want to make use of the extraordinary amounts of fatty flesh, but eventually the corpse itself becomes saturated with seawater and begins to sink. After days, or even weeks, the killer whales return to continue consuming the whale. A healthy humpback adult might be forty-five feet long and weigh upward of as many tons: bones, blubber and meat. The bones, when exposed, are saturated with fatty oil. After the killer whales are satiated, they leave the now dismembered carcass to slowly sink to the bottom.

If the carcass falls into the deep bottom off the edge of a coastal plate, the rich nutrients trigger an ecological event. Most of the ocean's nutrition comes from the river systems and estuaries where sunlight mixes with virtual compost heaps of nitrogen to create rich feeding areas. This is why most fish and mammals are found near shore. But the dark depths have a host of sightless and terrifying-looking creatures. When a whale falls into their world, it creates a new microenvironmental community that includes different kinds of octopi, giant isopods, squat lobsters, hagfish, goblin sharks, lampreys, vampire squid. The stuff of nightmares in the lightless deep.

"Let's go to the police," Jenny said.

"Hold on," Starlight said. "In my experience going to the police is rarely a solution to anything."

"This is a murder," Delphine said. "This is not *Murder She Wrote*. The police will see us as suspects in the death of this guy. No way should we go to them."

"No way," Jenny said.

Delphine cleared her throat and said, "From where I'm sitting, the short list of suspects includes all of us, Tyler and the 88's. Speaking of which . . ."

Two big, customized Harley-Davidsons rolled up to the lot. Big men with swastika tattoos turned off the bikes and lifted their legs over the machines. One unholstered a large semi-auto handgun and stood by his bike. The other was the leather-clad biker who had followed Delphine out of Seattle. He had worked on his Vandyke since they had met near Marblemount.

The Vandyke man walked along the periphery of the lot. He paused at something that looked like a trail camera with a cell phone taped to the side, then unhooked the device from a battery pack and made his way to the women. Without speaking, they considered running to their bikes, but noticed that the men's bikes were cutting off the easiest access out.

"You are thinking about going to the cops?" the man with the camera asked.

"We're just discussing our options. You know anything about this?" Delphine finished with a question and as she did, Starlight reached inside her boot.

"You the little dyke who stabbed Mouse through the foot at the information fair?" The Vandyke man was smiling at the three women, but his eyes lingered on Delphine.

"I might have, but I also might have had a good reason. I don't like being pushed around," Starlight said.

"I guess. You got him good." The man was smiling broadly. "I don't think he is ever going to live it down."

He walked over and stared down at the pile of bacteria and protein that had once been the body of the Babysitter.

"I told you I'd see you over here," he said to Delphine. "This is a mess; we better get out of here. The buzzards will start drawing people's attention and the cops will be here soon enough. Listen, over by where we placed our surveillance camera is a broom. Push your rides to the pavement and sweep up your footprints and tire tracks."

"You want us to clean yours, too?" Jenny asked more sarcastically than she had meant to sound.

"Naw," the big man said. "My tracks are all over this lot. Cops know that. We're going to call the police anyway. We'll say we found it. You didn't do anything but unroll him, right?"

"What the hell?" Delphine began to say something more by way of demanding an explanation. "I think I should be able to provide a little more information to the cops when they inevitably come to talk to us about him." Here she nodded to the corpse. "I mean, 'we just found him here'? You think a two-bit explanation from me is going to satisfy anyone?"

"All you did was walk around out here, looking for something, then you saw the tarp and you unrolled it. Nothing more our camera didn't catch. Right?" As the Vandyke man was speaking, he was looking around the lot, replaying the scene in his mind.

"That's right," Delphine said, beginning to understand the man was trying to do them a favor.

"Listen . . . Tye was either setting you up or he is going to have you killed, too. I'm telling you the cops are going to be involved here in a few minutes and we don't just want to be standing around teaching you a class in Tyler Dearborn's tomfuckery."

"Where do you suggest we go?" Jenny asked, clearly getting angry now.

"Follow me. I'll take you to a guy with answers." He pointed to the man holding the gun. "Hurricane will follow to make sure the three of you don't get lost."

Delphine wished she could go somewhere and think, but

now she was clearly in the action part of the investigation. John often said, "Do everything you can to remain an observer; it's when you start taking action in a crime that your life can turn to shit." But she was now an actor in events, not just an observer. She was feeling more and more trapped and she knew this was when people made disastrous mistakes.

The women covered their tracks as best they could, then they fired up and followed Vandyke without the visible gun. They ran down the paved road and turned off onto a hard rock-and-sand lane. They came to a tavern with dozens of bikes parked under a barnlike structure. Their guide shut down his bike and waited for the others to do the same.

"We built this parking barn to protect us from drones. Law enforcement thinks they are really cute, tracking us. You can drive different scooters back to where you are staying."

"No fricken way . . ." Starlight began.

"Listen," the guide said sternly. "We will bring your bikes to you and trade them out once it gets good and dark and late for the cops to be surveilling. They are not running triple shifts now, and they sure as hell haven't approved any overtime. And by the way . . . you're welcome."

"And what do we have to be thankful for?" Delphine asked.

"For letting you know that you will be going home at all."

BEHIND THE tavern was an office that looked to be converted from a storage room. The entire structure was made from prefab log cabin kits pieced together on-site. Kegs and taps lined the north-facing wall, which had windows placed high up so no one could look in or look out. A pinball machine with old Sailor Jerry–style pinup-girl graphics sat against the opposite wall. Beside the pinball machine were four gray file cabinets with large locks on each drawer. On the western wall rested a flag of the Confederate states behind a black wooden desk carved with death's-heads and an SS insignia. Sitting at the desk was an almost unnaturally small man. He had two pairs of glasses, one in place on the bridge of his nose and the other perched up on his forehead. He wore a sleeveless under-shirt, and the women could not see his pants under the desk. While most of the bikers they had seen were large and meaty, this man seemed almost elfin in contrast. The speakers near the filing cabinets were playing a Beethoven piano piece. Above his desk on the outside wall hung a large elk head with dusty glass eyes.

"Please, sit," he said. "I hope you were treated well by my associates." He was looking at Delphine.

"Yes," she said.

"I understand you are involved with Tyler Dearborn. Is that correct?"

"Yes, but in fact I was looking for the three children he traveled here with."

"Ah . . ." the little man said. "Why? If I may ask."

"I felt they were in danger."

Later, the world would learn the little man's name was Andrew Miller, who had grown up on a big ranch in eastern Oregon and had gone into the service only to wash out before he could be deployed. In the room with Delphine, he picked up a remote control and waved it at the stereo to bring down the volume. Beethoven receded into the background noise of the Southern rock being played in the tavern. The elk on the wall did not change his expression.

"I regret every moment I spent with Tyler. I want to assure you that we did not kill the big man you found out in the turnaround this morning."

Delphine said calmly, "And who are you?"

"I prefer not to use names. I never really know to whom I am speaking and I'm not all that sure who might be listening in to our conversation. But let me just say that I am a man you should trust."

"Ah . . ." Delphine sat forward while the other women leaned back in their chairs, seemingly happy to let her do the talking. The man who led them into the office had walked out, but he appeared again with a platter of drinks from a cooler. Delphine chose a bottle of water and her friends decided on beer.

"What is your interest in Tye?" Delphine asked.

The man behind the desk poured himself a cup of coffee from a thermos and leaned back in his chair. The chair seemed to be consuming him.

"Tyler arranged five adoptions for myself and two of my other associates. He made the bold claim that the children's blood was one hundred percent pure."

"And you were not satisfied with the . . . children."

"Within a year, all five children became seriously ill. They all developed measles. Two children died, one of my own, and another became deaf as a result."

"I suppose by one hundred percent pure you mean that they had not been vaccinated."

"Naturally, they were of pure white heritage and free of invasive medicine." The little man spoke softly, as if he was intentionally trying to restrain himself from justifiable rage. "Vaccination is a Jewish conspiracy to introduce disease into the bloodlines of the European races. All these diseases were first developed in the Russian villages of the Jews. All these diseases—measles, smallpox, diphtheria—were unknown to the Aryans."

"Then how was it that your children became sick if they were otherwise pure?"

"Obviously their blood was not pure or, more likely, they were infected in Tyler's facility in Seattle."

"Infected by whom?" Delphine set her water bottle between her legs.

"Immigrants coming over the border. I could see him hiring Mexican help, can't you?"

Delphine drank deeply from the water bottle. "I'm sure we could have a long conversation about immunology, but I'm not sure it would help us."

"You yourself are dying from cancer. Haven't you ever considered where all the money goes? Who profits from this current plague of your disease?"

"Please . . ." she started, but he waved her off. He pointed to the oversized computer monitor on the side of his desk.

The little man turned it so she could see his screen as he began typing. Then he began scrolling through pages about Big Pharma, Big Medicine. Words blared at her from the screen: INTERNATIONAL JEWRY CONVICTED OF MASS MURDER; JEWISH DOCTORS, INDIAN DOCTORS FILL THEIR COFFERS

WITH BLOOD MONEY MADE FROM THE DEATHS OF WHITE CHILDREN. Delphine turned her head away.

Delphine could not take her eyes off of the eyes of the taxidermy elk. An oppressive silence seemed to flow from the dead eyes into her brain. "Listen, junior, what are we doing here, and what do you want from me?" she finally asked.

"You and I are going to prove to the cops that Tyler killed his associate, the one who others called the Babysitter."

"You want to do this as part of your civic duty, peewee?" Delphine asked.

"No," he said flatly. "Though we do operate under a code of ethics. We are an organization dedicated to cultural purity. We are not criminals. And I'm not rude enough to make jokes about other people's stature."

"Oh, I'm sorry," Delphine said. "I assumed you were used to it. Why don't you stand up on an apple cart and I'll give you a peck on the cheek?"

The three women stared at him wordlessly. Starlight wiggled in her chair as if her body was demanding to get up and leave but her mind wouldn't let her. "Why the camera on the Babysitter's body?" Delphine demanded.

"We were hoping to see Tyler come back to check on the status of the police investigation. We have sources in the police department. They tell us that a man called in and told the cops, just about an hour before you appeared, that two women were going to dump a body in that lot. The police were in fact on their way when we scurried you out of there."

"Tyler killed the Babysitter, then?" Delphine asked.

"Yes." The little man twirled a pen across the knuckles of

his right hand. He cleared his throat and stared hard into Delphine's eyes.

"Listen, let's speed this along. It's simple. I know you believe the Babysitter murdered the woman who took care of the babies in Seattle. You just have to go to the cops and convince them that Tyler killed the big man you found in the lot."

"Why would any of us do that?" Jenny said. "Why would we go to the police?"

"Do you have tender loyalties to Tyler Dearborn?" he said.

"Not at all," Delphine said. "But right now I have no idea who killed the big guy in the Hawaiian shirt, and circumstances would certainly go bad for us if we lied to the cops about it, particularly if the Rolling 88's have film of us discovering the body and then immediately coming to you about it."

The man with the Vandyke stood up from where he was sitting in the back. He put the trail camera on the little man's desk.

"I am going to arrange for you to talk to the cops and you are going to take down Tyler Dearborn for killing the Babysitter."

"Why don't you just do it yourself?" Delphine asked.

"Just as I said, we are a cultural advocacy group."

"Okay then, just tell me, why would Tyler kill his own associate?" Jenny asked.

"Tyler is a criminal and a murderer. He steals babies and sells them back to the highest bidder. The Babysitter didn't want to get taken down when Tyler goes down."

Starlight piped up. "Junior makes a good point there . . . At least about Tyler being a dirtbag."

The little man had a tired smile on his face as if it was clear that he had heard every short joke in creation. "It would be a mistake for any of the 88's to talk with the police, and I think your friend here knows that already." The little man nodded his head toward Delphine. "You spoke to the Babysitter last night. You accused him of murdering the nursemaid."

Delphine was grim and becoming angrier. "Listen, shrimpy, the only way you would know that was from talking with him. You certainly didn't get that information from any of us. You were the last person to talk with him alive."

The little man flipped his pen into the air and caught it. "It would be a very bad idea to involve us in any way. Because we have a recording of you unrolling the body, looking for all the world as if you were dumping it there. The rest of the recording can be creatively edited to make our narrative all the more believable."

"More believable than ours?"

"First, there are several officers who used to ride with our club and are still quite loyal. Second, you are all in a beef with the deceased."

"Now wait a minute," Jenny said, but the small man interrupted her.

"Let's not argue."

"We just want the other two children," Delphine said. "Give me them and I'll stop with the jokes and get out of your hair."

"All of you had reason to want the big man dead. He was a thief. He had brought you a baby back that turns out to have . . . how should I say this? A tricky provenance."

"Okay," Delphine said. "How do we do this?"

"Find Tyler. We'll help you with what we know, but you will

do the actual hunting. Then you drop a dime on him. I'll give you the number to call."

"Are the police interested in finding him?" Jenny asked.

"Presumably. He robs people, he sells babies and steals them back, he beats defenseless women and he sells motorcycle gangs defective white babies. He robs motorcycle gangs of their rightful possessions. He's not going to win many friends from any quarter acting that way."

"You didn't like the quality of the children you purchased, so you paid him in fake gold," Delphine said as a statement of fact.

"How could you possibly know that?" he asked.

"I found his notes in his Seattle apartment. I found evidence of the faked bricks of gold."

"The less you know about that the better it is for you. The existence or nonexistence of any gold has nothing to do with Tyler going down for murder."

Delphine sat forward. "But if we are linked to you and finding him for you, won't we be on the hook for the presumably imminent murder of young Tye?"

"If this all goes according to plan . . . and it will . . . no one will worry about what happens to young Tye." The small man with two sets of glasses on his head moved his face within inches of Delphine's nose.

Delphine directed a question to the biker chief. "So, you are saying that Tyler killed both the girl and the big man he called the Babysitter."

"I'm not just saying it, but I'm asserting the scenario is true." He brushed the air in front of his nose in a swatting motion as if to visually change the subject. "Now, you will hang around here until dark. You will each be given much better bikes than you rode in on to ride to the places you are staying. Leave the keys in the saddlebag on the left-hand side. Then, in at least forty-eight hours, your own bikes will be returned to you."

"I'm not well and I need to lie down," Delphine said.

"Of course. We have rooms upstairs with queen-sized beds. You can have anything on offer to eat and drink on the house, then you can go."

Jenny leaned toward the desk. "I need to call my boys."

"Of course. We are not animals, and no matter what you think we don't mean you harm. We will listen in on your calls."

Starlight and Jenny chose to go with the man with the gun to get some food and make a couple of calls to their people. Delphine went with the much taller Vandyke guy. They walked up a musty staircase with wooden steps that flexed under the old shag carpet. Off to the side, under a dormer, was a small room with three locks on the outside. Stacked outside the door were four large ammo cans on a plastic sheet that was spattered with various shades of paint. The cans were unlocked and their lids were open. Two were flecked with gold. As they walked past, Delphine looked down inside these two open cans. They stopped and the Vandyke guy seemed comfortable letting Delphine have a good look around.

"My mom died of cancer," Vandyke said. "That's what you have, isn't it?" His tone was concerned. "Liver cancer was what my mom had. It was terrible. It must be a terrible way to die."

He opened a small bedroom door and showed her the bed.

"None of this life is good," she said.

"Did the boss talk about the Jews and their so-called scientists?"

"Please don't," Delphine blurted out. "I was almost ready to believe that you weren't the spawn of Satan."

"Yeah . . ." He smiled almost sweetly. "Fair enough. The sheets are clean and I will make sure everyone knows not to disturb you. And no one will." He said that last phrase with a tone of seriousness that made it seem like a matter of personal honor.

"I'd be careful about teasing the boss about his size," he continued.

"What's he going to do? Build a nest in my hair?" she said, and for some reason she thought for a moment about the brown finch back in Seattle.

He looked at her quizzically with his eyebrows arched. "No, I suppose not. But he is a violent man, is all I'm saying. I think you can only push him so far."

"Duly noted," she said, and closed the bedroom door between them.

DELPHINE SAT on top of the bed. She decided to call her son, but her call went directly to his voicemail. She lay on top of the covers and closed her eyes. She was so tired that deep sleep seemed to rush upon her. Owls hooted in her dream, and she was anxious that her son was in some vague but lethal danger. Her skiff was broken down on a white sandy beach. Her old dog who was with friends in Sitka was hurt. Dot was whimpering, licking her right hind leg. Her son Bertie had gone out in the skiff with her that morning, but he was not on the beach with her. Dot was badly injured. Bertie was missing. The lower unit on the outboard for the yellow skiff had been sheared off. Brown bears moved back and forth just behind the brush along the beach fringe. She could not see them, but she heard them grunting and saw the brush move. Bears, a hurt dog, and her son in peril. Even from the depth of her sleep she knew she wasn't going to be rested when she eventually woke up. She tried to call upon the face of Leigh simply to confront the anxiety, but all she could see was blood on white skin and blood soaked into blond hair, then the dark red-black of what John and the cops used to call brain blood.

She started to cry in the dream and her body that was her own and beyond the reach of the dream registered the anxiety by breathing hard. Her shoulders tightened as if she were try-ing to hug herself.

She heard bar music from downstairs. A bass thump and a nails-on-chalkboard guitar part. Was that Dot whining? Did she hear Jenny's voice crying out? Delphine tried to wake herself up. She rolled back and forth, trying to wrap Dot in her arms. The movement brought her closer to the surface, but every time she came close to shaking off the dream, she saw the image of Leigh once again. The bears let out a bellowing grunt.

"Stop," she said aloud in a way that made her think she was rising to the surface. Someone was shaking her arm.

"Don't die," she said aloud.

"Let me help you, sweetie." The voice belonged to Jenny.

"Don't die," Delphine said again.

"I'm not . . . not for a long, long time. Long after you and I have survived this whole mess with these freaks. I won't die."

Jenny held Delphine in her arms for a moment. Delphine's heart beat through her ribs and her fireman's coat. The coat was lumpy to Jenny's touch. Every pocket was stuffed with supplies.

"Were you ever a Girl Scout?" Jenny asked. "I mean damn, girl, you have a ton of stuff in here. You are prepared."

"Maybe," Delphine mumbled. "I can't shake myself out of this bad dream."

"Yes, you have. I'm here and I'm not dying," she said into her ear.

They lay down in the bed, and below them Bob Seger thumped and wailed. Jenny wrapped a quilt around Delphine's shoulders. She scooted an arm under Delphine's neck and held her trembling body close. Soon, they were both asleep.

A hard rap on the door shook them awake. "Dark enough to take off." It was the voice of the Vandyke man. Jenny and Delphine sat up on the spongy bed. Delphine was rubbing her eyes. Jenny tried to straighten her hair.

"We slept a good long time," Jenny said.

"Yeah," Delphine yawned. "Thanks for staying."

THEY WALKED down the stairs, and Delphine saw that the ammo cans and the painting tarp were gone. Then they came down to the ground floor and met Starlight at the end of the bar. She had been drinking boilermakers with some of the members of the club, which appeared to be a northwestern branch of the Rolling 88's. They had been laughing and swapping stories about Dyke biker gear and her preference for shorter Harleys.

They walked out to the barn where the bikes were parked. The Vandyke man never offered a name or even a nickname. Everyone in the club appeared to be on a "Hey Dude" basis with the women. Vandyke pointed to a very clean Sportster with an elongated front fork and a low-slung seat. "You can take this. We'll get you your bikes soon. Don't worry. I know it's silly sounding, but our boss is paranoid as shit."

"Thank you," Delphine said. "But I'm still feeling rough. My balance feels off and I've never ridden a bike like this."

Vandyke looked around. He turned to another man in the club. "Dude, she is going to ride bitch with me. She is sick. Okay?" The other man nodded in agreement. "Just make sure when you go drop off their bikes, you will have to take someone on bitch coming back with you. Whoever it is will be driving three bikes down and two bikes back." The club mate didn't understand the logistics but dutifully agreed anyway.

When Delphine climbed on back of the chopper, her phone began to ring. She saw from the contact information that the caller was her principal doctor, Dr. Walters. Delphine spoke into the ear of the Vandyke man. "It's my doctor, I really should talk with him." She looked through her call log and noticed she had missed three calls from Dr. Walters already. Vandyke shook his head, then pushed himself forward on his saddle, making it easier for her to dismount.

She walked over toward the bike barn and answered.

"Hello Delphine, this is Chuck Walters. I'm calling because I'm worried about you. You have missed two appointments."

"Yes, I'm sorry but I got caught up in some kind of . . .

difficult business with a friend. I'm over in Eastern Washington now."

"That's all right. How are you feeling?" Dr. Walters was kindly. Genuine concern inflected his voice.

"Truthfully, I'm feeling sick. I can't really eat much, and I'm tired all the time."

"How are you getting around? Are you driving?"

"Well, I started off driving a motorcycle, but that's getting more difficult."

"But you were able to work the motorcycle all right? That's something."

"Yes . . ." Her shoulders slumped down. She imagined the doctor sitting in his brightly lit office, surrounded by monitors and light tables and accordion files of very old cases, talking on the phone while staring at photos of his grown children when they were just toddlers.

"Really, Doctor, I've been thinking about finishing up my treatments. I feel like it's getting toward the end."

Dr. Walters was quiet on the other end of the line. Delphine suspected that he was reading over his notes and thinking about what more to say.

"Delphine, you and I have talked about how long you wanted to work at all this, and just as I said at the beginning, it's always your choice."

"Thank you, Chuck. I appreciate you telling me that."

"You have lived with this cancer about three years, maybe a little more. I will be here anytime you want to come back. Let me ask you a couple of questions. Have you been depressed?"

"I think I've been appropriately sad and perhaps anxious about dying of cancer, but I'm not depressed. I feel like I'm realistic."

"Yes . . . you always seemed realistic and, well, frankly . . . courageous. I just ask because I wouldn't want you to stop treatment if you were just temporarily depressed. Because you know, we could treat the depression."

"I know, Chuck." Delphine was remembering how direct and honest Dr. Walters could be, compared to all his young associates.

"One more question. Do you need to start hospice and get someone over there who can give you palliative care to handle your pain?"

"I'm sure I will, but right now I feel strong enough to handle the situation I'm in."

"Well, good. I trust your judgement. But just remember you can contact me anytime. I will be with you so you get what you need. I would like to see you again if you make it back to Seattle. But I'll help you with whatever you need from there."

"Thank you, Doctor. I appreciate your help. I'm sorry if I didn't express my thanks before."

"You've had other things on your mind, Delphine."

"But I should have thanked you."

"Take care of yourself, Delphine. It's been a pleasure working with you. Let's talk again in another week. Okay?"

"Okay. I will be in touch."

She dropped off the call. A few tears sprinkled her cheeks as she turned back to the Vandyke guy. She was dimly aware that she had told her doctor that she was ready to die, but really, was she?

The Vandyke guy looked straight at her. "Tye can't be that hard to find. We just can't be the ones that do the finding. But right now . . . what's going on with you?"

"I'm just sick, but it looks like that's all wrapping up soon."

"Well, I hope so."

"Okay," she said, and she walked over and threw her leg over the big bike and wrapped her arms around Vandyke's leather coat. She found the foot pegs up high on the rear end. The engine rattled up from her hips all through her shoulders.

"Thanks," she said into the back of his dirty neck. "Were you following me in Seattle?"

"I was following Tyler," he said. "It's complicated."

"Oh," she said.

Delphine leaned into the turns and mostly kept her eyes closed. Vandyke drove smoothly around the sweeping corners out in the country, but the chopper rattled and shook as he downshifted coming into town.

CHAPTER TEN

When they pulled into the single-wide courtyard, Delphine clambered off the back of the chopper. Vandyke offered her his hand to shake. Delphine stood back, not really wanting to touch his skin.

"Come on," he said in a deep voice, "I won't bite."

She shook his hand. He held her grip for a long moment, pulling her close. "Don't kill him," he whispered. "And don't go to the cops just yet."

"Just yet?" she asked. He clucked at her twice as if he were asking his horse to move ahead. "Don't kill him. Remember that." He clucked again and the chopper lurched ahead before the two other women had their borrowed hogs shut down.

She lifted her hand as if to wave. "It's all going to turn out fine," Vandyke said, and he drove away.

Jenny walked over, rolling her shoulders as if she was doing an impression of a cowboy. "You got a love interest there?" she said with a smile on her face.

"Oh, please," Delphine said. "He just told me not to kill Tyler."

"Were you threatening to kill him?" Jenny asked.

"I didn't think I was." Delphine had a puzzled look on her

pale face. "I don't know what the hell is going on with that guy; he feels like a cop more than a creep."

Jenny stretched her arms and her shoulders, standing next to Delphine in the dirt. "Well, I think we should just leave. I'm sorry honey, but I think we should split and avoid any more meetings with outlaw bike gangs. You can stay with us up in the mountains. We will be safe."

"But will we?"

Starlight walked toward the trailer house, and she overheard the other two talking. "Let's just talk about things for a minute," she said while opening the door.

The three boys were lying on their stomachs watching TV, arms and elbows propping up their heads in the quavering blue-and-red light from the set. What Delphine noticed first was that Starlight was not looking at the boys. Jenny walked in and also looked past her sons, farther into the room where a man in a black suit was sitting in the recliner.

"Hello ladies," the man said, "I'm Sergeant Murphy with the State of Washington Anti-Gang Task Force."

"We're not in a gang," Jenny said in a quavering voice.

Starlight stepped forward. "I am kind of in a gang but actually we are a 501c3 charitable organization."

"Oh my God," was all Delphine said.

SPERM WHALES have a documented dislike of being spied on. Researchers in the lower latitudes once attached a video camera in a waterproof housing to the back of a sperm whale in a pod of six. The housing had a radio tracking device that allowed it to be found and followed. The footage was telling.

The whales dove in a tight group. All were in touching distance of each other. The camera captured the whales plummeting into the darkness. One whale drifted back in the group and stuck an eyeball right next to the lens, clearly watching whatever this thing on his pod mate's back was. Several whales made clicking sounds during the dive. The lead whale spent many long moments looking into the camera. Then, the whale drifted out of camera view and into the upper frame. Moments later, the camera housing was bumped off the whale and floated to the surface, where it was recovered by a researcher. The inquisitive whale had clearly knocked the camera off his companion.

It's tempting to think that it was no more than a friendly gesture akin to brushing a piece of lint off a companion's jacket just before walking into a restaurant, and maybe it was, but still, the clicking noises indicate that there seemed to be some actual consideration of what the object was and what it was doing there. Not to say we have any real way of knowing what the whale was thinking.

But let's consider this: Delphine had studied how sperm whales take black cod off fishermen's longlines. At first, she simply mounted cameras on the line with their lenses looking up toward the surface, toward the baitfish. She had put black cod from the fisherman's catch on the line to help bait the whales in.

But when the camera was mounted openly on the longline, whales would scan the camera casing with their clicks. They could do this scanning and remain mostly out of sight of the camera. The sperm whales would investigate the object on the longline for several minutes, keeping a good distance away, then, satisfied they knew that it was some foreign object, they would not come close. But when the object was camouflaged inside of a large tangle, the whales would come directly into view and begin taking the fish off the line.

Again, Delphine is loath to draw any inference or lay claim to knowing what the sperm whale was thinking, but it's clear the whales don't like to have cameras, or perhaps any foreign object, in their surroundings.

In discussions around the galley table at night, Delphine would speculate on what accounts for this camera shyness. It's possible that an animal that was old enough to have survived what has been described as the holocaust of commercial whaling might naturally be wary of any man-made object coming close. But what is vexing is that on the surface, the whales don't appear shy at all. Feeding whales will come within arm's lengths of a fishing boat as the crew is setting their gear or as the gear is coming up. Whales will bump the fishing boat while they wait for the fish to come up the line. Nothing about the whales' behavior on the surface seems shy. The sperm whales appear supremely confident. "Scared of you? Why would I be?" seems to be their attitude.

Jenny moved in front of the TV and snapped it off, looking sternly at her boys. "What are you doing letting this guy in the house?"

Dwayne squinted up at her. "Mom, he is a powiece officew. He had a badge an evewything." The other two looked up at her with sleepy eyes.

"What's the big deal, Mom? He said no one was in any trouble. He just wanted to ask a few questions."

"Don't be so trusting," Jenny said. "You guys should watch more slasher movies where the bad guy pretends to be a cop."

"Okay," Gudger moaned. "We'll watch more slasher movies." Dwayne jumped on Ned's back as if in celebration.

"Don't need to be hard on them, they asked me a lot of questions before I came in. I think they vetted me pretty good."

Ned looked up. "I asked if he was going to take you to jail, Mom, and he said no."

"Well, next time tell someone to come by later when one of your parents is home."

"We only got one parent," Ned said.

"I know that!" Jenny snapped back. Now she was crying.

"Okay," Sergeant Murphy said as he stood up and held his open palms in front of him. "We shouldn't get emotional now. Nothing bad is going to happen here. I'm not here to make arrests, I just want to talk. Give me a chance. Boys, can you give me the room here for a minute?"

The three boys got up and walked out into the other room, a bedroom with another TV. As soon as the door was closed, the TV in the bedroom snapped on.

Starlight stood by the door leading outside. "Well, officer, if I'm not under arrest, I think I'm going to get back to my place. I have a lawyer who usually helps me out with these kinds of things."

"What kind of things are those?" Murphy said in a serious tone.

"The talking to police officer kind of things."

"What I wanted to talk with you about was how the whole

transaction went when your friend got baby Hank back from his first adoptive family."

Starlight smiled and twisted the knob of the outside door. "And I look forward to that conversation with my lawyer."

Murphy smiled as if butter wouldn't melt in his mouth. "Then who is the best person to talk with?"

"It was nice talking with you, Sergeant." Then she stepped out into the night and shut the door.

Jenny had never been in trouble with the law, and now was thoroughly fed up with this adventure. She was choking back tears. "I'll tell you all I know. My husband and I knew Delphine from the hospital in Seattle. They both had the same kind of cancer. When my husband died earlier this week, Delphine came to my house. We tried to find this guy Tyler at the weird-ass biker meeting. Tyler told us we could meet two of his babies at an abandoned lot. We went there early, and we found a big man dead and wrapped in a tarp."

The more she talked about these events, the harder she cried. "Delphine told me he had worked for this man, Tyler. He went by the moniker of the Babysitter. Then some weird guys with motorcycles showed up and said that they were looking for Tyler. They were assholes and paranoid as shit but they wanted us to find Tyler, too. I mean really . . ." Here tears and snot sputtered from Jenny's face. "How hard can this guy be to find? And why does everyone suspect that we are the ones to find him?"

Jenny stopped now. Her chest was heaving. "And that's all I know."

"Okay," Murphy said. "Thank you. Okay, I just want to ask you something . . ."

"Lawyer," Jenny blurted out. "I told you what I know. You want to ask me more questions, I want my lawyer. If you want to arrest me, then tell me what's going to happen to my boys and get me a lawyer."

"No ..." Murphy said. "You've done great. I appreciate it, I really do. I'm not going to arrest anyone tonight ... I mean, not that I know of." He smiled at this. "But instead of a question, I just want to tell you that I suspect that Tyler was coming for you today. That it's a good thing you got to the meeting early because I suspect that Tye was planning to kill you there."

"Kill me?" Jenny was disconsolate now.

"Kill everybody. I believe that Tyler is closing all accounts today and plans to disappear."

"Well, I don't know anything about that," Jenny said. "I'm going to go watch TV in the other room."

"All right," the sergeant said. "Thank you for your help. I'm sorry if I upset you."

"That's all right," Jenny said, and wiped her eyes with a bandanna from her back pocket. "It's just been a hard week." Then she got up and went to the other room. The sound of canned laughter swept through the room as she went in and closed the door behind her, leaving the sergeant and Delphine together in the quiet room.

"Here's something that worries me—" Murphy started to say.

"Don't you want to ask us our names and contact information?" Delphine interrupted.

"No, I have that already. We've been working on your angle for a while now. Even before you turned up at the information rally, where your friend stabbed that guy in the foot."

"You had people at that place?"

"You wouldn't believe how many people. Your friend was lucky the guy she stabbed wasn't one of ours, but what concerns me is that you have thrown in with the 88's and are going to deliver Tye to them."

"Are you kidding me?" Delphine said with a little outrage in her tone. "You are concerned that *we* have thrown in with the 88's?"

"What do you mean?" Murphy asked.

Delphine looked at him as if she couldn't believe what she was hearing. "I mean you were sent here by the Rolling 88's. They want anyone to take the fall for the death of the big guy with the Hawaiian shirt. Anyone but one of the 88's."

"Yes. I do talk with people associated with the 88's. They said you could help us."

"Help you with what?" Delphine asked.

"I tell you, I don't need any help with the murder you stumbled across today. What I'm interested in is being able to find out what Tye knows about the 88's finances. Specifically, about the fifty pounds of gold."

"I don't know anything about fifty pounds of gold," she said, nearly exhausted from this conversation already.

"Please, Delphine, you have come so far already. I believe what you tell me about just wanting to protect the babies and the girl in Seattle. There are some that don't, but I do."

"Well, it's true."

"You sure you don't know anything about gold?"

"Not a thing." She was sitting on the threadbare couch now, directly across from Sergeant Murphy. "Tell me about it." Her eyes were closed, and she felt exhaustion sucking at her brain. She thought of a dead black cod drifting toward the maw of a sperm whale.

"I'll try and make it quick. There have been three recent robberies in the basin here. One of a remote farmhouse, and two banks that had their safety-deposit boxes blown and looted. In each robbery, large quantities of gold were taken. The farmhouse had exactly fifty pounds of gold taken and we are still trying to track down the contents of the safety-deposit boxes."

"Fifty pounds of gold seems pretty specific." Then she remembered the T-shirt read 50LBSAU at the biker fair.

"Back during the Nixon era when he was trying to deal with inflation, he tried price caps. He tried manipulating the fed bank. But this is a conservative part of the world. Wheat was king and wheat farmers feared losing all their cash to the government. It became . . . let me see . . . fashionable for a farmer to buy fifty pounds of gold. That's eight hundred ounces. Back in the early seventies, gold went for somewhere around one hundred twenty dollars an ounce. Since then, more and more people started believing in gold as a way to hold off financial disaster. More people want it even at the higher price. You know what gold is going for today?"

"No idea."

"More than eighteen hundred dollars an ounce. So, fifty pounds of gold is worth about a million and a half, and that's quite a few children even in Tyler's racist valuation of human life."

"Okay. And how does this concern me?"

"I'm getting to that. Stay with me." He leaned forward and looked into her sleepy eyes. "I'll make it simple. Fifty pounds of gold does not take up a bunch of space. Two medium-sized ammo cases twenty-five pounds each can hold it. Farmers just squirreled it away, buried it in the barn or under their house. But as gold went up, the farmers got nervous and they started talking to friends in the coffee shop. 'What do you do with your gold?' And people started digging up the ammo cans and putting the gold in the bank. Now people are talking, some of the farmhands find out. Some of the farmers' kids find out and some of these people are getting into painkillers. So eventually guys like the Rolling 88's know about the fifty pounds of gold. Now none of these farmers were showing any of these investments on their taxes. It was all off the books. So the first few robberies went unreported. So."

"So . . ." Delphine opened her eyes. "How does this affect you and me? The 88's think you are thinking only about the two murders and the cops are going to take care of Tyler Dearborn for them."

"I suspect it's the other way around. I suspect that it's the 88's who are going to take care of Tyler."

Delphine sat thinking. Coyotes howled in the dark. She was thinking like a ticking clock.

"Here is what I'm thinking, what I suspect," she said. "I suspect that the 88's wanted to buy kids from Tyler. I suspect that they paid Tyler off in counterfeit gold and this pissed Tyler off more than anyone expected."

Sergeant Murphy cracked his knuckles. "Now, see, that is interesting. True believers like the 88's consider themselves to be the real philosopher kings of the underworld, but the truth is, people like the 88's aren't nearly as smart as they think they are. I know all I need to know about murder and I know every word that was said during your meeting today. You were right that the 88's were the last to see the Babysitter. What I really need to know more about are the gold thefts and how they relate to Tyler's next move."

"Next move?" Delphine asked.

"Well, we believe that young Tyler wants out of the baby business. We believe he either has or is about to steal gold from the Rolling 88's."

"This makes sense to me," Delphine said cautiously. "I saw counterfeit bars back at Tyler's place in Seattle. The Rolling 88's must have paid him in counterfeit. But it had nothing to do with me so I didn't think much about it. All I want is the babies back with their moms."

"Seems like a big step up for a punk who beats women and steals babies," the police officer said, "to take a million bucks from some heavy hitters."

Delphine was thinking about this information. The baby business had to be hard; diapers, crying, feeding. Not things Tye would have been good at, especially without Leigh to help him. Not enough money, either. Then she remembered Leigh talking about his "golden parachute." She just shrugged her shoulders and let her interior clock keep ticking.

"It's a major step up and a very dangerous move," Murphy said. "What worries me the most is whether he is actually willing to clear the decks of anyone who could snitch him off."

"Leigh spoke with you, didn't she?"

Sergeant Murphy went dead eyed. "I can't tell you that."

"I've got to go to bed," she said. "I feel terrible."

"Listen, Delphine. We're going to get Tyler. Why don't you help us?"

Her stomach tightened as her mind returned to the meeting with the 88's. Who was working with whom? Who could she trust?

Murphy cracked his knuckles again and leaned forward with his elbows on his knees, then said, "It's better that you tell us everything you know. Better by far than letting Tyler or the 88's talk to us with the benefit of their lies. These guys will dump everything on you and if you don't tell us first, we'll have nothing to do but believe them. Don't just jump on that crappy bike and try and disappear."

"It's not a crappy bike."

"Be that as it may. There are some who think you were connected up with Leigh. That you purposely insinuated yourself into their fight on the street in Seattle because you wanted info about the gold. I mean, you have done an awful lot just to do some kind of welfare check on a bunch of poopy babies."

"Now you are accusing me of wanting the 88's gold? I didn't know a flipping thing about real gold until about five seconds ago." She stared at him for a long moment. "I'm going to bed now."

"If you are in on it, you are in danger. If you aren't in on it, you are talking to me and the 88's and you are still in big danger." He handed her a cheap burner phone. "There are three numbers here. First one is my private cell. The other two will know all about your predicament with the 88's and Tyler. You see him, you talk with him. You call me. I can trace your location if you have this phone. You call me and I'll keep you safe."

"Unless you want to arrest me."

"What you do from here on out will determine that."

"Fine. I need some rest."

Just as Sergeant Murphy walked out the door, Delphine's cell phone started to chirp. She answered the phone without looking at the name.

"Hello," she said, sounding short and out of patience.

"Mom? I just got your message," Bertie said in a worried voice.

FOR MOST people, all of nature is shrouded in mystery. It probably wasn't always that way. Before human beings developed language that could be codified and written down, it is likely that they saw the world with more immediacy. There was the now of feeding themselves and reproducing. Memory was likely an important aid. The worlds on both sides of our eyes were attached by the small bridge of what we remembered. Some people deny that animals have this dual nature. But an important question for researchers is, what is the nature of animals' memory? Does it exist in the same quality of dual worlds: what is happening now, and what happened in the past? So, an important question is, do large-brained animals have a capacity for memory that's similar to human beings'?

Delphine's research touched on this question. Individual sperm whales came to the Pacific shelf for the riches of black cod being brought up by fishing boats. Perhaps they could sense the "dinner bells" of the boats cycling in and out of gear from a distance. So, could sperm whales be simply hunting for food in the "now," when they heard the dinner bell? But this might argue against a consciousness-like memory. After tagging some of these large males, Delphine's team could follow them via satellite technology. This showed single whales, perhaps followed by one other, traveling to other locations on the inside waters where black cod appeared in great numbers. There is no indication as of yet that the oily fish send out sonic clues as to where they are. The fish have a sonic signature: if a whale gets close enough, they can "ping" on the fish and recognize them as food. But tucked up in the inside waters, it is unlikely the whales would be able to sense the fish were there. Yet tagged whales have been detected leaving the offshore sites and traveling directly to these feeding areas in the inside waters. Sperm whales have been known to travel as far north as Skagway, in Klondike country. Why? No one is sure, but it could be they are scouting for food. Which is probably how the whales first found the black cod in the inside waters. But the track line of the satellite data suggests that the whales were not scanning but traveling directly, which argues, but not conclusively, that the whales knew the feed was there from memory.

Do mothers remember how to care for their young? Or is that skill somehow just hardwired into their behavior? Observation done down in the equatorial waters suggests that there is some form of "groupthink" when it comes to protecting young from predators. The groups are multigenerational, and the older mothers and nursemaids seem to act in accordance to pre-established patterns to protect their young. When whalers discovered that groups of moms and nursemaids would gather, head in, to protect an injured calf, they began intentionally wounding calves to trigger this behavior. The whalers then would target the amassed group with their harpoons and the slaughter was complete.

But after several years, the moms and nursemaids learned to change their strategy. When the whalers wounded a calf, one adult whale would tend to the wounded calf and the other cows and calves would dive very deep and stay under for as long as possible—perhaps more than an hour—and then come up far from the first point of deadly contact. Sometimes they were still in sight of the whalers who would give chase, leaving the injured calf being tended by the lone cow. This new strategy, if not entirely successful at protecting the group, cut down on the number of kills and made the whalers work harder for their catch.

The moment Delphine heard her son's voice, she was flooded with memory. Bathing with him in the little cabin at Bartlett Cove. Carrying him in his car seat down to the covered skiff where, as soon as the engine started, he would almost always fall asleep. Sewing Halloween costumes every fall—Ninja Turtle, Wolverine, Spiderman. It should have been obvious that even though they didn't have broadcast television or cable TV, young Bertie's imagination had been captured by the lure of pop culture. He had married well to a beautiful and articulate young woman he had known in college in Walla Walla, and together they were raising a funny young boy who had always been a delight to Delphine. As she thought of his life in that instant, she heard his voice and wondered to herself what she was doing wandering around Washington State in the service of someone she didn't really know or care about.

"Mom? I just got your message. I've been thinking about you. When are you checking out of the hotel?"

"I've already kind of checked out, sweetie." Delphine heard the electric thumping of modern dance music in the background on Bertie's end.

"Kind of checked out?" Bertie asked, then yelled, "Reggie can you turn that down? I got your Grandma Delphine on the phone."

"Hello, Grandma," Reggie said. Delphine could hear his feet bouncing on the wood floors.

"Hello Reggie. How are you, sweetheart?"

"Good," the little boy said. "When are you gonna come visit us?" The music thumped on.

"Soon, baby, just as soon as I can." There was a catch of emotion in Delphine's voice.

She could hear Bertie walk over and turn the dance music down. Though the boom, boom continued as Reggie's feet kept dancing.

"Is that true? Are you gonna come down to Monterey?"

"I'm just wrapping up a project over in Eastern Washington. I'm about done, then I will go back to Seattle and pick up my stuff. Any chance you might want to do a road trip with me?"

Bertie was writing for a TV show that was on hiatus. She knew he had some time. "I'd like to spend some time driving with you," she said tentatively into her phone.

"Of course. I'll talk with Camile; I might have to bring the little man," Bertie said.

"Perfect," Delphine said.

"How are the treatments going? What's your doctor say?" She could hear the dread seep into Bertie's voice from across the distance to Monterey, California.

"Oh sweetie, I think my treatments are done."

"Is that a good thing?"

"Yeah, it's good. It's good. Even Dr. Walters thinks so."

The electric silence, merged with the thumpy dance music, quavered between them for several moments. "Mom? You okay?"

"Oh yeah . . . I'm running around like a crazy woman. I've even been riding a friend's motorcycle. A Harley Sportster. I'm great. We'll talk about it when I see you."

"I'm still listed on your release of information, right? I mean, I can talk with your doctors?"

"Sure, if they ever call you back. Listen, don't worry. We'll have a good long drive to talk about everything."

They said their goodbyes and made some flexible, tentative plans. Reggie came to the phone to give her a big smacking kiss into the receiver, and then Bertie hung up.

There was actual silence. There was no traffic outside. In the next room, the boys and Jenny had turned off the television. Her hands trembled. The thing about making loose plans, plans not pinned down, was the underlying assumption that she would be alive to honor any promise. She went to the door leading outside. She wanted to listen to the night's own silence. But in the distance she heard a big engine downshifting several blocks away, and woven into the fabric of the night she heard the clipped yipping of coyotes seemingly just around the corner, out of sight.

CHAPTER ELEVEN

Delphine lay in bed, shivering. Trying to puzzle out all the information the sergeant had given her. Her head was splitting now. She felt weak as a feverish child. With each breath, she seemed to pump her small heart deeper and deeper into the gloom. She wanted to sleep but everything she had learned bothered her. Had she gotten Jenny and the boys into this intractable mess? And for what reason? Leigh was dead. Her body in a dumpster like a snarl of line that threatened to entangle them all. It would be best to cut themselves loose with their sharpest knives and leave this sad country. The cops and the Rolling 88's would figure out their own revenge fantasies without her help. And yet, there were still the babies. The idea that they were in grave danger clung in her guts, particularly if Tye was going to come into a fortune and would need to travel far and fast to escape the 88's. But Tye was a brutal coward it seemed to her. Let the 88's have him.

Her phone rang. Tom Foster was calling from Seattle. He called to tell her to stop working on the case. The clients would stop paying for the investigation because Tyler had agreed to give the baby back to his mother in San Francisco. They threw some more money at Tyler, and Tyler had relented.

"Money," she thought. "There is almost no problem that money can't address."

LATER THAT night, she dreamed of a canoe made from hammered gold. It was made in the style of a Tlingit craft hollowed out of a golden log. It sat heavy on the sand of a white beach somewhere in the north. She lay out inside the canoe. She had long hair in the dream, auburn curls, and her body was strong. The gold had that dull yellow luster that made her hungry with greed. Gold made men salivate and she was cupped like a pearl inside the mouth of the golden canoe. The gold was warm in the sun that played upon the sand. The world seemed heavy, or rather pressed down onto her body, so that the soft gold took the shape of her back, her buttocks, and her thighs. In the dream she was becoming golden. The object of earthly desire, wealth that she would never be able to spend.

Deeper and deeper she sank into the bottom of the canoe. Deeper and deeper her body drifted away. Soon enough, five men on each side of her came alongside the canoe and lifted it up, letting it slide along the sand. As the stern, where her head lay, eased out into the water, the gold became cold. She took a big breath in and gulped for air. The canoe rested on the water for only a moment but then sank away into the grey green of the world of whales. The world where she was never meant to be. Deeper and deeper she sank away, and now she was dying. She would rest on the bottom to be encrusted with barnacles and urchins. Ten strong men had lifted her off the shore and put her in the icy sea. One of the men had on two pairs of glasses and one of them wore a Vandyke beard.

"No. Not now, goddamnit."

She woke up and the littlest boy was under the covers with her. Dwayne saw that her eyes were open and he said in a sleepy voice, "Mom said we awe going home. But I want to stay with you."

Delphine was wide awake now. She was happy to have shaken herself free of the sinking gold canoe and swum to the surface.

Jenny was standing in the doorway. "Dwayne, come here, baby, and let Delphine rest. You have to pack up."

"I'm staying hewe with heuw."

"No, Dwayne. You are coming home with us."

"Thewre bad guys all around hewe. I'm staying with Delphine!"

"I'm gonna get something in my stomach, big boy. Let's go out into the kitchen." And Delphine ruffled his hair.

Jenny finished feeding her boys breakfast while Gudger loaded up the truck as he ate a folded pancake in his left hand. When two hands were needed, he carried the pancake in his mouth. Soon they were packed and fed, and they left. Jenny did not apologize but said only that she had to go. Delphine was free to come with them and she hoped that she would, but Jenny did not press the point.

"It's all just too much for me and the boys. Bikers . . . cops . . . a dead man in an abandoned lot. It's just too much for the first week after Robert's death."

Soon, they were gone. Delphine was alone again, with the Sportster and a full tank of gas. Apparently, the Vandyke guy from the 88's had stopped on the way to grab their bikes back and topped it off. It upset Delphine that he seemed to go out of his way to be nice to her. Her stomach continued to hurt from the cancer, but the thought of the Vandyke guy liking her added another level of nausea to her symptoms.

She ate some dry toast, then went to the apartment of the woman who appeared to be renting the room she was staying in. The woman did not speak much English, but Delphine paid her enough money to stay another week. *Una semana, por favor.* Or so she thought. Delphine left the woman in her apartment where food was frying, and the kids were propped up at the kitchen table watching Spanish-language television. Delphine walked across the makeshift courtyard and lay back down in her bed and began dreaming the dream of the gold canoe.

What could I do now? she thought to herself. She had no idea really. Tye had left Seattle with three babies. One had been returned to Shirley. That left two, who were most likely still with Tye. Tom had called off the case. She just knew she wanted to find Tye and these two babies and sort out how to get the babies back to their mothers, who Delphine assumed were in Seattle. She had more data than she even realized, but she wanted more, so as the warm gold canoe sank once again into the ocean, her brain kept chugging away, trying to put the data together into one clear picture.

ONE OF the most interesting things about sperm whales is that because they are so remote, they have made very few appearances in lore. Tlingit and Haida had clan crests borrowed from killer whales. A few baleen whales made appearances in northwest coast stories. One such story describes the creator, Raven, flying out of the blowhole of a dead humpback whale found on a beach. But sperm whale appearances were rare. They were often seen in folk stories as vague "monsters of the deep" with blocky heads and long teeth on narrow jaws. Delphine knew that her recent dreams were being influenced by the whale. The golden dream canoe was really a coffin. This was from Queequeg in *Moby-Dick*. Delphine loved Melville's book, partly because the writer preserved the mystery of this great beast of the distant ocean along with its role as a monster. She knew that gold was the real threat behind her circumstances now. She knew, like Queequeg, she needed a coffin, and so her shadowy mind provided her a coffin made of gold. The white whale may or may not have been God in the book's allegory, but Moby Dick was the great source of awe and like all whale stories, this one took her down into the immense pressure of the deep.

Delphine went out to the scrubby grass yard and kicked over the Sportster. It ran a lot smoother, almost as if someone at the 88's had tuned it up. It was time to stop dreaming and to travel out in the world and find some more information.

The bike glided into the cottonwood and sage morning. She leaned into the turns and slowed down at the stop signs just enough to necessitate putting her toe down to the pavement. Dogs looked up and woofed at her as she breezed through the neighborhoods. There were three tall structures in the downtown area and one of them was the spire of a church. The streets were quiet and as the morning warmed up, the air changed and gradually became heavy with the smell of pavement and a strange odor of agricultural funk, as if something were composting under the well-fertilized soil. The songbirds retreated to the cooler parts of the valley as the day progressed. She drove in wider and wider circles from the downtown area. She was nominally looking for the old airport shuttle with the car seats strapped into it. But mostly she was trying to think through what she could reasonably expect to happen. How would she get the babies back to their mothers?

Near an avenue that seemed like a secondary main street for the outskirts of Yakima, there was a lot filled with old American cars and trucks. Parked on the edge was an old shuttle bus with no lettering on its side. She pulled over, took out her phone and checked her texts. Sure enough, there was the one from Tom that had the license plate of this very van.

When she entered the van, she took two steps and the crying began. She walked toward the back and two babies, each about a year old, were just opening their eyes from what could have been a nap. Instantly, the babies were crying in chorus. Then sparks flew in what Delphine thought could have been a hallucination.

Beneath the floor, rising up from the dirt, she heard a man's voice: "Goddamnit, Lupe, keep them quiet. I've almost got this done."

Sparks showered through a hole in the floor where the man was using an acetylene torch for welding. The babies howled, and the torch spit fire.

"Lupe, fuck . . . come on. Do something about the crying. Did you run out of cough medicine? Jesus."

"There doesn't seem to be a Lupe here," Delphine said. She

unbuckled one baby and bounced it in her arms while she let the other one suck on the knuckle of her index finger. The welder underneath the bus went quiet.

For a long moment, he was silent.

"Who is that?" he finally asked.

"Who are you?" Delphine spit back. There was a backpack leaning against the driver's seat and inside she found three bottles filled with unknown white liquid. Usually, she would have assumed it was some kind of milk. But everything about this situation was sketchy, so she wasn't sure. There were ugly brownish-red smears on the floor of the van. She gathered up one of the babies and put a bottle with the other, who seemed drowsier than the one she held.

Soon, the crying subsided a bit and the inside of the bus filled with the sound of doped-up babies sucking on bottles. One of them kept up a sleepy cry, hiccupping along as she fed.

Delphine heard the man drag himself out from under the bus. The two children were blond and blue eyed, of course they were. They were most likely the demo models that had made the trip with Tyler to Yakima.

Suddenly a dirty man stood in the bus's doorway. Tyler.

"So it's you," he said.

Delphine sat with the two babies in the driver's seat. "Who is Lupe and what did you do to Leigh?"

"I don't know what you're talking about and I don't know what right you have snooping around in my business."

"I know you killed Leigh," Delphine said in a soft voice, so as not to disturb the feeding baby.

"Then you know more than I do," Tyler said.

It surprised her that Tyler didn't look more like some kind of monster. He was a punk. He was the same punk that he had been in Seattle when he was slapping Leigh around. She was thinking he had a soft baby face for a criminal. How could he expect to rob gold from anyone, let alone the Rolling 88's?

"I doubt you killed Lupe, since you were calling her."

"I didn't kill anybody, Ms. Busybody," Tyler said.

Jesus, he needs to work on his patter, Delphine thought to herself. What she said was, "Then where is Leigh?"

"She split town. I guess she didn't like being around the kids this long."

"Did you sell little baby Blue Sky back to his mother? Did she threaten to go to the police back in Seattle? Is that why you killed her?"

"That is my business. Listen," he said as he ran a dirty hand through dirty hair. "I'll give you two thousand dollars to take care of the babies here with me while I finish the job."

"You have the money on you now? Give it to me." Delphine wasn't in the mood to dicker.

"Naw, I got it out of town a bit. You get it after the job is done. You can't leave the bus. I'll get you some more milk and solid food and some diapers and shit. You'll be fine."

"Give me the babies and a car to drive and I'll take care of them," Delphine said.

"Really?" he said, appearing to think about it.

"Yes, really. That's all I want. To take those babies back to Seattle."

"Yeah . . . well so what?" he said. "What happens to these babies is none of my b . . . I mean none of your business."

Delphine didn't know if Tyler was now brain injured or simply stupid.

"Another question, Tye, about the day we met over here at the information fair. Why did you want me to go to that meeting with the babies and the new families the next day?"

"Ah ... jeepers ..." he said like a sneeze. "I wanted to scrape you off on the 88's. I was hoping to get these two kids here"— and he nodded to the towheads in the bus—"I was hoping to get the babies all hooked up with the 88's and recoup my investment in them. But things changed. You know, plans changed and I—"

"Never mind." Delphine waved her hands at him as if she were dismissing him. "Just give me money, a car and the two babies, and I won't get in the way of your business."

"None of my business is your business," he said petulantly.

"I don't want to even think about your business," Delphine said.

A van pulled up outside the bus, but Tyler didn't seem upset. She looked at him carefully. He had his right hand wrapped in a dirty bandage.

"What did you do to your hand?"

"Oh, shut up," Tye spit out at her.

Later, Delphine tried to replay the scene in her mind several times, but she couldn't see it clearly. Maybe she was involved in feeding the baby or perhaps she had been so indifferent to what Tyler was doing or saying that she completely missed when the hand of the Vandyke man reached up into the bus, pulled Tyler by the hair and slammed him down onto the pavement.

"Nungggg," was all Tye could manage to say.

"What the fuck man?" Vandyke said. "You think you can steal from the club?"

"Nungggg," Tye repeated.

"What are you doing?" Delphine said through the door, staring at the two men on the ground. One of the babies started crying. "You are scaring the children!"

"I'm sorry," Vandyke said. "I had a tracker placed in your Sportster because I knew you would be looking for him. I came by just after you got here. I called back to the club and let them know we had him and asked them to send a truck out so we can get you and the babies out of harm's way."

"Out of harm's way? So you are rescuing me, like some kind of musketeer?" she demanded.

"Hey, easy now. I'm protecting you." Vandyke looked a little hurt.

"Just let me have the babies and a rig. I'll take them back to their mothers in Seattle."

"I can't do that," Vandyke said.

"Listen, I don't care about him or your gold bars. Just let me take the babies to their moms, then I'm all done."

"It makes me very sad that you know about the gold. Now I really can't let you go. Come on, girls." Here, Vandyke turned around and was speaking to two women in tight pants and tank tops who were standing over by a black truck. "Let's load the babies up and get back to the barn. The boss is going to want to know about all this and he is going to want to check out these kids."

The girls came on board and the heels of their cowboy boots made a threatening clatter on the thin floor.

"I'm sorry," he said, looking again at Delphine with his sad eyes.

The women from the 88's walked toward the van with the babies. Vandyke loaded Tye onto the back of his Road King and Delphine threw her leg over the Sportster. Tyler was conscious but loopy as he rode behind, clinging to Vandyke, his broken-down boots not on the pegs as he tilted dangerously to the side. Snot and blood dripped from his nose and his eyes could not hold focus. They sped away and the big bike fishtailed down the road. One of the girls in the van showed Delphine her AR-15 before she got in the bus. There was staining on the front barrel.

"We'll be right behind you," was all she said by way of a warning.

BOB SEGER'S song "Against the Wind" was still playing on the jukebox in the tavern when they arrived. Above the bar was a full mount of a small black bear, its mouth open in a snarl, with a plastic tongue the color of a fake flame in a trailer home fireplace. The biker girls, who looked like they were still in high school, unhooked the car seats from the seats of the old van and brought the two kids inside and set them directly on the bar. A bartender reached into her garnish tray under the lip of the bar and started feeding each of the babies blood-red cherries. Each child puckered their lips and cooed softly as they sucked on the juice.

The small man came out of the back room, still wearing his two pairs of glasses.

"I'm not giving any speeches. You stole our gold. Where is it?"

"You're crazy," Tye said. "You paid for your kids in coun-terfeit."

"The kids were defective. I gave you defective gold. Where is the pure stuff you stole? Lay him out on the bar," the little man said.

Two big men lifted Tye up as he was squirming.

"I worked on my dad's ranch growing up. I used to cut cattle as a kid. Cut, dehorn and brand. It was dirty work, wres-tling those yearling steers down in the dirt. Dehorning was the bloodiest work. I know you're thinking that the testicles must have bled the worst. But surprisingly . . . no." Here, the little man unsnapped a pocketknife from his belt.

Tyler was openly fighting against his captors now. Delphine was easing toward the babies in their car seats.

"The key is to have a good sharp knife and not to cut the seminal cords directly, but to scrape the blade across the cords so that when the testicles break free, the blood vessels do not open up and allow the blood to flow freely. There is a little blood from cutting open the scrotum but not so much from the seminal vesicles themselves."

The knife must have been very sharp because he had no trouble slicing up the inseam of Tye's blue jeans. With just a light tug, he opened up the cotton briefs.

"I have a suggestion." Delphine cleared her throat. "As much as I don't care for Tyler, I think I'm beginning to see the picture here and I think for once you men should stop being stupid and consider where you are. Your only real choice is to give me the children and let me take them home to their moms."

"Why should anybody do that?" the little man asked.

"Because if you don't, I'm going to tell the authorities what I know about where you are right this minute."

"And just where are we, little missy?" the boss asked.

"You are all in a world of hurt."

He lifted his top set of glasses off his head and lowered them onto his nose.

"I really don't see it that way," he said, with not quite enough confidence.

Tyler was still squealing on top of the bar.

"You want to know how I see it?" Delphine asked.

"You have the floor," the little boss said.

"First, I'm tired of all this bullshit and acting like you guys are all some kind of criminal masterminds."

Tyler yelled something incomprehensible through his snot and his tears.

"The first dumb thing you did, Tyler, was selling babies to Nazis. You have no clue how to take care of babies. It is dumb to sell babies to the 88's. They weren't happy with the shipment. Which is more evidence of their stupidity, but that's neither here nor there . . . They paid you in the counterfeit gold I saw in your apartment.

"This, of course, you saw as a sign of disrespect. You agreed to sell Baby Blue back to the birth mother and you, being the dumbass you are, still wanted gold. Real gold. So you and the Babysitter made a plan to rob the 88's of their gold. Another bright bit of thinking. But what really upsets me is that, back in Seattle, Leigh didn't want to give Blue Sky back. You beat her mercilessly in the bathtub in your apartment. That's how you hurt your hand, Tye, and finally, when you couldn't get her to submit, you killed her. You dumped her in the trash, while the Babysitter took Blue Sky in another vehicle.

"You couldn't appreciate the value she put on the baby and you insisted on converting the baby's value into the only primal worth you understand. Gold."

"You got no proof," Tye squealed.

"You are a slob, Tye. Stabbings are messy. Both you know and I know her blood is all over your van. Leigh was dead for at least a half hour by the time I saw her in the parking garage. Lividity had started to affect her corpse. She wasn't killed in the garage, she was killed in the van. I saw blood stains there, or your pathetic attempts to wipe the stains up. Her blood is on your clothes and, I'd say, on everything you touched."

"Now you're going to tell me that I killed the Babysitter."

"Good point. The 88's clearly killed the Babysitter. During the robbing of the gold the night of the Grease Monkey Dykes party. The ballistics will match one of the rifles here in the clubhouse right now."

"Why would we do that?" the little man asked.

"In the larger sense, you did that because you are big dumb men. See, mammals with large brains and a high degree of dexterity in their environment have what you might think of as imaginations. You want what you want and you grow impatient when you can't get it right away. So, big-brained animals like you tend to imagine getting what you want first, before you come up with a sensible strategy to get it. This short sightedness can cause confusion and panic, particularly when it's being pushed along by hormones. There is no good reason to kill anyone, but still you wanted what you wanted and you had to make stupid decisions like murdering the Babysitter."

"How do you know we killed the Babysitter?" the little man said. "You don't."

"It's obvious, Gollum, that the same person didn't kill Leigh and the Babysitter. Leigh had all the hallmarks of being killed by someone she knew well. Stabbing is intimate, sometimes sexual, sometimes fueled by pure hatred, but up close. The Babysitter was killed by a gun that wants to distance itself from the victim, like an AR-15."

Here, she turned to the young woman with the staining on the barrel. "Ballistics will match the gun you are holding in your hand."

"After this is all done we'll have everything cleaned up by the time your blood dries on the floor. The cops are going to want some physical evidence," the little man said.

"Please be quiet," Tye blubbered. "Shut up."

Tyler was screaming now. The girl with the semi-automatic rifle moved the babies off the bar and set them on the table near the door. Then she walked over to hold the rifle level with the bar, aiming it straight at Tye's head.

The short man pulled the one pair of glasses down to see through them and then with a deft flick of the blade, he opened Tye's scrotum.

"Now let me get back to this: instead of cutting through the cord, I'll just scrape the blade across until the ball just comes off. It takes longer but you won't bleed to death. Now, just tell me where my gold is."

The sounds from Tye's throat were again unintelligible.

Bright blood spattered down on the bar and on the torn pieces of white cotton drawers. "Faaaaaaa!" was all Delphine could hear.

"Wait . . ." Delphine said in a loud but steady voice. "You know your biggest problem? The cops already know about where to find the evidence. The gold in Tye's van and the blood spatter and the ballistics."

"The cops know?" one of the biker mooks stammered.

"Yes, I just told them, because you have an informant here in your own clubhouse. I'll let you figure that one out for yourself. But I'm sure the informant is working on getting the news to his boss right now.

"And what all the other pinheads are thinking is how to get their hands on Tyler's stolen gold. It was just this morning that I saw Tye welding under the deck of the old airport van. He was using a gas torch. He must have been welding a steel box to the frame. All the rest of the body is rotten sheet metal. My dad taught me to weld a little. He was welding steel under there. Welding it to the frame of the rig, I suspect. Your gold is in that metal box right outside."

With those words, the loyalties of everyone in the room exploded like a crystal vase at a shooting range. One of the men holding on to Tye's ankles let go for a second, thinking wrongly that he should go out to check on the gold. Tye grabbed the fork in the garnish dish and rammed it into the big man's eyeball. The screaming startled everyone. Tye kicked the man in the face. Then he reached over and grabbed the barrel of the AR-15. A short burst of fire blared from the muzzle and the bartender fell to the floor with a blossom of blood sprouting from his chest. Tye pulled the girl to the floor with the gun, jumped off the bar and kicked the girl in the face. The two babies were crying again. The sound hurt Delphine's head as if she were diving hundreds of feet underwater.

The small man had run back to his office lair, looking for his own automatic weapon, Delphine imagined. Vandyke was standing with his hands to his sides away from his weapon. The Gun Girl was whimpering on the floor. Other men in club jackets were scuttling around outside. Delphine could hear the metallic sound of high-capacity clips being rammed into place. She also heard big bikes being kicked into life as some of the soldiers prepared to ride.

"You. Sick lady. Come over here." Tye waved his gun around. "Stop this bleeding somehow."

She started walking toward him.

"Wait!" he yelled at her. "Take your coat off and leave it there. Who the fuck knows what all you got in those big pockets. I don't need any of your taser gun now."

Delphine ignored his command. The injured men tried to stanch their bleeding and pull themselves out the door. Two helped the big man who had been shot. The air was filled with a chorus of moaning and swear words.

"Hurry up now." Tye's voice was quavering with pain. His belt was still buckled holding his torn pants up around his waist.

Delphine kept her coat on while she ripped a damp and nasty-smelling bar rag into three strips. She walked slowly toward him. She took a bottle of vodka from the bar and said,

"This is probably gonna hurt," as she came near, then doused his scrotum with the alcohol. While he was screaming, she found a small first aid kit in her pocket. She stuffed dirty-looking gauze on the cut, then wrapped the entire sack with a strip of bar rag. She doused the strip with more vodka.

"Jesus please!" he burbled like a child.

"Be quiet, you big baby," she said. "Get yourself another nurse if you don't like my treatment." Then she took some gauze from the kit and took another wrap around his testicles. The bleeding didn't stop but it slowed and began soaking into the bandaging.

The door cracked open. Tye swung the rifle up and fired. Glass tinkled down onto the floor.

"Let's go." His voice was hoarse.

"What do you mean? Where?" She thought it was a reasonable question.

"You give me one of those babies and you take the other one. You walk right next to me. Hold these fucking kids up high next to your head and we'll go to the truck."

"No . . . that's stupid," she said. "They'll shoot our legs out from under us."

"Walk fast, take big steps. I'll hold a gun on the boy . . . the one dressed in blue, most likely Juris. These guys are thugs, but they have a soft spot for white babies, even if they are impure." Tye stood up and held his gun on her.

Soon enough they were by the door. He opened it to gunfire from two sides.

"I got two kids here. We are walking to the truck. Stay back, goddamnit."

Two of the 88's were under the bus banging on the metal box welded to the frame.

"I'm telling you, get the fuck back."

The little man stood between them and the truck. "Hold your fire," he yelled. Then he spoke softly, more directly to Tyler. "There is no way you are getting away with that gold. We will kill you for it. Why not be reasonable with us and you could live?"

"Are you kidding?" Tye said.

"Put the babies down and stop this foolishness."

"Kill the babies and the woman if you want. Or keep them if you want. I'm driving away in that bus."

"I don't have anything to do with this guy," Delphine called out. "I don't care about him. Just don't hurt the kids."

The little man holstered his weapon and raised his hands. "Let him get to the bus. Then saddle up. He can't outpace us."

Delphine turned her head and saw Vandyke speaking into a small burner phone on the edge of the commotion. What struck her for an instant was that it looked like the burner phone that Sergeant Murphy had given her.

They made it to the bus. Car seats were strapped into three of the bus's seats.

"You drive," he said to her.

"No," she said.

"I'm holding a gun on you, or don't you realize that?" he said.

"Kill me. I don't care. You'll still have to drive." She sat next to the closest child.

"Are you crazy?"

"How do you think I lost all my hair, you idiot? I have

cancer. I'm going to die soon anyway. Why should I waste what time I have left taking orders from you?"

"I'll kill that baby."

"Go ahead." Here, she truly was bluffing. As for what she was going to do to prevent Tyler from shooting the child, she was working on it.

"Jesus Christ!" He sat down in the driver's seat looking like he was sulking. Blood was now dripping from his bandages. Deep-throated motorcycles idled around the bus. The men on the bikes were all well armed.

Tyler fired up the bus and the well-armed men tucked up their kickstands, then Tye jammed the bus into gear and blasted the engine into full throttle, spinning the back tires in the dirt, and turned the wheel all the way to the right. The bus raised a cloud of dust as he did a drifting doughnut-shaped skid in the parking lot. He ran over two bikes and slowed his rotation. Others dumped their machines and hopped away from the swinging tail end of the bus, which had clearly been modified with a much more powerful engine and a sturdier racing clutch than it had ever had when making runs full of sleepy travelers from the Days Inn to the airport.

The babies had gone from crying hard to screaming. He broke off from his skid and drove into the back fence, which turned to splinters, then took off through the arid brown grassland behind the tavern. The bus bounced wildly on its stiff suspension, storage doors flying open overhead, loose diapers soaring through the air, the close chemical smell of a portable toilet spilling out onto the floor, engine blaring and rivets straining with each lunge, but deep inside

Delphine's brain was the wailing high-pitched scream of the little children.

The one unfortunate thing about the 88's motorcycles was that they were specifically designed for blaring up the highway, not for off-roading along the burnt-up grasslands. Of course, neither was the reconditioned bus. But the bus kept moving while many of the bikes lay sprawled out on the sand. The babies' screaming continued, their mouths forming large O's and their eyebrows arching upward in panic while their little heads bounced back and forth like toys. Side to side and forward and backward. One of the babies stopped crying as it turned blue from exertion. The two babies waved their hands in the air, giving the semaphore for "all done, all done."

Delphine tried her best to make sure they were not seriously injured. Their cheeks were flushed and their jeweled tears floated fat on their red skin. One was a towhead blond and the other had golden-brown curls, but in the panic Delphine could not make out any difference in their faces. All she could keep track of was their different outfits: one pink, one blue.

The bus found a relatively flat graded road in the brush. Tye gunned the engine, sending dust and small stones up into the air. Two bikes continued to follow but the dust made it impossible, and the bus gained greater and greater distance. Tye made a sharp turn and it appeared he had lost the followers. More swerving turns threw diapers and bottles from side to side until finally they turned onto a paved road. Now there was no more dust to follow.

Tires squealed on the pavement. Two more quick turns onto surface streets and a turn into an unpaved alley, past cyclone fences and yards stacked with wooden pallets, kids skipping rope and mean-looking dogs chained to fence posts that showed circular patterns of dirty claw marks. When at last Tye slowed down to collect his thoughts, there were no motorcycles in sight and the exhausted babies simmered into faint narcoleptic burping and tears.

"Let me out now," Delphine said. "I'll take the children and you will never hear from me again."

"Shut up," Tye said. "There is a guy out here digging a hole for this bus. I got to think—"

"Not your strong suit," she said.

"Shut up," he repeated. "Where is it?"

"Let us off."

"Shut up."

He drove for a mile and spotted a man with a front-end loader digging a hole and piling the sandy soil next to the pit.

"I only have a few minutes and this will have to do," Tyler said.

It was only then that Delphine reached into her coat and took out the burner phone that Sergeant Murphy had given her. Like it or not, it was time to give herself up to the cops, just as she had started to give herself up to death. She did not dial the cops first, but took a photo of a local street sign and texted it to another number with the message, **Dying here. Hurry.** Then, leaving the phone on, she placed it in her coat pocket closest to her shoulder.

Tyler got out of the bus and waved to the loader driver. The driver waved and smiled. Then Tyler shot him two times, once high in the chest and once low down in the gut. Delphine's head swam.

The driver fell from his seat and lay bleeding in the dirt. Tyler jumped up into the loader and moved the big machine forward with its bucket down. The dirt was soft; it took barely ten minutes for him to dig a hole that was about ten feet deep and twenty-five feet long.

Tyler scoured down a ramp into the hole. Delphine got the babies out of the bus in their car seats. She could run, or hobble, but where? The operator's truck sat near the driveway. She ran to the operator and checked for a pulse. He was still alive. She spoke with him and he gave her his truck keys. She was about to stand up with the keys when she went limp, as if the ground itself wanted to suck her body down. She rolled over. Tyler was standing over her with the long-handled shovel he had used to hit her in the back of the head. She started up again and all she saw was the end of the shovel handle coming down right between her eyes.

Delphine relaxed. Her body floated up into the warm air. Children crying louder. Still signing the words "all done, all done," as if they were waving like a queen. Delphine was being dragged by her feet. Head bumping up steps. The smell of gas inside the bus. Still floating, still drifting. Engine noise. Down an incline. Metal cracking, fiberglass shattering. Glass breaking. Dirt seeping in the broken windows and a different engine blaring.

Tyler had driven the bus with the children, Delphine, and the loader operator straight into the pit.

Was she hallucinating or was Tye actually starting to bury the bus in the sand? He got out and clambered into the digging machine. She could hear Tyler gunning the loader's engine and

the staccato of sand and rocks falling on the bus. He was bury-
ing them alive.

Delphine crawled along the floor between the seats. The
shovel with her own blood on it was on the floor. She could
barely hear the engine of the loader driving over the top of the
pit. Each time it passed over the roof, the van broke down a
little bit more. Sand flowed into the broken windows like
water, piling up on the inside. The babies were near the front,
where the roof was reinforced iron rather than the fiberglass
in the main cab. The voids where there was still air grew
smaller and smaller. Rocks thumped and clunked down on the
body of the bus.

She didn't know where she would get the strength to get
out of this. For a moment she considered simply lying down
with the children and comforting the two of them until they
all fell asleep and died. The operator who was also to be buried
with them appeared to be unconscious. Could she just give in
to the darkness of the situation and let them all die? Lie down
with the innocent babes and the poor man she didn't know
and make that decision for all of them?

Near the back of the bus there was a seam of the roof that
was torn open. Sand and small stones continued to pour into
the shrinking voids. She stood on the seat and then, with a
foot on the back of the seat, she lifted herself up into the current of falling grave material that was covering her.

She swam up into the flow. She kicked her feet to find solid
purchase to push herself up. Her body almost plugged the
opening that allowed the soil to fall into the voids, and as soon
as her body did that, the current slowed. Sand pushed against

her mouth wanting to fill her lungs. Sand filled her ears, her nose. She slashed her arms up above her shoulders. Pressure began to force in around her chest. She sputtered dirt out of her mouth. She pushed and pushed. Clawing her way up, using rocks as paddles when she could.

THIS WOULD be her death, then. The feeling of life being squeezed out of her took on a kind of intimate certainty. She wasn't *going* to die anymore. She *was* dying. Right that second. She began to give up. Relaxation started to soak through her body. And just as she started to sink back down into the shrinking voids of her awaiting grave, she felt a hand grab on to her forearm. Then other hands grabbing her elbows. Some strength other than her own began lifting her up. Soon she was at the surface.

Delphine had called the Grease Monkey Dykes and they had come. There was a strong hand gripping her forearm. The face of a spitting woman appeared inches from her own face. A gravelly voice coughed and the voice became clear. "My God, you don't give up easy, do you?" The voice belonged to Shirley, young Hank's mother.

THE QUEER ladies arrived just as Tyler had been flattening out the surface of his makeshift pit. They had arrived just moments before the cops had come upon the scene. Sergeant Murphy was there, and the Vandyke guy, who appeared to be comfortable around Murphy and the other cops.

When the Grease Monkey Dykes first arrived, Tyler lifted his rifle to cover his escape in the operator's pickup truck, but one of the ladies had her own weapon and promptly shot him through the biceps, causing him to drop the gun. They rushed the loader and when they turned off the engine, they could make out the keening sound of the babies crying from underground. The cops called in a 911 rescue unit, but without any discussion, the Grease Monkey Dykes formed a circle around a soft spot on top of the pit and starting digging with their hands. On their knees, they passed dirt from one to another and they all began sinking into the pit. It was a perfect daisy formation.

It was a matter of almost pure luck that they met Delphine on her way up. They lifted her up and passed her back from their circular formation around the hole. But they kept digging. Another stroke of luck turned out to be that Shirley was a gifted machine operator. She unwrapped a chain off the front hooks of the machine, rigged one end to the teeth of the bucket, and lowered the end down into the widening hole. Soon enough, one of the Dykes was in the void. She attached the chain to a solid junction of metal in the undercarriage, allowing Shirley to pull straight up to forestall a collapse and make a little more room for the other women to go down and heft the babies and the unconscious operator out of the hole.

Delphine was laid out on the stretcher. She was coughing up mud. Vandyke was wiping her face with a bandanna, and he poured water over her head to help clean out the sand in her eyes and nose. He looked down at her with his sad eyes.

"Just breathe in. Big breath in and then out. You are going to be okay."

"Who the heck are you?" she finally croaked out. "What the hell are you doing to the babies?"

"My name is Bob Stark. I am an undercover operative for a federal gang task force."

"What's with the pit?"

"Tye paid this guy to dig the pit. His plan all along was to bury his rig and any bodies he needed to bury."

"Did you get the gold?"

"Check it out. The gold is in the operator's truck. He took it out just before he decided to bury the van."

Delphine had more questions for him, but the EMTs came and lifted her up and put her in the ambulance.

"Where are you taking me?" she asked.

"To the hospital to get checked out."

"I'm fine," she said in an urgent voice.

"Excuse me, ma'am, but you don't look good at all. They would have our jobs if we cut you loose right here." The EMT held a mirror up to Delphine's face. There was a thick coating of dust all over her bald head. She had a deep cut on top of her skull and blood was spattered all down her head and shoulders. She was frighteningly pale and so thin that her brow and teeth stuck out in a way she didn't recognize. Brand-new Halloween masks looked less frightening than she did.

"See?" the female EMT said. "Honey, you just can't walk around like this. You'll be scaring the children."

"Okay . . . take me in," Delphine said in a tone of final acceptance.

AT THE hospital, they scrubbed her and stitched her, flushed her system with nutrients mixed with fluids. Then they got her medical records from Seattle and started in on another round of cancer treatments. They held on to her for two days before the doctors even mentioned letting her go.

On the morning of the third day, a young officer came by to tape-record a formal statement. The Vandyke man—a.k.a. Bob Stark—came with the young officer. Stark was clean-shaven and seemed to have washed all of the dye out of his hair. They spoke for a while, and he tape-recorded an addendum to her official statement. He even went through the rigmarole of placing her under oath to tell "the truth, the whole truth and nothing but the truth, under pain of perjury." He did not dance around the reason for this: they needed the cleanest, most binding testimony they could get right now in case she passed away before her testimony was needed at trial.

Tyler had given a statement while in custody, he told her.

"Did he admit to killing Leigh?" she asked.

"No ... he had a cockamamie story that I won't trouble you with. It's enough to say that he blamed everybody else for his problems. He blamed the 88's, the lesbian bikers, and even the babies themselves. Seems like all the crying got to him."

"I'm sure he didn't have good things to say about me."

"No ... you came into a fair share of his ire. He said he was deathly afraid that you were going to tase him."

They were just about to wrap up their conversation. Even though Vandyke had made a show of turning off his tape recorder, Delphine was certain that one or both of them were still recording every word she said. The two cops had gotten her statement and taken photos of her body, focusing on the injuries to her head and her hands. They took DNA swabs and bundled up the clothes she was wearing. One of the police officers gave her her fireman's coat. Delphine was able to wrangle the fireman's coat and almost all the contents of her magic pockets from Bob Stark. She had cooperated completely, but Delphine felt there was something that still made him suspicious of her. So, she asked him about that.

"I just have a hard time understanding why you cared so much about Leigh, and why you pushed yourself, as sick as you are, to come over here and keep pursuing this dirtbag. It just bothers me."

"I was worried about the babies," she said. "Nothing more."

He sat there looking down at his shiny cop shoes, surprised, probably, that he wasn't wearing his biker boots. Outside, the hospital sirens blared. Inside, tones sounded from the wall speakers and robot voices worried the air, calling people to attend to some small calamity or another.

"And as far as being sick goes . . ." Delphine paused and looked at his worried face. How could this guy be an undercover cop if he worried as much as he appeared to worry? "Being as sick as I am, I stopped worrying about myself a while ago." She said the words and she thought of her husband John and his pointless death out at the side of the road.

"I suppose . . ." He stood up and started to shake her hand. The young officer was already out the door and Bob Stark began to say something in the way of an emotional goodbye, when suddenly the door burst open and a whirlwind of boys' voices blew in and the ugly dog Booster jumped right up on her bed.

"Hey!" Dwayne said. "We dwove down here to give you a wide!"

CHAPTER TWELVE

It was two weeks later, and Delphine was at Jenny's place near the Canadian border. She had just woken up from a nap on a hillside a couple of hundred yards from the house, looking to the west into the Pasayten Wilderness. To the north was an old forest fire burn that had torched a thousand acres of wilderness land. To the south were some patches of bug-killed timber currently ripe for burning. A woodpecker was tap-tap-tapping on a dead tree nearby and a mockingbird improvised the songs of other birds while boys were laughing up the hill.

Delphine had spent part of that morning talking with the Ukrainian woman on the phone. She was still living with the other mothers and their babies in Seattle. Juris was home now. He was the golden-haired child with the curls. The other girl was back with her mother as well. Tye was in jail and the Ukrainian woman had taken over the lease on the apartment. The Department of Child Protective Services was finishing up the investigation into their living situation, and they would decide whether the children were safe, or if they would move to take over custody. Delphine gave testimony to the social worker, saying that the Russian mother had said nothing about being part of the scheme to sell the children and had expressed sadness that Tye had stolen them from the mothers. The social worker seemed convinced.

As long as there is no more evidence of criminal intentions brought into the home by manipulative men looking to exploit the situation . . .

The young Russian mother had written to Delphine on a postcard affixed to the social worker's official report. The postcard read, *Thank you, thank you, thank you. You protected my family and saved baby's life. With much love, Svetlana.*

Delphine found the note and the words reassuring, but what was most reassuring was the recent voicemail recording on which she heard plates clattering on a wooden table and women's voices speaking in easy conversation, with babies and moms both making sweet sounds as they began to eat. The babies had finally stopped crying.

Bertie was sitting next to her reading a book by P. G. Wode-house. He was sprawled out in the type of vintage lawn chair that sagged his butt down toward the rocky ground. The air was full of the smell of pitch and dust, blended with a tang of woodsmoke coming from up by the house where the boys, including young Reggie, were preparing a fire for a picnic and barbeque later that evening after the celebration of life for Robert.

When Bertie saw his mother's eyes were open, he waited for a few moments before asking her, "Mom, do you want anything?"

"No sweetie, I don't really want anything."

He handed her a glass of ice water. "I wish I could make it so you avoided the worst of what's to come next."

"You are doing that already, Bertie. I suppose I'm close enough now that I don't want anything more or need to avoid anything either." Above them, straight into the direction of the sun, came the broken song of a peregrine.

Bertie cleared his throat as if to keep his voice from breaking. "Do you want me to finish up your memos for your colleagues? I can do that. I mean, I think I know what you want and where you want the research effort to go."

"No." She stretched, with her tiny arms—emaciated, skeletal—spreading above her head, the joints showing, round and swollen. "No, I've given up on those. People know what to do. They don't need me to tell them. They just have to continue the work. Some will be like me. I was a plodder just gathering and gathering what was there to gather. I was more like someone doing a jigsaw puzzle. Putting little pieces together until a big picture emerges. Some will be more out on the edge. Taking some big swings at big gains in understanding behavior . . . but they know what to do."

"But you want me to help you write some sort of encouragement from you?"

"Naw . . ." she said, and her voice was weak. "If they need that kind of encouragement from me, they won't have the stuff they'll need to continue their work. I was just clinging on to ego gratification. We don't need any more of that in the field."

"But your former students . . . don't you think they would like to hear something from you? Something to keep them on track?" Bertie had laid his book on his lap. The bright sun showed round on each lens of his sunglasses just under his Seattle Mariners cap.

"They are all hard workers, and they know that I trust them. No, they know more than that . . . they know that I love them. They know they just have to keep finding ways to get out there and observe. Find new ways to observe, perhaps. But they know that for themselves. Put the animals first, and they don't need me to remind them of that."

The boys ran up on top of the little hills. Dwayne was still in his dark blue suit. Gudger and Ned had already changed out of their good clothes. Ned and Dwayne had long sticks with charred marshmallows dripping off the ends like ancient, desiccated fruit. Reggie ran behind them, only half changed out of his good clothes. He had a white shirt with a tie on and swim trunks pulled up over his sandals. Reggie was five years old, with long curly hair.

"Hey, buddy," Bertie said, "you having fun?"

"Their mom lets them cook candy on the sticks, as much as they want!" Reggie said, amazed.

"Not aww the time. Mostwe we can't eat this much candy . . . I think it's just because it's my dad's memowial," Dwayne said. "I mean that's pwobabwie the reason. We still must be cawful with the burning sticks."

"Thank you for that, Dwayne," Bertie said seriously. "We don't want to see anyone get hurt at the party."

A THOUSAND miles to the north, a male sperm whale hunted along the coastal ledge. He was in a small group and would dive for fifty minutes at a time. The darkness of the world's largest ocean did not seem to daunt him. Within the group, each individual used a full array of sonic tools to navigate into the gloom. As he dove, the male scanned the bottom and the boundless columns of light and water surrounding his body. Pressure gripped him, but the massive bulk of flesh and muscle was able to push back against the ocean. He stayed in a small group of males that often remained close enough to touch one another, until one lone male turned and broke toward the south. Alone along the edge of the great sea, this individual possibly used vision and sonic tricks, and possibly some near miracle of natural sensitivity to the mass in the stars, which possibly enabled him to orient himself on the earth's ocean. North, south, east, west. Delphine didn't know how it worked. She would never know now, but it pleased her to know that this one individual had broken away from the group and was headed toward the equatorial waters where his family was swimming off the Galápagos Islands: females with their calves, feeding on squid and small fish, bunched together protecting one another. In just a few weeks, the male would find his way to them, appearing one day out of the dark blue ocean.

Bertie put his book down and went to the house to see if he could help Jenny with anything. Reggie crawled up on his grandmother's lap. He had carried a book with him and she read to him for a half an hour. She kissed the top of his head as she read. Soon enough, he heard the other boys laughing up by the house. A great horned owl called out somewhere in the woods and just as the boy scrambled down off her lap, the owl took silent wing down the slope to the creek bottom. Delphine was breathing in and breathing out, as easily as the warm air rose and the wind blew over her skin. Then she took a big

breath in and let it out slowly as she smiled at how happy the
boy made her.

LATER THAT evening, that is the way Bertie and Jenny
found her. Slumped in her chair, the owl still calling in the
distance.

ACKNOWLEDGMENTS

Big Breath In is a novel. That is, it is a work of fiction. Yet I wanted to write an extraordinary female character, so I used the life of my wife, Jan Morrison Straley, as a model for Delphine. Delphine's history is Jan Straley's history with several notable exceptions: While Jan did work as a criminal defense investigator, she never investigated a child trafficking operation, and her husband did not die while riding a green bicycle in the dark. Also, Jan does not have cancer.

Jan Straley has suffered with Parkinson's disease for the last twenty years. Why didn't Delphine share that disease? I chose cancer for Delphine because Parkinson's changes its symptoms day to day and hour to hour for each individual. Different treatments have their own side effects and it's hard to predict or plan around, in life or in a novel. I may someday write a story that describes the capriciousness of Parkinson's, but this is not it.

The whole story came to me one night when we were both staying at an old hotel across the street from a hospital in Seattle. I noticed a yellow Harley-Davidson Sportster covered in grit chained to a lamppost. It seemed to have been there a long time and I wondered if a sick person had ridden it to the hospital and never made it out to recover the bike. That night in a wish-fulfillment dream I had Jan overcome her disease to tear up and down the streets of Seattle on a yellow Sportster. After months of thinking about the details of this story I asked Jan if she would allow me to write it and to use her as the model for the main character. She said, "It sounds like you really want to write it." The cost to me was that she got to choose her own name and she chose "Delphine." Which resulted in me giving Delphine a French ancestry that she does not share with Jan. The rest of my family also got to choose their names while I chose my own.

I am not a marine biologist, but Jan is. I got a great deal of the information about big animals from our conversations in field camps and various research vessels over the years. I also relied heavily on the book *Sperm Whales: Social Evolution in the Ocean* by Hal Whitehead. Any mistakes or crazy interpretation of facts are my fault and should not be laid at Dr. Whitehead's or Jan Straley's feet.

All praise and thanks go to my entire family who helped me with the book: my siblings, Mary Worthington, Hugh Straley, Jane Skrivan and Martha Straley. While a great deal of non-familial praise should be heaped on Alexa Wejko, Rachel Kowal, Janine Agro and Johnny Nguyen of Soho Press as well as copy editor Julie McCarroll for their incredibly hard work in helping me polish this manuscript in time to meet its release date, and many, many thanks.

I'm also indebted to Finn Straley, Emily Basham, Arthur Straley and young Walter Straley who kept me drinking from the fountain of love that kept me working on this book over the last four years.

To dedicate this book to Jan seems redundant because every page is soaked with her adventurous spirit.